CELEBRITY
SPOTLIGHT
ENTERTAINMENT, LLC.

INNOCENT BY
CIRCUMSTANCE

A NOVEL BY

C-Murder
AND EUGENE L. WEEMS

INNOCENT BY CIRCUMSTANCE

Published by: Celebrity Spotlight Entertainment, LLC
www.celebrityspotlightentertainmentllc.com
FIRST EDITION: 2015

Cover Design: Marion Designs/www.mariondesigns.com
Editor: Terri Harper/Terristranscripts@gmail.com
ISBN: 978-1503355798
ISBN 10: 1503355799

Library of Congress Cataloguing-in-Publication Data:

Celebrity Spotlight Entertainment, LLC

Printed in the United States of America

DEDICATION

We the authors dedicate this book to the following people:

To our parents, families and friends who are living or have gone on to a better place. The love remains unconditionally in our hearts.

To all our fans, we thank you for the love you shown us.

Sincerely,
Corey 'C-Murder' Miller
Eugene L. Weems

ACKNOWLEDGMENTS

Allah U- Akbar

For my Angels: Chelsea, Courtney, and Chanelle.

What's up to my boy and co-author, "Eugene Weems."

R.I.P Kevin Miller and Soulja Slim.

Everybody on lockdown hold ya head high.
FUCK the system.

Much love Sabrina. TRU Records 4-Ever

Much love to Chelsea, Courtney, Chanelle, Dionne, Noony, Janelle, Antoinette, Ronny, Devin, Lil Leonard, Kalil, Big Mama, Marie, Keli, Malika, Diamond, Moses, Montez, Momz, Moneteeezy, Wayngo, Juan, Boo, Corey, Teedy, Eyes, The Cutt Boyz, T-man, G-Money, Lil Jimmy, Black Jimmy, Grasshopper Tee, Bummy, Wayne, Kwame Teague, Lashonda, Koch, Karneil, Will Hornton, Demetrius AKA Fleetwood, B.G., Silkk, Germany, Bass Heavy, KLC, Serve On, Aish, Lisa Chana,No Limit Soliders.com, Corlissa, O-Zone Mag, Shyne, Ron Rakoski, Gail, Rick Joseph, Cardio, Fro, Bee in Angola.
And everybody I forgot.

Stay TRU
Corey 'C-Murder' Miller

ACKNOWLEDGMENTS

ALDINE WEEMS...My grandmother and mother, the woman who holds both titles, my world, my heart. The loving and caring spirit that intoxicates my soul. The foundation of my temple. The queen who remains at the top of the pedestal of my realm. The woman who raised such a handsome, respectful, successful man. How can I ever show or express my gratitude for being blessed with you? Such words of appreciation don't exist in this world. Memories of you, your unconditional love, kindness, and beauty remain alive through me. I will continue on my journey toward achieving all your unfinished goals as well as my own aspirations until I conquer them all. As you used to say, a person will never accomplish nothing with hopes and wishes, but only through believing in self, hard work, dedication and devotion to the things you want to see happen. My success is living proof of your teachings. Love you, momma, with all my heart and beyond my last breath.

My love goes out to the following people: My sister Melissa Gina Johnson, my niece Micaiah and nephew Micah.

Finally, my deepest appreciation and warmest friendship is extended to all those people who have been supportive. Thank you for the love. I will keep bringing you hot page turning novels. So if you missed out on any, go cop them and experience the excitement of an electrified heart throbbing read. Let me continue to take you into worlds beyond your imagination.

Eugene L. Weems

Contents

PROLOGUE

"No! You better not! I want you all to leave my house now!"

"Ese, grab her!" Joker demanded.

"Flaco, you better not touch me!" Big Dee shouted. "Why are you doing this to me, Joker?" she asked.

Joker smirked cunningly, "I'm goin' to teach you a lesson about goin' against your race," Joker barked, shooting a frown at Flaco and Stranger, nodding toward Big Dee's direction. "Now!" he ordered harshly.

Stranger and Flaco reached at Big Dee aggressively. She fought back furiously, wrestling and tussling with them both. They were no match for her. Her fighting skills were better than average. The style of fighting she learned from her best friend Boo, who taught her Muay Thai Kick Boxing.

"Man!" Stranger huffed while stumbling backward, then knelt to catch his breath. He looked up at Joker, "Ese, what you gone do, just stand there and watch? Help out," he said breathlessly.

Joker thrust his hand deep in his right front pocket and started moving toward Big Dee. When his hand came up he was holding a gun. He rammed the barrel rather painfully into the left side of Big Dee's head. "You want to fight, huh? Let's see if you can fight this."

CHAPTER 1

This is what happened.

At the age of fifteen, my life began to undertake a dramatic twist, like an unexpected scene in a mystery novel. I could actually feel the strength of my demise violently tugging at my soul and my physical being and the vital spirit of the godly ways that had been instilled in me since infancy.

When I was at the tender age of five, my mother had been killed in an automobile accident. I have only vague recollection of her physical presence and fewer actual memories of childhood events that include her. I can't recall my sadness at her loss. I doubt that I recognized the actuality of the circumstances at the time. I don't even recall what she looked like. I made inquiries about her for several years, but as time passed, so did my curiosity.

My grandmother stepped into the role and she upheld that title and responsibility unconditionally. She had been all that I cherished, the solid foundation to my basic morals and the shield that protected me from the sinful ways of the streets. She was beautiful in her effervescence. A person with a loving heart, caring personality, full of warmth, laughter and softness. She was extremely intelligent. I always felt she knew the answers to my questions and could easily solve all my problems. The big pearly white smile she constantly wore was more alluring and warming to a person's soul than the rays of the sun itself.

I was torn from my lovely black grandmother when she suffered cardiovascular trauma and went to an early grave. The doctor said she had bronchitis and emphysema and her lungs collapsed from continuous years of cigarette smoking. I promised myself then that I would never indulge.

The day of her death was also the day of my death to the life that I cherished. Then began my quest for survival in the fast-paced, treacherous and wicked streets of Las Vegas, Nevada. The ghettos, the hustling, larceny, robberies and burglaries committed just to maintain the necessities of life.

I had run away from the constant quarreling of family members who couldn't agree on my guardianship. It seemed they cared little for my welfare, but only about which of them would oversee the funds left in trust for me in my grandmother's life insurance, of which I had been designated sole beneficiary.

I cared little about the money, because it could never ease the pain of her loss. So I emptied my leather backpack of school materials, then stuffed a small lightweight blue blanket inside, along with my pet ferret, Squeegee, and a few of his things. I pocketed the loose change that was scattered atop my dresser and took one last inventory of the items I had gathered for the journey, realizing that I had forgotten Squeegee's ferret snacks. When I was satisfied that I had everything of importance, I took a deep breath, tossed the backpack over my right shoulder and launched myself into the night, never to look back in the direction of the life I was abandoning. I wasn't about to stay where I felt unwanted. Part of my mind was saying that I shouldn't run away, that my family did care for me, but those thoughts were overruled by my certainty that I should just leave, walk away. If they truly cared, they wouldn't be arguing over which of them would have to take me into their home.

Thus began my journey with no destination. I was clueless as to where I was headed. I figured I would walk as far away from the west side, where I had always lived, until I found a different world. I headed east, walking blindly, lost in thought and paying no attention to my surroundings. I felt no fear, for I knew almost everyone in the community. My grandmother Aldine and my Aunt Ruby were well-known. They had opened Operation Life, a non-profit organization that provided free medical aide to those in need, along with a WIC program, a day care center for low income families, and a job training center. I was compelled to assist in its operation from the beginning. I was appointed leader of a program called *Be Like Me, Drug Free*, whose goal was to steer kids away from the temptation to use or sell drugs.

As I walked, I could hear Squeegee hissing from inside my backpack. I could see him looking up at me from deep within the pack, his beady eyes shining like red gemstones. He was pure white, a birthday gift from my grandmother three years earlier, so tiny at only six weeks old. But boy, did he stink! My grandmother finally had the veterinarian remove his scent glands. I think Squeegee was as happy about it as we were, because he was never thrilled with the daily bubble baths and scented shampoos that were our only means of controlling his strong body odor.

Squeegee was easy to train, but, true to his breed, he had a fetish for shiny objects and was expert at hiding things. He kept my grandmother in a constant state of frustration because he always hid away her car keys and jewelry. It reached the point that she blamed Squeegee when it was actually she whom had misplaced an item. I quickly learned that this was just her way of showing her love for the little guy.

I had been walking for hours. I was nowhere near the west side any longer. My feet ached and I cursed the Jordan sneakers on my feet, having neglected to change into my Oasis running shoe before setting out. I squinted at the black plastic Timex watch on my left wrist, but its numbers were elusive in the darkness, the natural blue indigo had reached its demise months ago. The streetlights offered no assistance. The streets were virtually quiet.

I soon realized that I had walked to a familiar street where my best friend, Big Dee, lived. A few cars sped past me heading in the opposite direction, introducing gusts of pre-dawn coolness to my skin and face and sending chills up my spine. I rubbed my arms to calm the goose bumps that had appeared there.

As I continued toward Big Dee's apartment, I heard a growling sound close by. I paused to survey my surroundings and saw nothing that posed a threat, so I continued along my way. The growling came again, louder than before. I froze and squinted into the shadows around me, searching for the source. When it came once more, I slid the backpack from my shoulder so I could check on Squeegee, worried that he had heard the growl and might be afraid, as I was. I felt foolish when I recognized Squeegee curled into a ball, sound asleep and snoring loudly. I had never heard him snore with such deep resonance. I reached inside to awaken him and noticed the bag of ferret snacks was empty.

"Squeege!" He didn't budge, not even when I lightly plucked him on top of the head with my index finger. "See, man, Squeegee, you done ate up all your food and I don't have the money to buy you no more!" He might as well have been in a coma, for he didn't twitch at all at the sound of my agitated voice. I tucked the blue blanket around him snugly to protect him from the cool air, shouldered the backpack and started across the intersection toward Big Dee's apartment complex.

I ambled through a Kentucky Fried Chicken parking lot and into a small empty lot. As I approached the front of the gateless complex, I noticed a group of four well-dressed Hispanics standing around a royal blue Ford F150 pickup. Two men and two women. They each held bottles of beer. The ladies were dressed in sexy outfits. The low cut tight pants showed their curves and their halter tops displayed their flat stomachs. Both men wore black jeans with huge silver belt buckles and colorful long-sleeved western style button-up shirts, black cowboy boots with silver-tipped toes. One of them wore a snow white cowboy hat. I assumed they had been out partying all night and just didn't want the fun to end quite yet. They noticed me when I appeared out of the darkness of the empty lot. I waved a lazy right hand in their direction as I crossed the street to take a shortcut through the dirt yards in the complex. The man in the white hat gave it a little tip in my direction, acknowledging my greeting.

I strolled across the hard-packed dirt yards with an attentive stride, assuring myself that I would not become victim once again of the nearly invisible clothes lines that were everywhere. I had learned my lesson several years ago not to be in a hurry to get through these yards in the dark. I had found myself nearly decapitated and flipped onto my back on the hard dirt surface, left breathless and gasping with a nice welt across my throat where I had run into one of the invisible cables that had been strung. The dim yellow lights from back porches weren't much help, either.

When I arrived at Big Dee's flat and raised my hand to knock on the door, I suddenly paused when I remembered the early hour. It would not be a good idea to upset Dee's mother. I stood there collecting my thoughts, trying to devise a plan to get Dee's attention without waking her mom. I recalled that Dee's bedroom was just to the right of the door, so I eased my way to her window and tapped, loudly whispering her name. When there was no response, I decided she must be camping out in the living room, where I knew she felt more comfortable sleeping.

I was hungry, cold, exhausted, and my feet were killing me. Now I was wondering if it had been such a great idea to run away, as well. Silly me, I tongue lashed myself. Great. Now I was talking to myself. I sighed in frustration and lifted my face to the sky, inhaling a great breath of fresh air in hopes of clearing my head, trying to make some sense of my ordeal. I watched the new day begin to dawn, forcing the shadows back and the night away. Just as the sun began to shed its first rays across the land, I decided it was time to go ahead and risk waking Big Dee's mother. I had to get off my feet and get some rest and food! I knew she couldn't stay angry at me for long.

The door vibrated in its frame as I banged my fist. It sounded much louder than the effort I was putting into the task. My surroundings were so quiet and still, it was the only sound for miles, it seemed. I heard movement inside the flat and watched the peephole darken for a moment. Several locks were clicked open and the door opened only as far as the security chain would allow. I could see Big Dee's right eye as she peered through, trying to recognize who could be at her door at this odd hour of the morning.

The door quickly closed and I heard the security chain being released from its post, then the door opened wide. It was Big Dee, my best friend in the whole wide world, who I hadn't seen in weeks. She was Hispanic, very beautiful, with the most gorgeous transformational hazel eyes I had ever seen. Her jet black hair hung gracefully to the small of her back. She was very curvaceous with a tapered waist and humongous breasts, a real brick house. I estimated she was physically developed and matured ten years in advance of her fourteen years of age. Always quick to take up a motherly or big sisterly stance in my life. I was older than she was, only by one year, but still, I was older and felt I was the one who should be the advisor and protector. And man, I tell you. Big Dee was overly protective of me, so much to the point she insisted that I learn to speak Spanish, and you guessed it, she would be the teacher.

Her reason as to why I needed to learn the language, she said it would come in handy and it would help me be aware of those who might speak negatively about me and/or have ill feelings toward me. I really didn't know what she was getting at. I honestly didn't care about the meaningless opinions of others, but I decided to let her teach me her native language anyway, just to make her happy. Then, when I became fluent in Spanish, she tells me to keep it a secret, not to let others know I spoke the language. This damn girl had her nerve, demanding that I learn a new language and then turn around in the same breath and say keep it a secret, not to speak it. But what damn sense does that make if I can't use what I learn, I thought. There was a method to my best friend's madness and it was only obvious that there would be a hidden clause somewhere between her request and reasons, which was I was only to speak Spanish to her and out the presence of others. I didn't even attempt to contest her request, which was more demand than request. I was going to do whatever I wanted to do regardless, but out of respect and loyalty for her, I would honor her instruction. Big Dee stepped aside out of the doorway to invite me in. She closed the door behind me and secured the locks.

"Where is moms at, asleep?" I asked while heading toward the fridge to get a bite.

She must have been following my actions because she said, "I don't know what you expect to find in there 'cause ain't nothing to eat in there, not even a grunion."

I cracked the fridge door anyway to take inventory of its contents. I grimaced at the two items that shared the spacious icebox. A makeshift water jug made from a plastic gallon milk container sat on the top rack, half full, and a thin but tall glass jar filled with yellowish liquid was cradled on the inner side of the fridge door, its label read yellow chili pepper, but there was not one of the small hot pods immersed in the juice. It was unlike Big Dee and her mother not to have any food in the fridge. I couldn't recall ever seeing it so empty. It had always had at least some sort of lunch meat, TV dinners or leftovers from last night's evening meal. "Damn!" I mumbled below a whisper.

I assumed Dee must of heard me utter my disappointment or she had came to the conclusion that I was upset from the way I slammed the fridge door closed because she said sarcastically, "I told you."

I told you my ass! Why ain't no damn food in the spot? What the hell is really goin' on around here? Y'all on a hunger strike or some type of fast or diet? Maaan! 'Cause I told you shit ain't cuttin' it for my stomach, I mentally rambled off.

I turned to check the cabinets for canned goods. I was sure there would be a can of beef stew, fruit cocktail, refried beans, or at least a jar of peanut butter, if nothing else, collecting dust on a shelf for drastic moments like this?

I pulled open one of the cabinet doors above the counter top. A group of cockroaches must have been eavesdropping and waiting on me to open up the door, because when I did, they dove out as if they were sky diving. They hit the counter top and scattered for cover. The presence of the roaches didn't take me by surprise, not even their action, for I have had numerous run-ins with the brown vermin and witnessed similar performances on more than one occasion at a relative's apartment.

I ambled back into the living room and took up a seat on the small couch where Big Dee was holdin' camp. I removed the backpack from my shoulder and set it on the floor, then shed the Jordans from my aching feet and sank lazily into the rough wool sofa gazing about the unattractive living room that was familiar. A carpetless floor, one wooden end table against a wall with a mini stereo and one small speaker on its surface. The small couch that Big Dee and I occupied was the only substantial piece of furniture that decorated the room. The couch faced the front door but was positioned in the far back of the room only a few feet away from the huge glass patio door that led to a small porch. Dee broke the silence between us. "Boo, what time is it about?" she asked sleepily. I didn't bother to answer the question for I had questions of my own.

"What's up with no food in the spot?" I began, "And where is Moms?" I inquired, now staring at Dee's pretty, smooth face, mentally outlining the details that make her so beautiful and unique. She told me she hadn't seen her mother in weeks and that she was worried because mom normally would call to check in and drop off groceries and lunch money for school. I asked Dee if she knows where her mom was resting at. She said she didn't know and mom wasn't giving any information to her whereabouts or how she could be contacted. All she knew was that her mother was with a man who normally accompanied her when she would come home to drop groceries and money. This explained why there was no food in the house; or did it, I wondered?

I quickly became upset with Dee's mom for being so irresponsible and selfish, and for choosing some chump over her own daughter. The high level of respect I previously had for her quickly diminished 'cause I felt she has placed my homegirl in harm's way by leaving her alone and exposed to the sick predators that prowl the streets. But I was more furious with Big Dee than I was with her mother, 'cause Dee knew she should have called me and let me know she was living alone while her mother ran around with some dude. I knew in my heart Dee was capable of taking care of herself, but that wasn't the point. Dee is legally still a child and her mother's responsibility, and such responsibility was being neglected, as far as I was concerned.

It was Dee's turn to quiz me about what I was doing out and about at that time of the morning. I told her about my grandmother passing away and my relatives arguing about which of them was going to have to take me in, and so I had simply run away from the whole scene.

With tears in her eyes she rose from her end of the couch and pulled me into her arms, giving me a huge bear hug and practically smothering me as she crushed my face into her huge soft breasts.

I hadn't allowed myself to cry over my grandmother's death, but when I felt Big Dee's heart beating against mine and knew that I was finally in the presence of someone who actually cared about me, I lost all composure and cried like a little baby until I couldn't cry no more. Dee shared the tears with me while assuring me that everything would be okay and that she would be there for me through thick and thin, no matter what. In my heart I knew her words was genuine, for she has always protected me as though I was her newborn child. She was the only person on this earth I would allow to see my sensitive side.

She finally released her bear hug. I sucked in the air as though I had been under water. We sat facing each other. She wiped the tears away from my face then caressed my cheeks with the tips of her fingers. She told me I was always welcome to camp out at the house and demanded that I get comfortable, because I would be staying. I certainly didn't turn down her offer, because I did need a place to lay my head until I figured out my next move.

I heard the growl again, but this time it was my empty stomach. I removed the loose change from my front pocket and slowly counted it several times for accuracy, not wanting to accept the fact that I had only two dollars, sixty-five cents to my name. _I figured that I could buy a grab size bag of Doritos tortilla chips, a king-size Snickers Bar and a Big Gulp soda and share it with Dee. Yeah, that's what I would do, I figured. I asked Dee was she hungry. She shot me a most irritated look in answer to my stupid question.

"Why? You got some money to buy us something to eat?" she asked.

"I have two dollars and sixty-five cents to get us something to take the cheat off us," I replied, holding out the hand with the loose change.

"Boo, that's enough to get us something to eat for a few days!" She was excited.

Yeah? I wondered what in the world we could possibly buy with two dollars and sixty-five cents to last us for two days. If Dee said we could, then we could. She knew better than I did. I figured that I'd just follow her lead because she was the expert shopper. We decided to stroll to the store, but first I headed to her restroom for a quick pit stop. I was stopped in my tracks when I heard Big Dee screaming in fear.

I ran back into the living room to see what was wrong. I found

Dee standing on the arm of the sofa, her eyes as big as dinner plates. At first, I noticed nothing that posed a threat. "Girl, what the hell wrong with you?" My heart was pounding hard from being taken by surprise. She pointed to the floor. I looked down and had to laugh when I saw Squeegee, who had freed himself from the backpack and was attempting to make friends with Dee. He was sitting up on his rump and waving his little arms in the air. Dee had never met him and her reaction was perfectly normal, because ferrets are often mistaken for large rats.

I ambled over and lifted him into my arms, tickling his tummy. It took Dee several minutes to calm down before she attempted to get acquainted with Squeegee. I left the two of them alone while I finally hit the john, then the three of us headed out to the grocery store on foot. I wasn't happy about the fact that I had to put my shoes back on, so I tucked the laces inside and slipped into them, which was much more comfortable. I shouldered the backpack with Squeegee inside and we all headed out to our destination.

CHAPTER 2

The glass doors opened as we approached the front of the store. I followed Big Dee down one of the long aisles. She was obviously familiar with the store's layout, because she knew exactly where to find the items she wanted. She removed twelve packages of Top Ramen noodles from a lower shelf, handed them to me, then ambled into the refrigerated section. She snagged a package of 99-cent chicken hot dogs and then headed toward the produce section.

We stopped at eight huge wooden barrels that were filled with assorted candies. Each barrel had a clear Plexiglas lid. Big Dee began sampling the sweet treats as quickly as possible. I quickly followed her lead, plunging one hand in a barrel of gummy bears while my other hand was removing a half dozen sweet and sour gummy worms from the next barrel. I made my way down to the last barrel, which hosted my favorite candy inside, chocolate covered raisins. I scooped up a handful and stuffed my mouth as I followed Dee out of the aisle. We went to the quick checkout line, twelve items or less, which had a pretty long line of customers waiting to pay for their purchases. I ambled over to a candy and magazine rack. I removed the backpack from my shoulder and set it on the floor in front of me, then snagged the *Smooth* magazine from the rack and swiftly flipped through its pages to peep the centerfold honeys, then snatched up a copy of *O-Zone* magazine and began skimming through it, too.

In a couple of minutes Big Dee could be heard calling me to come pay for our items. I replaced the mag, shouldered my pack and quickly returned to the cash register and paid for the items. A total of two dollars seventeen cents for twelve Top Ramen and a pack of hot dogs. Not bad for a couple of bucks, I thought. We headed back to Big Dee's flat.

The sun was shining down full blast by then and I was exhausted.

I took up my original spot on the couch while Big Dee did her thang in the kitchen. I had just dozed off when she tapped my shoulder and handed me the bowel of grub she prepared. I didn't even growl about being awakened, which would have been my normal reaction. I must have been starvin' for I practically inhaled the food. I never realized just how good a soup with chopped up hot dogs would be. I guess anything is good when you're hungry. We ate hot dogs and Top Ramen for the next two days, just like she said we could. Even Squeegee nibbled on Bid Dee's concocted delicacy. But our food supply quickly dwindled. Dee's mom need to bring her ass home and drop off some ends, I thought.

I took up camp in Dee's room while Squeegee hung out with Dee on the couch. I was pretty depressed as well as grieving for my granny, so I stayed isolated in Dee's bedroom sleeping as long as I could until Dee felt the need for more company other than Squeegee.

I was awakened from a deep sleep by a bad dream I was having. I rose onto my elbows, held my face in my hands and debated whether I wanted to get up, still feeling a little sluggish. Coming from the living room, I heard the faint sound of music, laughter, and Dee's voice demanding someone stop doing something. I waited for a few seconds to try and make out what Dee was saying. I figured that Squeegee was giving her a hard time because she probably hadn't given him any attention. I laid back down until I heard Dee's voice rise a few decibels. I jumped up to go see what was going on. I entered the living room unnoticed.

Dee had a house full of company. Three of her female friends, scantily clad and with far too much makeup on, and two Hispanic adult males who were clearly members of the southerner Mexican gang, the tattoos on their arms and neck confirming their gang affiliation. One of the thugs was rough handling Squeegee, slapping him around aggressively as though he was training a pit bull to fight. Squeegee growled and fought back to the best of his ability but he was no match for the bully. I damn near lost my mind when I seen my little Squeegee being treated so crude. I was beyond furious and quickly took his place. "Man, what's your --" I swiftly darted in for the kill with a cruel overhand that found its target.

The dude squealed in pain when my fist introduced itself to his chin. He fell backwards to the floor before my left hook could do any damage. He was out cold. Squeegee ran up my leg and into my arms, breathing heavily, happy to see me.

"Nooo! Joker, that's my best friend!" Big Dee shouted, running over and stepping between us. The gang banger she called Joker had pulled out a gun. I frowned at him and tried to shove Dee out the line of fire with my right hand, but she didn't budge.

"Say Ese! You done fucked up by putting your hands on my boy, homes," Joker said waving the gun. "Ese, get out my way so I can smoke this fool," Joker ordered Big Dee.

She wouldn't budge. Joker attempted to move around her but she kept blocking him, pleading and explaining that I am her best friend, the one she had told him about and she was not going to allow him to shoot me. Joker demanded that I give his unconscious friend a fair fight. Big Dee accepted on my behalf as long as he promised not to involve any guns. Joker tucked his gun away. I took that as he accepted Dee's proposal.

"Flaco! Get your ass up, Ese!" Joker tugged at his friend's arm. "Get your ass up and represent the three SUR gang!" Joker growled.

Flaco was just coming to, still dazed. He managed to get to his feet with the help of Joker. "I'm gonna kill you, Ese," Flaco threatened and took a fighting stance.

"Hold down, Ese," Joker said placing an open hand on Flaco's chest, then gazed in my direction and continued. "Let's take this outside."

No problem fool! Let's go outside. Outside, inside, it doesn't matter where we do the damn thing at, it's all the same to me, you got to bring a ass to get some ass, I mentally expressed.

"Aight, let's handle that, then," I said, placing Squeegee on the floor.

"I got your back, Boo," Big Dee whispered into my ear.

I knew she did, no doubt about it. Big Dee was my best friend, my sister by another father and mother, and my mother of another lifetime. Of course she had by back unconditionally, a fact I've been absolutely sure of for several years now. I made my way outside. I knew if anything was to go down foul, Dee was able to hold her own, because I taught her good how to scrap and she was a beast when it came to chunking 'em. If I had to choose any one of my friends to catch my back, it would most definitely be Dee.

I stepped out the door and was cold cocked by Flaco and sent sprawling in the dirt front yard. I tried by best to regain my balance, but the unexpected blow to the head had dazed me to the point that my equilibrium wasn't able to recoup fast enough before I hit the ground. I lay there on the cold hard pack dirt yard trying to compose myself.

"Now that's what I'm talkin' about, Ese. That's how a true SUR do it," Joker cheered.

"Boo, get up and whup that fool," Big Dee cried out. "You know that's fucked up of you Flaco to dope fiend him like that. What! You afraid that you would get your ass kicked on a head up fade? That's why you had to blindside him. Huh?"

"Bitch, you watch your mouth and shut the hell up before I do your ass the same way," Flaco snapped back.

Big Dee squared up with Flaco, "Well, what's wrong with your doin'? Brang it!" She challenged. By that time I had stumbled to my feet and found my footing.

"Dee! Dee! Get out the way and let me handle my business," I grunted. She stepped to the side to let me face my opponent.

Flaco laughed and smiled cunningly and said, "You still want more, Ese?"

"I got a dub on my homie Flaco. Which one of you want to bet?" Joker asked looking in the direction of the three girls who was watching the action.

"I'll bet you," Big Dee announced. "I got a twenty spot on my boy Boo that he stomp a mud hole in Flaco ass," she said.

"Bet!" Joker accepted. "And I want my money right after your little boyfriend get knocked out."

I wondered what Dee thought she was doing, betting on her brown ass, because she didn't have money, not one dime to her name. If I lose, then what? Then there's really gonna be some shit. Joker gonna flip and most likely bust a cap in both of our asses. That was an issue I couldn't be worrying myself with at the moment because it didn't exist, for I hadn't lost yet and hadn't no intentions on losing.

Flaco made his move. A crisp left jab caught me on the bridge of the nose and left me teary eyed, followed by a deafening right hook to the ear. I howled in pain. Seeing that I was in distress, Flaco rushed in for the kill with a powerful leaping left hook. I tucked my chin and turned my right shoulder into the punch in the nick of time to give the blow a durable target. I countered with a straight right to the chest that backed him up a few steps. Dee cheered me on from the sideline. Flaco was no punk. It was obvious that he had some training in boxing because he held his hands up high, chin tucked, and he knew how to put his body weight behind his punches. The only flaw that I noticed was that he was a headhunter, a real big mistake when it came to fighting an experienced fighter. He delivered a well placed kidney shot that nearly folded me. I realized then I could no longer underestimate Flaco and if I was to beat him I would have to step up my A-game, which I did. I slipped a left jab then a straight right and pivoted out to his right side, releasing a four-piece combo, then dipped out to the left and fired a twelve-piece flurry of jabs, upper cuts and hooks to the head and body which folded him like a lounge chair. Flaco was down for the count.

Big Dee jumped in excitement shouting, "That's my homeboy, my boy. I told you my homeboy was gonna kick his ass. Let me get paid, break mine off!" She held out her hand toward Joker.

He slapped it away and growled coldly, "Bitch, I'm not givin' you shit, not one red dime. So you might as well chalk that up as a loss and get out of my face."

"What!" Big Dee was pissed off now. I knew that Dee was not going to accept that. She had a very serious problem with someone taking something from her, and Joker was refusing to give up something that she felt entitled to.

"Oh, you gonna pay me or get your ass whup'd out here real proper like," she said pointing her finger in his face.

He shoved her aggressively, the wrong thing to do in front of me. She threw two haymakers at his chin that hit nothing but air. I launched in to take her place with a right body shot that followed a gruesome left upper cut that put Joker on his back. He swiftly leapt back to his feet. I got ready to deliver another attack, one more grisly than the first, but found myself staring down the barrel of a gun. Joker wiped at his bloody mouth with the back of his left hand, keeping aim with the other. He spat a wad of the bright red fluid, glanced up with his eyes full of hatred and growled, "Bitch, how about tryin' that Mike Tyson shit now and see if you can stand up under the seventeen blows I'm gonna hit yo' ass with." Then smiled a ghostly one, stepping forward.

Dee pleaded for my life, but her words fell on deaf ears. I knew I was a dead man so I took what might be my last chance for survival. I could only hope my martial arts training and speed would pay off. I swiftly pivoted, grasped his wrist, turning my back in toward his chest. I snapped my elbow back into his face, pivoted back out, twisted the hand that gripped the gun and bent him over backwards. I snapped a consecutive flying knee to his jaw that knocked him unconscious.

I removed the gun from his hand and tucked it in my waistband, then searched his pockets and came up on a small wad. I shuffled through the bills. "Thirteen funky ass dollars," I grunted. "Dee, this, chump only had thirteen lousy ass dollars," I said and handed her the singles.

"What!" She frowned and recounted the bread. Joker hadn't the money to cover the debt from the beginning, just as Dee hadn't, but does that make them even? No! I thought. Regardless, right or wrong, that thirteen bucks belonged to Dee and we were going keep it because I had to knock the chump out for disrespecting my homegirl. Plus, we needed the money badly. I knew she would accept the thirteen bucks and be cool with it considering the circumstances. There was nothing she could do about it anyway, right? Joker didn't have more money or anything else of value on his person. It's only common sense that you can't squeeze water out of a dry rag.

Dee's girlfriends had split after the action was over. No goodbyes, no I'll see you laters, no I'll holla at cha's, no nothing, just a magician's trick, vanishing in the air, the three girls had broke wide into the wind. Dee and I strolled back inside the flat, leaving our adversaries laid out in the yard.

I secured the locks on the door, washed my hands, then retrieved Squeegee to give him a thorough examination to be sure he had not suffered any broken bones or serious injuries. Once I was satisfied that Squeegee was okay, I removed the weapon I had taken off Joker, dropped the clip from its sleeve and jacked the slide to extract the loaded round from its chamber. A nice piece of metal, I thought. Just what I needed in case Joker and Flaco returned with a slew of their gang member buddies to retaliate. I assured myself I wouldn't hesitate to use it to protect myself, Dee and Squeegee.

Dee must have had a similar fear of them returning, for she flopped down next to me and rested her head against my shoulder while clutching tightly to the handle of a huge butcher knife. I'd never seen such a cruel design. Just the look of it frightened me, but I knew that knife would be no good if Joker and his crew was to return, because they would most definitely be packing guns. Dee and I sat in silence as she watched me reload the weapon.

Squeegee had made himself comfortable on my lap. Several hours passed. I assumed that was a sign that Joker and Flaco would not be showing up for revenge, so I broke the silence between Dee and I. We chatted for a long while and decided that we would sell the gun. She knew of a fence who would take if off our hands. Although I didn't want to let it go, we needed the bread for immediate necessities. I had planned to head out in the morning to the union hall for a job, and union dues would hit me for forty bucks that I didn't have. Dee made the call to her fence. He swooped through and offered eighty bucks for the piece. I nodded to Dee and she accepted the offer. She slid me two dubs for union dues and held onto the other half for groceries.

Squeegee wouldn't let me out of his sight. Everywhere I went, he stayed on my heels. He made it clear that he wouldn't be doing no more camping out in the living room with Dee when he dragged his blanket into the bedroom where I was holding camp. I grabbed the backpack to get his water bottle. To my surprise, it was crammed with candy bars, bubble gum and a grab bag of open potato chips.

What the hell? Then I realized where the goodies came from and how they'd gotten in the bag. I thought back to the store at the candy and magazine rack were I was thumbing through the magazines. I recalled sitting the backpack on the floor in front of me. "That little thief," I said to no one other than myself with a smirk on my face as I eyeballed the goods. There was no doubt in my mind who the shoplifter was. Who else was so attracted to shimmering and colorful objects? Who else had a long track record and tendency of tiptoeing away with property that didn't belong to them? Who else was so cute and innocent looking? Who most likely would never be suspected of having the capability of committing a crime? Squeegee, of course, my little white furry pet ferret friend.

I called to Dee and she came rushing into the room with a worried expression plastered on her face. "What's up?" She huffed, heart pounding against her chest like a bass drum as her right hand clenched tightly around the handle of the butcher knife. I played it off like I didn't notice her paranoid behavior.

"Come an' get you some of this candy and chips compliments of Squeegee," I said with a smile. She moved over to the bed and picked out the items she desired. I couldn't help but eye the knife. Just the sight of it sent chills up my spine. "Girl, won't you put that Friday the thirteen lookin' ass machete up somewhere before you hurt yourself?" I teased.

She shot me a devilish smirk before turning toward the door and said, "Good night Boo. Go on and get you some rest if you plan to go job huntin' in the morning." She flicked down the light switch and closed the door behind her.

"I love you too, girl," I whispered.

CHAPTER 3

The smell of homemade flour tortillas and the strong spices of fresh salsa awakened me from a deep sleep. My eyes fluttered open as I yanked away the sheet to rise before noticing Dee standing in the doorway holding a plate of food. "Good Mornin' sleepy head. You must have been tired because you were dead to the world when I came back in," she smirked. Came back in? Came back in from where? I know good and well she can't be talking about coming in the room, 'cause if she had I would have heard her 'cause I'm a light sleeper, as I thought to myself.

"Huh, I made you some breakfast and laid you out some fresh clothes." She handed me the plate of food and nodded her head toward the end of the bed. I glanced in the direction to find a neatly folded and pressed pair of jeans that looked like my own and a white T-shirt that belonged to her. I then returned my attention back to the plate of grub and greedily eyed the scrambled eggs and cheese, grits, refried beans, turkey sausage, tortillas and salsa.

I hadn't realized that I was wearing nothing but my No Question boxers until Dee mentioned she had washed my pants and left a few dollars in the right pocket for bus fare. I snatched at the bed sheet to cover my lower half out of embarrassment. I was now feeling a little upset with myself for sleeping so hard that allowed Dee to easily strip away my clothes from my body. My mind began to wonder off with questions. How did I sleep through the removing of my pants? Did she sneak a peak of my thang? Was it on swollen at the time or was it in a deep sleep also? I reached under the sheet with one hand and gently gripped my swipe and traced its length to ease my thought of being under privileged in that department. Which that thought quickly vanished and my confidence was restored for I was gifted with more than enough length and thickness. I smiled within. Dee had been saying something but I hadn't been paying attention. "What was that you were saying?" I asked.

She frowns down at me. "What! You didn't hear what I said the first two times?" she snarled. "I'm not about to keep repeating myself 'cause you not listening."

"Girl, come on now an' stop tripping, I'm listening. Tell me what you were saying."

"If you was listening the first time instead of playing with yourself you would have heard what I said." She paused for dramatic effect, then added, "What I said, Boo, was what are you going to do, stare at the food or eat it?"

Ain't this a bitch! Is this what she's catching an attitude over by asking me such a stupid ass question like that? "I'ma eat! What you thank?" I glance up to probe her face before returning my attention back to the plate of food and asking, "Where you heading off to dressed up looking all good?"

"School."

"School," I echoed her answer.

"Yeah, school Boo! I do still go to school you know," she said sarcastically.

I had forgotten all about school, which I had quit going when I decided to run away from home. A reality check that had just begun to clear the fog that had been impeding my vision of what type of future awaits me if I choose to give up on life, my education, and most importantly, myself. "Yeah that's cool girl, I dig that about you, how you staying down with getting that edgumacation," I smiled, "'cause dropping out is for losers, like me," I said more to myself than to Dee.

It was the truth. We needed money to keep a roof over our head, food in our mouth and all other life necessities, seeing that Dee's mother wasn't stepping up to her responsibilities. It was only right that I be the one to sacrifice my schooling to support us than allow my homegirl to. Although I had no intentions on going to school no time soon anyway because I was getting my runaway on and that would be one of the first places the police would look for me once my family reported me missing. Dee had informed me she had spent all the money on food, detergent and hygiene products except for five dollars she planned to use for lunch money for the week. Do you know how much high school lunches cost these days? But knowing her, she most likely had a hookup with one of her friends that worked in the school cafeteria and could hook her up with free food, I assured myself.

"Boo, I'll look after Squeegee while you're gone," she offered. "You can't be toting around a pet job huntin'. I'll take good care of him. He can go to school with me, if it's okay with you?" Big Dee asked. She noticed the dirty glance I shot her way when she made such a suggestion. She rolled her eyes and said, "Whatever Boo! You don't trust me to take care of your ugly ferret?"

I offered a phony smile to ease the tension that I so wrongly created between us two. Dee was right. It wouldn't be appropriate for me to be dragging around Squeegee while I was on the hunt for a job. The fact was, I felt uncomfortable leaving Squeegee in the care of someone else for any reason over an extended period of time, but Dee was not just anyone. She was my best friend, the person who I trusted wholeheartedly. So I came to my senses and agreed with her suggestion. She smiled and leaned over, palmed my cheeks and kissed my lips softly, then tapped the top of my nose with her right forefinger before turning on her heels to leave. "Good luck finding a job. I'll see you when you get home, okay?" She waved over her shoulder.

"Bye. And don't be letting all your nasty ass friends play with my ferret either," I yelled out to her jokingly. I quickly wolfed down my breakfast, took a quick shower, groomed and headed out to catch the city bus that would take me to the union hall. The line was long as hell, but my turn had finally come to approach the oval shaped, freckle faced brunette who stood behind the counter smiling from ear to ear.

"Good morning sir. What may I assist you with today?" Freckle face asked.

"A job that requires little effort and pays a high salary," I teased.

Freckle face arched an eyebrow. Her smile had vanished and was lost somewhere in the depth of her new expression that clearly said, yeah right! You can't possibly be serious?

No, I'm not serious I'm just pulling your leg and being a little sarcastic at the same time, my cunning smirked indicated. Freckle Face's smile resurfaced bigger than ever. She slid a clip board my way that contained an application. I filled out the application and handed them back along with two dubs to cover the union dues. She swiftly eyed through the documents with the tip of the pen as her guide, then glanced up at me and requested two forms of identification and a parental permission slip. It never crossed my mind that I would need such documents. If I would have known, I would have had Dee to write a forged note giving me permission to work, but I still would have ran into a problem with the identification. "Damn!" I cursed underneath my breath steaming from the long hours I spent waiting in line just to be turned away because I had no identification or a stupid note.

I made a move to persuade Freckle Face into letting me slide through, but she must have read my mind because she held up an open palm to halt my attempt. I was heated and had chosen a string of choice words that would have punctured holes through her heart if I had allowed them to flow, but I chose to take the middle course and gigolo the defeat. So I just smiled and swooped up my bread from the counter, shoved it deep into my right pocket, turned on my keels and strolled out the door. "Ain't this about a bitch!" I cursed out of frustration. The next bus wasn't due for an hour and a half and I wasn't about to sit around and wait that long. I decided to foot it back to Dee's house since I had nothing else to do.

I had walked a great distance. I decided to stop and rest my aching feet. The Jordan's were not doing my feet any justice. I ambled toward a slum looking motel and took a seat on its staircase and scanned my surroundings while loosening the laces of my Jordan's. It was typical scenery that I was all too familiar with. I eyed a bag lady searching through a dumpster for aluminum cans before turning my attention to a group of crackheads probing the asphalt with their hands as if they had lost something so small that it couldn't be seen by the naked eye but only recovered by physical contact. I shook my head in disappointment watching them tweak and knowing the cause of their illness. I was beginning to understand why the white man introduced crack cocaine to the black and Latino communities. It was an effective weapon in their armory that would effortlessly and quickly weaken and destroy the races on their own accord. A real brilliant manipulation scheme, I figured before erasing the thought.

"Julia, when you see that mother of yours tell her to stop by," the voice of a woman uttered to someone named Julia. I turned in the direction of the voice to see the person it belonged to. Damn! My mouth dropped wide open at the short woman who stood in the entryway of her motel room casually smoking a cigarette. I could smell the heady aroma of perfume that mingled with the breeze outside her room. Her blond hair was in huge rollers and a red scarf was wrapped around her head. She wore a light brown bra and panties, a brown garter belt and black nylons. Her red lipstick looked shiny and wet. She seems bursting out of her skimpy lingerie, a heavy buxom lady, five-feet-two- inches tall in black ankle strapped sandals with stiletto heels, curvaceous hips and taper waist. She had to be somewhere in her early thirties and a prostitute, I supposed, I tried to resist the temptation of staring but my eyes seemed to have a mind of their own. So they took in their fulfillment before parting from the woman's body and turning toward the female structure that was heading my way in an oversized dusty pair of jeans, a sweatshirt, worn down black Nike shoes and a baseball cap pulled low over the eyes. As the person brushed past me I got a good glimpse of the face that was hidden beneath the baseball cap. I was astounded. She was beautiful. An angel dressed like a boy in filthy clothes. I shifted my position to watch her ascend the steps when she halted her climb, turned toward me and spoke. "I don't recall seeing you around here. Did you just move into the motel?" she asked with the sexiest voice I had ever heard. She had a foreign accent that I couldn't quite place.

I could feel my heart pounding against my chest. I tried to speak but my voice was lodged somewhere inside my throat. She descended the steps until she reached the one I sat on. I tilted my head and glanced up at her with admiration in my eyes. "Cat got your tongue?" she asked. "What's your name?" I didn't know anything about no cat having my tongue but I knew something had it. Whatever had it I knew I needed it back.

"Boo," I blurted finding my voice, "My name is Boo." I repeated it more for myself than for her, assuring my ears that my voice had returned.

"Hi Boo, I'm Julia Monevilay Perez" she offered. I repeated her full name mentally. "Julia" I recited allowing her name to roll off my tongue. "Your name should have been Jewel instead of Julia," I said honestly. She arched an eyebrow; it was obvious that she was searching her mind for an answer to what I meant about that before she decided to ask.

"Why is that?"

"Have you ever looked in a mirror?" I asked. She giggled and shook her head yes. "Well then, you should know why. You're beautiful," I complimented, "You're like a rare piece of jewelry that is hiding from the world and waiting to be found." I saw her face soften up. My words had touched her heart, but she kept her shield up, not falling weak to the slick talk. "You look like a very expensive beautiful jewel that is most definitely unique."

"Ooh, thank you, that was so sweet of you to say about me." Her eyes became glossy, "No one ever said anything like that to me before. I don't see myself as being beautiful," she admitted.

Julia seemed sweet, down to earth and there was no doubt about it, she was gorgeous even though she was scruffy looking in her tomboy attire.   There was something about her demeanor that struck my attention but I couldn't quite place a finger on it. That very moment Julia and I became friends and I asked her if I could call her Jewel instead of Julia because I thought it fit her better. She didn't have a problem with that. It was destined to be a name that would forever be a part of her.

She sat down next to me on the step and we talked for hours. I shared my story with her about running away from home and what had landed me on that step. She also felt the need to vent. She told me her mother was Puerto Rican and they were originally from New York and moved to Las Vegas. She went on to say her mother left one day and never came back, leaving her to fend for herself and five younger siblings. She told me about how she has to hustle the streets to keep the rent paid and food for her family. She also informed me she was only sixteen years old and had just returned from hustling, but needed to check up on her brothers and sisters before heading back out to the game.

I began to wonder what type of hustle she had. My mind took on many possibilities and the first was that she was selling her body. Nah, I pushed that thought out of my mind because Jewel's persona and demeanor didn't portray her as a prostitute.   Who would want a prostitute that dressed like a boy and was visibly filthy in appearance? I contemplated. So I figured she had to be getting her thievery on, but then also began to doubt that. Such occupation didn't fit her style, but who was I to assume what type of criminal behaviors a person was capable of just by looking at them? I was no specialist in criminology, or a psychic for that matter, so how would I know?

I mentally scolded myself and decided I'd just ask her exactly what type of hustle she's involved in. Before I could get around to inquire, a big old fat black man heaved out her name, "Julia, let me holler at you for a minute."

Jewel spun her head toward the fat man, then rose to her feet and called out to him, "Just one minute Clayman, I'm on my way. Boo, I'll be right back, just let me go over there and see what fat ass wants. That's my connect," she said before descending the stairs. My mind began to race again. Her connect? Connect meant two things to me, either he was her drug dealer or a fence. She returned quickly. "I can't stand his fat funky ass. One day he's going to get his." She went silent as if she was contemplating an important thought.

"Who is that nigga?" I asked.

"He's the dope man. I spend with him when I have the cash. He hooks me up with double ups."

"Girl, you smoke crack!" I frowned and hoped she would tell me she didn't.

"Hell no! I don't mess around with drugs. That's just one of my hustles. I cop from fat Clayman and shoot down to Lady Luck Casino to get my serve on, but it's risky down that way, too many undercover pigs patrolling that area."

"Why you just don't get your serve on right here at the motel? All these smokers around here you can make a killing."

"'Cause this is fat Clayman's spot. Plus he has workers up and down this street selling for him and that fat bastard don't play fair. So Boo, what you about to do? Just kick back here for awhile or what? I have to be bouncing to go get at some money; my family hasn't eaten since yesterday, plus we need soap and toilet paper."

I was starting to feel sorry for Jewel and her family. I hated to see kids without something to eat. I still had the forty bucks I was going to use for the union hall. I could give that to Jewel to get her sisters and brothers some food. She did seem genuine, but how do I know her story is not just an act? This could all be a performance here that is part of her hustle. I have seen some of the best of them and been taught by the best of them, and if she was popping some game then she was doing a hellava good job because she got me just about believing her. Everything was starting to come together like a puzzle. The dirty clothes she wore and the sob story she told went hand in hand if she was playing the con game. Even that accent of hers could be part of her performance. I decided then not to offer my forty bucks, but ask if I could accompany her to hustle. I needed bread also. My sole intentions wouldn't be about the hustle, but to make sure that those kids got something to eat. If what Jewel had told me was the truth, I had the forty bucks I could fall back on to make sure they ate if push came to shove.

So I asked Jewel if I could bounce with her on the grind. She excitingly welcomed me. She asked me to wait for one minute while she went to check on her family. I watched as she sprinted up the flight of stairs and tapped a code on one of the motel room doors. The door opens a crack held by a security chain. I see a partial face and a figure in the narrow crack of the open door. The door quickly closes and opens wide. Jewel darted in and within a matter of seconds she steps back out and thundered down the steps to where I now stood awaiting her return. "You ready?" she tapped me on the arm with the back of her hand. I nod and we headed out.

We strolled down seven blocks and I had become hungry after passing by an elderly white woman sitting at a bus stop bench enjoying a chili dog. Damn! That chili dog looks good, I thought. I looked over at Jewel and seen she was thinking the same thing. I know her stomach had to be touching her back. She hadn't eaten since yesterday, at least that's what she claimed.

"Jewel, I got a couple of bucks, let's stop at this corner store and get something to snack on." I held up the two dollars I had left over out of the three Dee gave me for bus fare.

"Aight" she smiled with a new pep in her step. We entered the small corner store that was owned by Asians. I told Jewel she could get something worth up to a dollar. I snatched up a grab size bag of chili cheese Fritos, she came strolling from the back of the store with two 25-cent cans of soda and a honey bun. I paid for the items and we shared the snacks as we ambled back out to the street and continued on our way.

I still didn't know what type of hustling Jewel was supposed to be doing. We were doing more talking and enjoying each other's company than anything. The elderly woman who we had passed on our way to the store was now standing hunched over the back of the bench resting on her forearms talking to a white man dressed in a white Arizona bomber jacket and matching baseball cap. The elderly lady was shouldering a huge white handbag that looked to be packed with her life's belongings.

The man drew a deep drag from his cigarette and then flicked it into the street, smoke seeping out of his nostrils and mouth simultaneously. He looked over his shoulder suspiciously and then made his move. He snatched the old woman's handbag sending her violently crashing to the ground. He took off running, heading in our direction.

Jewel uttered a wail

"Oo...ooh!" the elderly woman cried in pain. "Someone please help me. He has my purse, he has my purse. Somebody...please...."

"You bitch ass muhfuka." I gave chase. Jewel was already in

pursuit before me, and that girl was fast. Before the man realized that we was heading directly toward him it was already too late to change his course for Jewel was already on him like a ferocious pit bull. The man struggled hard to break free of Jewel's hold. He shoved her violently to the ground, but she managed to break the fall and swiftly bounced back to her feet. The man reached in his front jacket pocket. Just as Jewel began to dart in with another attack, he brought out a sharp blade. Jewel swiftly halted her attempt to strike. The man had pulled a switch blade knife and had every intention on making good with it. He lunged in with a thrust then an outer swing that poked and sliced nothing but air. Jewel's movement was too swift for him.

I leaped into the air in a three hundred and sixty degree spin. The jumping round house kick met its target. The man jerked up in the air like he just pulled the rip cord on a parachute. Somehow he managed to stumble back to his feet, never once losing possession of the woman's handbag. He was determined to get away with the purse. He made his move to escape, but I sent him back crashing to the ground with a left round house kick to the leg that shattered his right shin and then an outside crescent kick to the face. He dropped the knife and laid there breathless. He touched his nose wondering if it was broken. He had to be in excruciating pain, I assumed, from the twisted expression he had in his mug. The man looked up at me as I loomed over him.

"God damn man, you broke my freaking nose dude." The man sniveled. I wondered, Was this guy a comedian or what? Or was he just plain stupid? What was he thinking? He just tried to rob an old woman and stab my friend and now he's crying about a broken nose. I thought while reaching down for him, twisting my hands into his jacket.

"Hey, watch it man….come on I give up," the man whined.

Yanking him to his feet, my eyes convinced him that I was about to put a hurting on him very badly for his disrespect. Then I free my right hand and smash a closed fist into his mouth. "So you want to rob old ladies and then try to hurt people, huh." I kept repeating as I continued to introduce my fist to his face. He tried to cover up so I slung him back to the ground and savagely pounded heavily and insistently on the chump until I got tired. I had decided to rob him now for what he had. So I stripped him of the new white Arizona jacket, his cigarette lighter and smokes. I searched his pockets thoroughly for anything else I could take. Removed the old lady's purse from his clenched hand, swooped up the switch blade and pocketed it. Turning on my heels to leave, I applied a couple of stomps to his head for good measure. All because of his disrespect. I returned the purse back to its rightful owner. Jewel had been attending to the old woman while I was putting hands and feet on the perpetrator.

It was getting chilly out so I gave Jewel the jacket I had taken from the man. The old woman had suffered minor abrasions to the knees and hands. She continuously thanked us. Jewel insisted that we wait at the bus stop with the old woman to see her safely on the bus, but the woman told us she lived up the street across from the corner store, so we offered to walk her home. She agreed. It quickly became obvious that she was starving for conversation, because she walked at a snail's pace just rambling on about events that happened before we were even born. We finally reached the retirement home where she lived. We walked her to her door and waited until she entered. She invited us in, but we assured her we must be going. She told us we were welcome to visit her anytime and she would love to have the company. I promised that if we were back in the area we would drop in to say hello. She thanked us again, but this time with big hugs. She reached in her buxom and pulled out a twenty dollar bill and tried to hand it to Jewel.

"Here baby, this is for you two. I don't have much, but I manage on the little I get monthly from my social security check."

"No…we…" Jewel began.

"Ma'am, we can't take that," I interrupted. "Keep your money. We appreciate the offer. We helped you because you needed help, not for any reward."

"Darling, please, I insist. I will not take no for an answer," the woman said sharply.

Jewel looked at me. I nodded and she accepted the money. We thanked the woman and I got going again. The night had crept up quickly. I knew Dee might be getting worried since I hadn't come home or called to check in. Hustling would have to wait until another day, I figured. Jewel had a fresh dub that would be enough to get her family something to eat and the toiletries they needed. I told Jewel I had to go but I would walk her home first. Her cheerful expression immediately vanished as she looked up at me with her puppy dog eyes and her mouth parted to speak. I seen the sadness that formed within them.

"Why Boo?" she asked in a kid's voice. "Can you just hang out with me a little longer?"

I shook my head no. She sighed pouting.

"Come on Boo, please at least come with me to get something to eat, plus, I have to get change for this twenty so I can give you your half."

"Half? Come on now. I don't want half of your money, that's your bread…"

"No, it's both of ours, you heard her, she said it's for the both of us Boo, not just me."

"Well, I'm giving you my half, you can have it all."

"No! I don't want it all. You need money too."

I chose not to argue anymore about the money. I learned a long time ago from Dee that it is no use to argue with a woman because a man will never win.

"Aight. Whatever. Where you have in mind to get something to eat at? I'ma bounce with you and then walk you home, then I have to go," I said. She said she knew of a chicken joint two blocks away that stayed open late. And they had a daily dinner special for $9.99 that consist of 16 pieces of fried chicken, eight dinner rolls, a family size potatoes and gravy, coleslaw and four corn on the cobs. Now that sounded like the lick, for $9.99 a person can't beat that with a stick I thought.

We entered the chicken joint and Jewel placed her order. I stood at the video games reading the monitors of the highest scores and watching the game advertisement display. Jewel waited at the counter.

The eatery was in fact rather cozy with a great deal of mahogany and brass, red leather booths with framed pictures of black leaders and entertainers hanging on the walls. There was the murmur of voices from the customers. Two Hispanic men strolled inside, both short in height. The men shared a laugh about something they found amusing. One of the men approached Jewel and whispered to her in Spanish. I had only caught the words "How much."

How much what, fool? You better back your rusty nut ass out of her face, chump, before you find out how much whoop ass I'ma open up on you, I spoke to myself.

Jewel looked over at me with a devious look. I raised an eyebrow. She turned her attention back to the man, "Uh… I hate to ask you this," she says with tearing eyes, "but could I have it now please? That is the only way I would agree."

What the hell is this girl up to, I wondered as I watched the man take out his wallet and hand Jewel a hundred dollars, just like that. She whispered something in his ear and a smile lit his face. They both ambled toward the door. She glanced back over her shoulder and winked at me.

Aww…this little bitch a ho. Frowned up at the thought, I was now steamed, hot as the devil. This little punk ass bitch. I shuffled through my thoughts but only for a moment. I had to ask myself what was I so upset about? It was her own body she was abusing, not mine. If that is what she chose to do, then who was I to get mad at her? That didn't change the fact that she was a good hearted person and cool peeps to chill with. I guess I just forced myself not to believe that she would take that course of degrading herself and risking her life to the possibilities of diseases and psychopaths. I was also hurt because I had taken a liking to Jewel. I decided to follow them.

Jewel looked up and down the street to see if anyone was watching them before stepping into the dark alleyway. The man pulled at Jewels arm and began kissing her neck greedily. She gently pushed him away. "Slow down poppy, let me treat you good," Jewel said as she un-buckled his belt and allowed his pants to drop to his ankles. As she knelt before him, he rested one hand on her head and the other on his hip awaiting to be serviced with the pleasure of oral copulation.

"Oh…! You….!" The man grunted in pain with cupped hands now over his scrotum. Jewel had shot a hard upper cut into the man's crotch that folded him. She sprung to her feet and delivered a punishing left hook that crushed the man's jaw. He tumbled to the cold asphalt unconscious. I had just turned into the alley and caught the ass end of what was going down. Jewel had her back to me and swiftly turned when she heard my footsteps. She smiled at me and I frowned back. She rushed over to where I stood.

"What's all this about?" I asked sharply.

"What?" she asks innocently, knowing damn well what I was talking about. "Oh, him?" she points toward the unconscious man. "That's just a fast hustle. I'm always clipping a trick like him for their money, making them believe they about to get some, then I beat they ass once I get their pants down." She laughs. "You ever seen a mother fucker trying to fight with his pants down around his ankles? It's some funny shit," she giggles.

"Girl, your ass is crazy," I smiled, "Come on and let's go get this food and bounce before this chump wake up and we have to kill the fool."

We walked back into the eatery, grabbed our order and headed back out. I had been wrong about Jewel. What I had assumed she was doing wasn't even like that. She had been capitalizing off of men's sexual appetite and lust. What she was doing was still dangerous, but what wasn't when hustling in the streets, I wondered.

We made it back to the motel. I waited on the steps while Jewel ran the food upstairs to her family. When she returned she had two paper plates in hand. She hands me the one with the larger portion. I wasn't about to refuse the grub. I was hungry and I love fried chicken. She also slipped me half of the loot she peeled for plus the ten spot from the old lady. I pocketed the bread and dug into the plate of food. I asked Jewel if she knew what time the last bus had run. She shook her head and said buses don't run this late. "I'll call a cab for you when I finish eating."

And she did. I gave Jewel a hug and promised that I would come visit her soon before entering the taxi cab. "5239 Eagle Brook Court," I requested of the driver and sunk lazily into the back seat and began reflecting back on the wild day I had. Jewel was weighing heavily on my mind.

"Sir, we're here," the taxi driver announced.

I raised sluggishly, paid the driver and stepped out of the cab, yawning while reaching to the sky to stretch my tightened limbs. The cab driver must have been looking for a tip because he didn't pull off. He just sat there after he had given me my change. The only tip I had for him was he better get to pushing' before I decided to take my bread back and kick off in his ass.

I trotted up to Dee's flat and knocked on the door. There was no answer so I tried the knob and found the door unlocked. This was feeling all wrong. I stepped inside. It was unlike Dee to leave the door open. The taxi finally pulled away from the curb, tires skidding. I stood in the doorway for a few seconds feeling somewhat frightened. I stepped inside, closed the door and put the chain in place, then secured the double locks.

I heard a faint sound coming from behind the bathroom door. I walked over there and slowly pushed the door open. I couldn't believe my eyes. I blinked slowly, trying to clear my head and be sure I wasn't dreaming. I hadn't been.

"Dee...Squeegee..," I cried, rushing in to untie the twisted bloody body of Squeegee that was hanging from the shower pole.

"I'm sorry Boo, I'm so sorry," Dee cried, balled up in a corner. "I tried my best to stop them."

I fell to my knees next to Dee, clutching Squeegee's bloody body to my chest. I sobbed and sobbed like a baby. "What happened Dee?" I turned to her and she lifted her head for the first time. I noticed her lip was swollen and there was a cut on her right cheek and blood crusted inside her nose. There was a big blood stain between her legs. "What the fuck happened here Dee? Please tell me who did this. I promise I will make them pay. I promise you that." I stroked her face.

"Boo I'm sorry I couldn't stop them."

"Baby girl, there's no need to be sorry, I know you did your best. Just tell me who did this?"

"It was Flaco, Joker and his cousin Stranger," she said.

"Them bitch made muhfuckas," I said through clenched teeth. "We got to get you cleaned up and to a hospital."

"No Boo, I'm okay."

"Dee, listen to me. You trust me, right?"

"Yeah."

"Well, trust me on this, you must go to the hospital and get checked out."

I know the reasons why she didn't want to go. She didn't want to risk involving the police and being placed in a child protection facility as well as being embarrassed about being raped. I started to blame myself for what happened to Dee and Squeegee. If I would have just brought my ass home like I was supposed to, then I could have protected them. I scolded myself viciously.

I phoned a taxi, then ran down the spill to Dee that we would run on the medical stuff at the hospital. I helped Dee clean herself up. A horn honked. I knew it had to be the taxi. I peeped out the bedroom window and sure enough it was. We stepped out of the spot and entered the taxi. I told him our required destination and rested back into the seats with Dee in my arms.

The taxi dropped us off at the emergency room. I flipped him a dub and told him to keep the change. Dee and I entered the packed emergency room. The lady at the counter pushed a stack of paperwork toward us to fill out and gave me a number. I filled out the medical forms with false info to protect Dee from any future humiliation. It only took five hours before she was called to be seen. Damn a person would be dead by the time they could get some medical attention at this hospital, I thought.

CHAPTER 4

Big Dee was admitted into the hospital. She was diagnosed with bleeding of the rectum and had to undergo an immediate operation. She had been sodomized. Them bastards had done all they could do to my best friend except for taking her life physically, but mentally they had. I was going to make each one pay for it dearly if that was the last thing I ever did on the face of this earth.

Big Dee had convinced the doctor that she hadn't been raped and just when the coast looked clear it quickly became cloudy again. The internal bleeding in the rectum had re-awakened the doctor's presumption. He was no longer buying her story anymore. He knew all too well that Big Dee was the victim of a sexual assault and his professional practice and the test results from the examination could prove his analysis without a shadow of a doubt. There had been two distinctive types of semen found inside of her.

I sat in the waiting room for hours waiting for her to come out of surgery, talking to an old white man who I assumed was in his early seventies whose wife had suffered a heart attack for the second time in one month from what he had told me. He introduced himself to me as Professor Shelton. He was a small man. He had a full head of gray hair and sported a neatly trimmed beard and had a classical style about himself. A person of aristocracy, I assured myself. He spoke with words I found myself asking him what they meant. I had begun to think he was doing it on purpose so I would be inquisitive when he realized I wasn't shy to ask questions. I guess that was his method of teaching indirectly and plus a conversation builder so he could continue to ramble on with more of his fancy words that wasn't used in normal people's conversations.

He excused himself and headed toward the men's room and

promised he would be back shortly. That was my cue to rest my eyes because the old man was long winded. Man, I'll tell you, old folks can talk, I said to myself and hoped that Professor Shelton stayed gone long enough that I could fall asleep.

I was sound asleep when he returned. "The young lad must have been exhausted," Professor Shelton said in a whisper to himself as he laid his Mister Rogers sweater over me and added, "Sleep tight and dream well thoughts, young lad."

When I awakened I felt fully energized, I yawned and stretched my arms. For a moment I almost forgot where I was. I looked around and noticed Professor Shelton sitting in front of the television watching the news with his long fingers wrapped around a cup of coffee. He turned toward me when he heard me wake. "Gentle evening lad, I was wondering if you were ever going to wake. I begun to worry about you." He glanced toward a Styrofoam cup with a lid on it that sat next to a bagel on the end table next to me. "That will put a pep in your step," he added with a smile and returned his attention back to the television.

"Thanks Professor Shelton," I said gratefully. He didn't turn to give me a response. He just lifted his hand in the air to acknowledge me. I removed the plastic lid from the cup and took a sip. I had never been a coffee drinker, and this stuff was terrible. I replaced the lid and set the cup down.

I hadn't realized that I slept so long. My watch read 3:05 pm. I was sure big Dee had to be out of surgery by now. So I made my way to the front desk of the intensive care unit and asked if I could visit Big Dee. A nurse who I recognized from when me and Big Dee had come in, informed me that Big Dee was in room 107-b, that the surgery went well and she was going to be fine. I asked if I could see her. She told me not today because Big Dee was heavily sedated and needed plenty of rest. That was an answer I didn't want to hear. I just wanted to see my home girl because seeing is believing, that's what I was always told. There was no way I would be able to sneak in to see her due to the double doors that lead to the rooms that had to be buzzed open by a medical staff that worked behind the nurses' station. I checked the list for the visiting hours for tomorrow then turned toward the exit door. I hadn't said goodbye to Professor Shelton, but I left his sweater neatly folded on the chair where I had been sleeping. He was the coolest white man I ever met, he just wasn't up to speed with the new generations' ways of communication. At least that's what he may have wanted me to assume because it didn't seem like he had a problem understanding me.

I took the bus back to Dee's flat. The door was unlocked as I had left it. I put Squeegee's lifeless body inside a shoe box that I had taken out of Dee's closet and placed a rubber band around each end of the box and went to the back yard and began unearthing the soil with a cooking spoon making a hole big enough to place the box in. After I gave Squeegee a proper burial and said my goodbyes, I headed back inside the flat to clean up the place. It was spotless when I finished. I needed to make sure that there wasn't any evidence that could be found to support the doctor's presumption if he decided to involve the law and they decided to engage an investigation and come snoop around the house. I have always been the paranoid type, always thinking about the possibilities and covering all aspects of a situation.

I took a hot shower and dressed in the same jeans I've been wearing and put on a pair of Big Dee's white footy socks and one of her black hooded sweatshirts that she had in her dresser. I slowly slipped on my Jordans and tied the laces, checked my pockets to make sure that my money was still inside, pulled a wallet size picture of Big Dee from her dresser mirror and placed it in my back pocket and headed out the door to visit Jewel.

I exited the bus a half a block away from Jewel's motel room. There was a lot of traffic around the motel. People were entering in and out of rooms, cars pulling up and the dope man's workers ran up to it to score a sale. Crack smokers walked fast back and forth stopping to fumble with anything on the ground that resembled a crack rock and twitching their mouths uncontrollably. A homeless person with a basket dug in garbage for aluminum cans. There were a few kids running up and down playing on the stairs while a young boy who I assumed wasn't any older than thirteen sat on the floor of the middle of the door way of a motel room watching the activity around him.

I looked up at Jewel's room door and noticed it was closed as always. I ran up the steps after I was approached by a female crack head if I wanted to turn a trick with her for five dollars. I frowned at her sight. Her hair was nappy, her breath smelled and she was missing all of her front teeth and she had open sores on her face where I could tell she had been picking the scabs away because there were dark marks that indicated the sores were not fresh wounds.

I knocked on Jewel's motel room door. No one said anything but I heard footsteps inside moving around. Someone peeked out the curtain soon after, the sound of the bolt lock unfastened and the door knob jiggled then is swung open. Jewel greeted me with a smile, but I didn't match hers. She still had on the same dusty pants and wore down black Nike tennis shoes but a different shirt which was three times her size that fitted her like a night gown.

"Hey Boo" she said reaching out her arms to hug me. "I see you came back to see me." She invited me in, but I declined and asked if I could talk to her outside. She could see something was on my mind and agreed after she introduced me to her little brothers and sisters, Kevin, Jewlean, Benny, Tasha and Lisa. Tasha was the only one who waved with a smile that showed a live spirit in her eyes. She would soon become my number one road dawg and downiest little comrade.

Me and Jewel stood leaning on the rail of the balcony talking. I told her what had happened to Big Dee and Squeegee and I was at a loss as to what I should do about the situation. I showed her the picture of Big Dee that I had in my back pocket.

"She's very pretty," Jewel admitted, still staring at the picture as if she were studying Big Dee's features and comparing them with her own. I told her that I didn't believe that Big Dee would ever be the same after what happened to her and Jewel told me that Big Dee would never forget about it, but if she was a strong person she would be able to go on with her life. Then she began to tell me how Fat Clayman, the dope man, had once sexually assaulted her. Fat Clayman had locked her in a motel room and attacked her. She said the assault was interrupted when Samantha was trying to enter the room. Fat Clayman had orally sexually assaulted her and threatened if she told anyone that he would kill her brothers and sisters. She admitted that every time she sees him that her mind's eye replays back the attack and she feels ashamed as if it was her fault why she was sexually assaulted and that is the reason why she dresses like a tomboy with baggy clothes and stays looking dirty all the time in order to avoid people like him from trying to sexually abuse her.

I was at a loss for words. Here I was telling her about a situation which she had already lived and was facing on a daily basis and the fat son of a bitch who hurt her. He was smiling and walking around as if nothing ever happened. His day would come when he was least expecting it. I couldn't help but to feel sorry for Jewel. She had been going through hell and it seemed like she was never offered any mercy to the hand of life she was dealt.

"Boo, would you walk with me to the corner store so I can get some milk and cereal. We haven't ate breakfast yet."

I was thinking to myself, does Jewel know what time it is? She was talking about breakfast when actually it was close to dinner time. But I didn't say anything other than I would stroll to the store with her to pick up the items. Jewel opened the door just wide enough so she could stick her head inside, she uttered something and removed her head and closed the door, locks fastening from the inside.

The street lights blinked on and the light in the sky was quickly fading away. We ambled down the street toward the store where we came to an alley where three Italian men stood spread out facing the street with their hands in their sweatshirt pockets. They weren't noticeable from the streets unless you were approaching the alley. When we came into the alley path two of the men stepped out and cut me and Jewel off. The man in front of us had a butcher knife in his hand holding it in a threatening way toward us. He directed us into the belly of the alley. I only cooperated because Jewel was with me and I didn't want to risk her being hurt. The man who stood in the alley while his comrades blocked us out seemed to know Jewel.

"We meet again, huh little lady," the man said walking toward us with a black automatic handgun pointed at us. I thought, damn, what has Jewel done now? How were we going to escape this? I couldn't think any further than the barrel of the gun that was being aimed at us. My common sense told me to remain cool, but my pride said to try something, anything to get the gun out of the man's hands. But my street smarts told me to listen to the common sense and let pride be ignorant by itself. So I stood silent and played it by ear.

"What's up Franko?" Jewel said to the man. "What's all this about?"

Franko bent his head and rubbed the side of his face with his free hand and then looked up at us and said, "You should never forget the people you con out of money."

Jewel said she didn't con him out of any money, that he offered to loan her mother some with the promise of paying it back, which had nothing to do with her because she didn't borrow any money and she shouldn't be held responsible for what he gave her mother.

"Well, that's where you're wrong little lady," Franko said calmly with his deep Italian accent.

"Since your mother is nowhere to be found, then the debt falls on the next of kin, which happens to be you. So you owe me money and I would like to be paid in cash or blood, but I must be paid," he said.

"That's not fair Franko, you know I don't owe you anything and I don't have any money. You see me out here hustling to feed my brothers and sisters," Jewel pouted.

I noticed that tears of pain from people taking advantage of her had built up in her eyes. She was tired of the struggling and being the scapegoat for everyone else's problems. From where I stood, I could see she had been getting dealt the worst hands in the deck.

Franko said he didn't give a damn about what's fair or not, he wasn't concerned about that, he just wanted to be paid. I spoke up for the first time and asked Franko how much money was owed to him and that if it wasn't outrageous Jewel and I would get him his money. When he said seventy five dollars my heart started beating normally again. I told him don't trip, we could clear the tab with him right now. His eyes lit up at the offer of money, but they quickly went cold again and a frown came over his face.

"How is she going to pay me and she doesn't have any money?" he asked me.

"I'm going to give you the money out of my pocket."

"No, Boo you don't have to do that." Jewel turned to me and said "You need that money yourself!"

"Yes, he does have to pay it if you both want to walk again," Franko threatened.

"Be quiet and let me do what I want with my money," I said gently.

"Yeah, be quiet little lady," Franko remarked.

I gave Franko his money. He counted it several times to make sure that he had seventy five dollars. Once he was content he smiled and said, "What about the interest for the long wait?"

I instantly became angry. I knew where he was now taking this and I didn't like one bit of his low down dirty scheme. He just wanted to stay in Jewel's pocket and push his weight around. If him and his boys didn't have weapons, I would knock him and his home boys out and stomp a mud hole in their asses. My pride was already bruised for allowing the wanna be gangsters to intimidate us, but there was nothing I could do about it but play along so I could see another day. Hopefully the cards would flip and I would have the upper hand. But only if they knew they were playing around with live dynamite with a fuse that was already lit.

"I don't have no interest for you homie, neither does she," I said harshly

"Oh yes you do, tough guy. Now empty out your pockets, both of you," Franko demanded.

"Franko, why are you doing this to us?" Jewel pleaded.

"Be quiet Jewel and just do what he says," I said with a stern look.

"Yeah Jewel, do what your little boyfriend says because he knows right from wrong," one of the other men said, laughing.

We emptied out our pockets onto the ground. Franko had one of his boys search us to make sure we had nothing else in our pockets. He took out Big Dee's picture from my back pocket and looked at it, then crumbled it up and tossed it in the air. They taken every dime that we had plus the switchblade knife I had taken off the white dude the day before. We were told we were free to leave, but when I turned to leave Franko kicked me right in the ass as hard as he could that brought me to my knees.

"Now that's what you call an ass kicking Franko," one of his boys said and then they all laughed.

Jewel helped me back up to my feet. I didn't even look back, I just bit my tongue and got out of there for I was at a big disadvantage. I said nothing to Jewel as we headed back toward her house. She did all the talking. Mostly pleading to how sorry she was for getting me involved with her problems and promising to pay me back. But honestly, I wasn't paying her any attention. I was thinking about how I had just been robbed and kicked in the ass like a punk bitch by some chumps to top it off. I didn't even have the money to get back to the hospital to visit Big Dee and that was weighing heavy on my mind. I asked Jewel if she had any money put up at her house and she said no. I asked if she still had the Arizona state jacket I gave her and she said yes. I told her we need to sell it and go buy a double up from Fat Clayman so we could make some money. She was down with it and ran up the stairs to her room and came back with the jacket in her hand. She asked me who were we going to sell the jacket to and I suggested we might as well pay Fat Clayman a visit and see if he would give us two twenty dollar stones for it since he liked to have first access to all the merchandise.

I noticed Jewel's skin crawl every time she heard the mention of Fat Clayman's name and she wasn't fond at all to being in his presence. I followed Jewel to Fat Clayman's motel room. She knocked on the door and he opened the door after looking through the peep hole and seen who it was.

"What's up Julia? Who's your boyfriend? You ain't going to

introduce him to me?" he said.

Jewel turned to me and smiled, then said, "His name is Boo." I started to wonder why everyone was thinking Jewel and I were boyfriend and girlfriend and she didn't deny it.

"Yeah, I seen him the other day sitting on the stairs, he seems straight laced," Fat Clayman said.

"Yeah, he's straight, Clayman. You know I ain't going to bring no one to your spot if they wasn't all the way straight," Jewel assured him.

I noticed Fat Clayman's motel room looked like a hotel suit. All plushed out with the best of furniture and a big screen TV. Much different than the one Jewel and the kids shared in the same hotel. Fat Clayman had a room with a kitchen, living room and bedroom and Jewel's motel room only had a bedroom. He even had a hundred gallon salt water fish tank. I had to give him his props, the room was spotless and smelled good and suitable for a king. I noticed he was the only one home.

"So, what brings y'all over to the spot?" Fat Clayman asked looking at Jewel with lust in his eyes.

I spoke up before she could answer, "Folks, we got a new Arizona jacket that we trying to get off of so we can get our hustle on. We thought you might like it so we giving you first dibs at it since it's the only one like it around and the top dawg should always have first dibs on anything that come around his turf. So we giving you first dibs out of respect for a boss player like yourself," I said shooting drag just to stroke his ego so he would buy the coat and we could get our hustle on.

"Julia, I already like your boyfriend, I can see right now that if you listen to him, y'all going to have big things together cause I can tell that he's smart and don't have no problem with congratulating a playa in the game and not hating, plus, he's respectful. But I can tell that he has an evil side about himself that he keeps hidden also," Fat Clayman said.

The fat chump was catching himself analyzing me. This fool didn't know that I was way sharper than him in the game and I was just only stroking him to get what I wanted and hating on him all at the same time for what he had done to Jewel.

"Say Boo, tell you what I'm going to do for you since I like your style. I really don't need the jacket, but my girl might like it so I'm going to take it off y'alls hands since y'all trying to make a few ends. I'm going to give you four twenties for that jacket, but you have to promise that you will only spend with me when you need some more work," Fat Clayman said.

Jewel spoke before I could get my words out. "Clayman, you know I only spend with you anyways, and me and Boo is hustling together so we are going to come back to spend with you every time."

"That ain't what I asked you, Julia. I was talking to Boo anyways, if I believe," Fat Clayman snapped harshly but with a smile.

"Yeah Jewel, Clayman wasn't talking to you, he was talking to me, so be cool and stay in a woman's place when two men is talking business," I said cold bloodedly, then turned toward her and winked my eye.

"Yeah Boo, I like your style, I see we going to get along just fine, youngsta, and maybe once I get to know you a little better, I would put you on the team and you could work for me."

"Yeah, that sounds like a plan, Clayman, but the only thing about that is I have a problem with bosses. I always been the one to run my own show and at my own speed, you feel me folks?" I said, not knowing how he was going to react to that statement.

"Yeah Boo, I understand that and I don't knock it either. So what's up on that deal?"

"It's all good, I can promise you that. That's not a problem. Plus, I don't know anyone else around here that has work for sale other than you," I assured him.

Fat Clayman smiled and told us to wait right here until he comes back. He wobbled off into the back room and came back within a few minutes with a small plastic baggy with four cocaine rocks in it and gave them to me. Jewel gave him the jacket and I placed the dope in my pocket. I thanked him for his generosity and extended my right hand toward him. He gave me the old school soul brotha hand shake that started with a palm clap and hold around the thumb, then a clench of the fingers into a fist and then a solid fist tap together all in one motion. As soon as our fists touched, I fired a straight left to his face that caught him right on the bridge of his nose and brought tears to his eyes. I followed up with a leaping right hook on the side of his neck that brought him to his knees.

Jewel stood in shock watching. She had no clue that I was going to take flight on Fat Clayman. He tried to grab hold to my shirt. That's when I took hold of his hair and yanked his head toward me and thrust out three consecutive flying knees smashing into his face. I released my grip from his hair and he fell to the floor like a sack of potatoes. He was knocked out cold. Blood was oozing from his nose and mouth. I turned toward Jewel and seen she was frozen in place. I snapped at her to bring her out of the trance.

"What the hell you standing there for, find something quick so we can tie this fat bastard up and hurry it up."

Jewel snatched the telephone cord out of the wall and swiftly handed it to me. I hog tied the chump to where I knew he wouldn't be able to get loose. Jewel gagged his mouth with his own socks. I locked the security chain on the door to keep any unexpected visitors from walking into the room.

"Boo, what are we doing?" Jewel asked me looking up at me with her big beautiful eyes.

"What you think we're doing, we're about to jack this fool for all of his shit. Now let's toss this house up until we find his dope sack and the money he got up in here. It's got to be in the back room somewhere because that's where he went to get the dope for us."

Jewel didn't say anymore. She was down with me on whatever I decided to do. But I assumed she thought I was crazy by the look she gave me before we went into the back room. I saw some lady's gloves laying over the dresser mirror. I snatched them down and gave one single glove to Jewel and told her to put it on and use the hand with the glove on to move things around to avoid leaving any fingerprints behind. Then I placed the other glove on and began searching the room.

"Bingo!" I said excitedly.

The first place I looked I found Fat Clayman's stash spot. I figured anyone could have found it if they had known what they were looking for. There was a small size vent in the lower corner of the wall behind the bedroom door. It was only obvious that it could have been a possible hiding spot because the sockets were missing its bolt nuts that fastened it. So I easily removed the small vent cover and reached my hand inside the wall and felt a plastic bag. I removed the bag from the wall. It was a large sandwich bag that was half filled with different sizes of crack rocks. I searched the hole again and found two more large sandwich bags, one with money and the other with weed. I took a pillow case off of one of the pillows on the bed and stuffed the three sandwich bags inside and continued to search the room.

"Boo look," Jewel said in a whisper holding up two handguns by the handle. One was a chrome .38 caliber sub nose Taurus revolver and a .45 caliber automatic.

"Ha ha." I smiled at the sight of the weapons with evil thoughts.

"Give me that one," I said reaching for the .45 automatic. I dropped the clip as if I were a gunsmith to see if the clip had any ammo. Although I was a professional gun handler, certified by the ghetto street society.

"Boo, look whatcha call this one?" Jewel asked holding up a Heckler and Koch semi-automatic. My eyes grew big at the sight of the weapon. I tried not to show my excitement so I calmly said, "That's an H-K, let me have that."

I moved over to where she was and noticed a pistol grip shotgun and a .30-30 rifle lying on the floor next to the bed. I bent down and looked under the bed and there was a black duffle bag lying next to some shoe boxes. I pulled them out and opened them. The shoe boxes were filled with letters from some woman in prison and the duffel bag had extra clips and boxes of ammo for all the weapons. I stuck the pillow case with the drugs and money inside the duffel bag, added all the handguns except the H-K, zipped the bag shut and swung it over my shoulder. I held the H-K in my hand and told Jewel to come and get the other two guns so we could go.

We walked back to the living room where Fat Clayman was laying on his stomach, now trying his best to free himself. I stomped on the back of his head as I walked past him to the front door and looked out the peep hole to see who was outside that might be able to see me and Jewel walk out of the room with the merchandise. Jewel stopped and picked up the Arizona jacket we had just sold to Fat Clayman and put it on, then zipped it up.

"I might as well take my coat back since we taking everything else," she said.

I turned toward her as she walked over to where I was. She looked up at me softly. I frowned at her and said, "Don't you and fat ass down there got some unfinished business to take care of?" I pointed at Fat Clayman with the H-K in my hand. "I don't know what you're looking at me for with those puppy dog eyes, take care of your unfinished business," I told her.

She turned toward Fat Clayman and untied the gag from his mouth.

"Hoe, I'm going to kill your ass. You and that punk boyfriend of yours. You just wait, Julia. Just wait till I run across you niggas. I'm going to kill both of y'all sho as my name is Clayman. You think I put my finger in your pussy last time; this time I'm going to see how you like a hot curling iron up your ass, you little bitch," Fat Clayman snarled at her.

"You will never get the chance in this lifetime to ever hurt me again," Jewel said cold bloodedly.

I turned my head and peeked out the peep hole again when I heard the shotgun being cocked. I turned back toward Jewel and watched her force the barrel of the gun into Fat Clayman's mouth and pull the trigger. Fat Clayman's brains went flying everywhere.

"Now you will never hurt anyone else, you fat punk!" She then turned toward me and picked up the 30-30 rifle and asked softly, "Are you ready to go now Boo?"

I stared into her eyes for several seconds and saw that a heavy burden had been lifted off her chest. I didn't say anything, I just smiled at her then turned around and began unchaining and unlocking the door. Jewel stuck the guns underneath her jacket and allowed the rest to hang down in front of her. No one paid us any attention when we came out of Fat Clayman's room, not even the little boy who was sitting in front of the doorway of his room. He had his mind in a place far beyond reality. We were in the clear as far as we knew.

She followed me closely as we swiftly made our way up the stairs to her motel room. She tapped on the door with her special code and the sound of locks unfastened and the door opened. We ducked inside.

"Hi Boo," Tasha politely greeted me with a smile. She was a pretty little girl. A spitting image of Jewel but just a smaller, younger version.

"What's up little momma? What you up too?" I asked knowing she wasn't up to nothing because they had nothing to do in the room but stare at each other. There was no television to watch, only a small AM/FM radio to listen to. I saw a coloring book on the floor but there wasn't any coloring crayons in sight. They were living in a prison, confined to a small room with no entertainment of any kind and depending on their sister to score the meals or they would go hungry for that day.

I didn't like the sight of their living situation, but I knew Jewel was doing the best that she knew how. I saw that the kids were happy to have company over and they seemed to overlook the fact that I was standing in their room with a gun in my hand. I guess they could feel that I wasn't there to do any harm to them or Jewel. Jewel took the guns she had into the bathroom and came back out and told her brothers and sisters that they weren't to go near the bathroom.

Tasha asked me if she could read to me, she held an old newspaper in her hand studying it as if she were trying to decide what article she would read to me if I were to say yes.

"Not right now little momma, maybe later, but you can read that newspaper?" I asked in curiosity because I didn't know any seven year olds who could read the newspaper.

"Yes, she can read very well," Jewel said, intruding into the conversation.

"Oh yeah? Well, I guess you will be the smartest little momma I know then," I said to Tasha and gripping the top of her head with my free hand and moved it gently left to right in a playful way. She giggled sounding like Jewel did when I first met her.

"Jewlean, I need for you to do me a favor. Stand by the window and peek out it and tell me if you see anything unusual or a lot of people hanging out in a crowd," I said. Jewel looked at me strangely why I wanted Jewlean to keep watch for a crowd of people. But I knew what I was doing. I was really having him to keep an eye out for the police just in case someone called them and heard the shot and seen us leave Fat Clayman's room. I didn't want to alarm the kids by telling Jewlean to watch for the police because I figured if he had seen the police anyways he would let me know. He wasn't stupid, the police weren't liked in this area.

I turned toward Kevin and told him to pack up their clothes, that we were moving to a better place.

"Is there going to be a TV at our new house?" Lisa asked.

"Yeah baby, I'm going to make sure you got a TV," I said.

"Yippee," she shouted in excitement and jumped up and down in circles.

There was no doubt in my mind that I wouldn't be able to keep my promise because I had the drugs and money to keep good on my promise to her and if all else fails, I had the H-K and .45 to pick up any slack in my slipping.

"Jewel, let's go to the bathroom and check out what we came up on," I said leading the way.

I emptied everything on the bathroom floor that was in the duffel bag. Jewel pulled from her pocket six gold chain ropes and three men's rings. One of the rings had diamond studs in a horse shoe. I told her to put that junk back into her pocket because that's all it was to me. My mind was on the money that I had found. I removed all the bills from the large plastic sandwich bag which was mostly all tens and twenties and the rest hundreds. I smiled up at Jewel while stacking the bills by their denomination and then counted each of the piles quickly. I was like a mathematician when it came to money, my mathematical skills were guaranteed to be precise. We had five thousand eight hundred and thirty dollars. I gave Jewel half of the money, but she told me to hold onto her part. So I stuffed the wads into both of my front pockets and we looked at the drugs and estimated that we could make an easy four grand off of it.

Life was now looking a lot better for the both of us. I examined the guns and gave Jewel a fast safety and operation lesson and then reloaded the guns.

"Can I keep this one too Boo?" Jewel asked holding up the pistol grip twelve gauge pump shot gun.

"Of course you can have that one. You can also have that thirty thirty if you want it. I have the ones I want."

"Thanks Boo," she said.

Jewel was sweet. She just needed someone to love her and have her back and she would be content.

"Jewel, we must be going so go get everything you want to keep because you're not coming back to this dump."

When Jewel and I walked out of the bathroom, Kevin didn't have anything in his hands. I asked him if he picked what he wanted to take he said "Yeah." And then I asked him what he was taking. He opened both of his hands and lifted his shoulders and said, "We don't have nothing." He was right, there wasn't much inside the small room.

Jewel packed a brown grocery bag full of clothes. I rambled through the dresser drawer. Jewel told me she wasn't taking anything in the dresser and that everything belonged to her mother. I searched anyways looking for pictures so I could see how Jewel's mother looked. I found nothing but some old letters in the bottom drawer. I figured I would hold onto them and read them later. Maybe there would be some addresses or phone numbers inside one of them that would help Jewel find her family.

I tried to close the drawer back, but it seemed to be falling off the track so I pulled it all the way out so I could set it back on course. I bent down on one knee to line the drawer up on the rollers and to my surprise there was a soft brown leather book laying on the floor. I removed it from its hiding spot. It was thick and heavy and kind of resembled an appointment book until I unbuckled its leather button strap and read a few lines of the first page that assured me was a diary. I looked around to see were Jewel was and noticed she was straightening up the bed and not paying me any attention. I quickly fastened the strap back and stuffed it into my duffel bag along with my

H-K semi-automatic gun. I wanted to read through the diary first just in case it had something that might hurt Jewel dearly. She was already hurting enough and didn't need anything to add onto her pain.

I was positive that the diary I had just found belonged to her mother. I placed the dresser drawer back onto its track and it slid right into the slot without a problem. Jewel finished cleaning up the place. I hadn't noticed that Tasha had been standing directly behind me watching the whole time I was fumbling with the bottom drawer. I was now sure that she had seen me find the diary but she didn't say anything. She just stared at me with a smile on her face while biting on her index fingernail. I smiled back at her and winked and she giggled.

"Boo, we ready to go?" Jewel announced standing with a knitted brown blanket underneath her arm where she had wrapped the guns up in.

She took one last look around the room then peeped out the window and assured me the coast was clear. I lagged behind everyone else so I could keep them in my full view. Tasha had done the same wanting to walk with me.

Jewel and I looked like two grown-ups on Halloween escorting the kids around the neighborhood to trick-or-treat. Jewel waved down a passing taxi before we made it down the street close to the alley we had been robbed at just an hour ago. I opened the door of the taxi so everyone could get in and then I followed closing the door behind me.

"Star Dust motel please," I requested to the driver and leaned back against the seat and stared out the side window. As we drove past the alley I saw Franko and his two friends still standing in the alley way. I leaned back to hide my face as if they would have recognized me watching them as we passed them by.

The taxi pulled up at the Star Dust motel parking lot that was just four blocks away from Jewel's old motel room. The scenery was a big change from where we had just left. There was green grass and huge trees that was neatly manicured. Its parking lot was well lit and the outside of the building was nicely decorated. There was two swimming pools and a club house available for the renter's use and there was twenty four hour security that patrolled the estate premises.

"Everyone wait in the car until I come back," I said.

"Can I go with you Boo?" Tasha asked softly. The sight of her innocent look found my heart's weak spot and I couldn't deny her.

"Yeah, you can come," I said opening the door and stepping out.

Tasha and I walked into the office of the motel. Two beeps sounded off as we entered the door. It was the alarm that alarms the employee that someone was entering or exiting the office.

The office was made of glass windows, but at night from the outside it looked as though the windows were tinted. There was a small waiting area with three love seats and two lazy boy chairs for customers and a counter that was enclosed by Plexiglas window. I walked up to the window and requested to rent a three bedroom motel room for a month. The heavy set white lady said that it would be six hundred and fifty dollars and a one hundred and twenty five dollar deposit. I pulled out my wad and peeled off eight franklins and pushed it toward the hole that was in the glass.

"I'm going to need to see I.D. sir," the woman said.

I knew that was going to be a problem. I didn't have any I.D. and if I did I wouldn't have presented it to her so she could see my age and notice that I was too young to rent a motel room. I played it off by patting my pockets as if I may have misplaced it. I replied with a disturbed expression on my face, "I'm sorry ma'am, but I must have packed my wallet in one of my luggage's which has my I.D.s in it. Little momma, have you seen daddy's wallet?" I said trying to sound convincing to the lady as I looked toward Tasha. Tasha shook her head no. I saw that she was taught well because she played right along with my deceitful tactic.

"What a pretty little girl you have, I wouldn't never guess you were a father." I gave a cold stare toward the woman wondering what she was trying to say before she could clean it up.

"I'm not trying to insinuate anything other than you look too young to have a child, but don't worry about the I.D. just fill out the rental forms and sign here." She pointed at the end of the paper that was marked with an x that she wrote on the form. I quickly filled out the paperwork in a fictitious name and slid it back to her. She tore of the carbon copy and pushed it toward me with my change and two keys that was connected to a blue hard plastic hexagon shaped key ring that featured the room number. I swiftly grabbed the items and gave Tasha the change, her eyes widened at the twenty and five dollar bill.

"That's yours little momma, put it in your pocket." She thanked me with a hug around my waist and we thanked the lady and headed out the door.

The taxi driver was sitting patiently with his meter running. I pulled out my wad and peeled off two twenties and told him to wait until we came back. I motioned for everyone to get out of the car and we headed for room 102. There wasn't any stairs to climb and I was glad about that, me and stairs just didn't get along.

I keyed the door and stepped into the spacious living room that was already furnished and had a thirty two inch color television sitting on a swivel on the wall. The kids went wild running to turn on the TV and to admire the room. I checked every room to assure myself that no one was lurking inside. That was just me, always paranoid about a lot of things.

I swung the duffle bag off my shoulder and onto the bed and told Jewel and the kids to lets go. Jewel threw the blanket with the guns onto the bed and we headed back into the taxi after I secured the door.

"To the nearest Walmart," I told the driver. I allowed the kids to shop for a few toys while Jewel and I shopped for the necessities. I forked out seventeen hundred dollars on all our items. We all had gotten three outfits each, two pairs of shoes, pajamas and underclothes to last a full week. Tasha wasn't interested in toys, she wanted books. So I got her an Oxford dictionary, two books on law, crossword puzzles and a coloring book with coloring pencils. I had also picked up two books for Big Dee since I saw they had her favorites in stock, "Red Beans and Dirty Rice for the Soul" and "Bound by Loyalty". The two books she had been trying to get a copy of for the longest time, but no book stores could seem to keep them on their shelves. I was sure the gifts would brighten her day. I got a PlayStation and a few games for myself. Jewel picked up two pair of gloves and all the toiletries and other necessities she felt was needed along with some food items.

On our way back to the motel room I had the taxi driver stop at Mickey-D's and we all ordered super-size Big Mac value meals. I even treated the taxi driver to a value meal. He dropped us off back at the motel and I paid him his fare. He looked up at me expecting a tip. The only tip he was going to get from me was to drive safe. I needed to hold onto every dime I had and being freely giving to someone who had a steady income wouldn't sit well in my heart being that Jewel and I were surviving off the fat of the land hustling.

I thanked the man after he gave me my change, then Jewel, me and the kids hurried into the motel room with all the bags in hand to get settled in. The kids were so excited about their new living quarters and gifts that they seemed to have forgotten about being hungry. Tasha eased her body right underneath my left arm with the dictionary in her hand where I was sitting on the couch leaning over the wooden coffee table eating and began reading the words and meanings from it. I was shocked at how well she could read. She stopped every now and then to ask how to pronounce a certain word and I even fumbled over the words pronunciation. Jewel sat at the small dinner table picking over her food. Lisa was knelt down in the middle of the floor with a Barbie doll between her legs brushing its hair. Benny and Jewlean were putting together an electric race track while Kevin played the PlayStation. Everyone had something to keep them entertained for the time being. I slurped the last of my soda and leaned back onto the couch. Tasha stuck to me like glue.

I started adding up all the money in my mind I just spent within the last few hours. Jewel's and I's wad was quickly fading away although I still had over two grand left, but my pockets were feeling a little light. I was ready to go hustle some of the drugs off, plus I really didn't feel comfortable having drugs laying around the house with the kids there.

It was getting late and Jewel cut everyone's excitement short and demanded that everyone bathe and put their pajamas on and get to bed. She saw to it that the girls took their bath first and led them into the room she picked for them to occupy and tucked them into bed. I had dozed off to sleep. She waken me when she began to unlace my shoes to remove them.

"What's up Jewel?" I raised up quickly. I had always been a light sleeper, especially when I wasn't sleeping at my own house.

"Boo, I was trying to take off your shoes so you could be more comfortable," she said. I looked around the living room and seen that the T.V. was off and everything was neat.

"Where's the kids?" I asked. She told me they were all in bed. She asked me if I wanted her to run me some bath water. I told me no, that we needed to try and go get off those drugs.

"Tonight?" she asked in a disgusted voice.

"Yes, tonight."

"Come on then, let's go," she replied calmly.

I went into the bedroom and put the wad underneath the mattress and grabbed the sacks of drugs and put them in my sweatshirt pocket and then felt the small of my back to make sure the .45 was still there. I relaced my shoes and put on a pair of the black leather gloves Jewel had got us. She put on her old beat down Nikes and the Arizona jacket and slipped her hands into a pair of gloves and then tossed a baseball cap on her head backwards. We headed out locking all the locks on the door. We walked toward where she used to live. We decided that would be the best area to sell the drugs since that's where all the drug addicts hung out and come to purchase their dope.

We both had forgotten about what we did to Fat Clayman, my mind was on making money and Jewel was content being in my company. I told her we were going to sell the ten dollar pieces of crack cocaine for five dollars and the twenty pieces for ten. Everything was going to be sold for half. That way we would get all the clientele and sell out faster because word on the streets would spread that we were giving up love. She was down with it and said she knew just the spot we could set up shop for the night.

As we approached the corner street just before the alley we saw Franko and his boys still hanging out. They were also hustling dope but a totally different kind than we had. They were pushing dog food better known as heroin. They didn't see us as we were approaching them.

"Boo, don't even say nothing or look at them fools. Just keep on walking even if they say something to us," Jewel said. She must have noticed that I had now become fidgety and my eyes stayed focused on Franko and his two comrades.

I knew me all too well. I wasn't about to let what happened to me earlier go. I had a major problem with someone taking or trying to take something from me and they had taken my money, switchblade, my picture of Big Dee and had humiliated me in front of Jewel and that was eating at my pride and dignity.

"Jewel catch my back, I'm about to see if Franko is interested in taking this dope off our hands for a cool price," I said.

"No Boo, you know he's going to try and take it from us."

"Don't worry about that. You just make sure you're ready to blast they ass if any foul shit goes down."

Jewel didn't like my idea of trying to do business with Franko. She knew how Franko conducted business and it wasn't on the up and up. So she rested her hands inside her jacket pockets and gripped the handle of the .38 tightly in her right hand with her finger resting on the trigger just in case she had to make a quick move she could shoot through the jacket.

I called Franko's name just to warn him that I was approaching. They all turned and looked up at me with surprised expressions.

"Say Franko, I have something you might be interested in taking off my hands," I said.

They all stared at me with caution. I knew Franko's kind too well.

He was greedy and the curiosity of needing to know what I had would only flare up his greed much more and bring down his defense to any potential dangers.

"So what brings you back to see me so soon? I'm glad to see that you're not harboring any bad feelings toward me about what happened earlier. You know that wasn't personal, it was only business. So what is it you have for me that's so urgent?" Franko said.

"Do you have a place where we can go and talk and I can show you what I have?" I said.

Franko paused for a moment and stared into my eyes and started back pedaling into the alley way.

"This is my office so let me see what it is you have for me."

I reached into my sweatshirt pocket and tossed Franko both bags of drugs. He smiled at the large amounts of the product and said, "Now, who you two done robbed for all these goods?"

"Never mind that, Franko, give me two grand for all that and it's yours. You know that's a cool price for all that I'm giving up. You will make four times what I'm asking for, if not more," I said.

"You right little man, I will. It's well worth what you're asking for, but the only problem is, since I already have it in my hands, then it must belong to me."

"What you mean about that, Franko?" I asked knowing exactly what he was saying.

"What's wrong boy, you can't read between the lines? I'm not paying for nothing that's already mines, that's what I meant," he snapped harshly at me.

I swiftly removed the .45 from the small of my back and pointed it directly into his face. His eyes widened with fear. Jewel brandished her .38 at the other two men keeping them from trying to make an advance from behind.

"Toss me my shit back bitch and while you at it, break yourself!" I replied cold bloodedly. "And you chumps get over next to this punk and do the same. And hurry up before I start feeding you a few of these shells!"

They quickly moved to stand by Franko and slowly emptied their pockets. I demanded them to get on their knees and cross their legs and interlock their fingers behind their head the way the police had done me several times in the past.

"Youngster, I was just joking," Franko said, "You can't take a joke, I was going to give you the two grand for the work."

I knew he was lying. He was only talking out of fear now. He hadn't expected for Jewel and I to have weapons. I'm pretty positive he thought we were empty handed and stupid for even coming back around to try and make a deal with him. He just knew he had a couple of marks.

"Sure you was chump, that's why I'm going to take it now. I never had any intentions of selling you shit anyways chump, that was just my tactic to get your greedy ass off guard so I could get up on you," I admitted.

I searched their pockets to make sure they had emptied out all the contents from them. I noticed neither of them had much money on them and I hadn't found the gun on Franko that he pulled on Jewel and I earlier. I punched Franko in the middle of his back with my left hand. His back arched as he yelled in pain.

"Where is your stash spot? And this is the only time I'm going to ask, then I'm going to start filling you with hot slugs!" I said angrily.

Before he could speak one of his comrades spoke up.

"It's right over there by the dumpster under a small cardboard box," he said turning his head in the direction to where the hiding spot was.

"Shut your damn mouth Raymond, you know I'm going to make you pay dearly for ratting off my hiding spot!" Franko exclaimed cold bloodedly.

I told Jewel to check up under the box. She lifted it up and immediately began filling her pockets. Once she got all that was there she brought me the gun that Franko pulled on us earlier.

"Well Franko, I guess you got the end of the stick this time. I believe this would make us even."

I hauled off and kicked him in his narrow ass as hard as I could, sending him crawling in pain. I placed my .45 back in the small of my back and released two consecutive kicks to Franko's side that flipped him over onto his back. He stared up at me with squinted eyes. I pulled the slide back on the gun injecting a round into its chamber and pointed the barrel down toward his face and said, "Apologize to me, punk."

"I'm sorry, man."

"That I already know. Now apologize to my girl for disrespecting her and her moms."

He apologized to us both and begged me not to kill him. I told him that I wasn't, but he kept on begging for his life and I got tired of hearing his voice so I popped four slugs into his face that brought him to a silence. The other two men tried to get up and run, but Jewel quickly domed them, not even giving them a chance to make it to their feet.

Jewel swooped up the items off the ground and we made our way back toward our motel room. Hustling was out of the question for the night.

CHAPTER 5

Jewel and I returned back to our motel room. We quietly eased our way into the master bedroom and shut the door behind us. Jewel emptied her pockets onto the bed and then liberated herself from the Arizona jacket that had her sweating underneath its thick lining. She let it fall to the floor where she stood now fanning herself with her gloves. I removed my sweatshirt and took the drugs from its pocket and set them on the bed, then balled the sweatshirt up and tossed it in the corner so I could wash it later to get rid of any gun powder residue that I was sure had gotten on the sleeve when I had fired the gun.

I dropped the clip and jacked the gun off to release the loaded round from its chamber and laid it down on the floor.

"I'll be back, I'm going to check up on the kids," Jewel said before exiting the bedroom. I hadn't asked her where she was going and really didn't care at that moment. But I guess she just felt the need to tell me anyways for whatever reason of her own. I noticed that about her. She always felt the need to tell me what she was about to do or thought about doing to see if I would approve or disapprove of her actions. I ambled to the bed to see what we came up on.

"Damn!" I cursed out loud to myself at the sight of all the heroin and money. I picked one of the four huge rolls of money and shuffled through it. Jewel walked back into the room and asked what was wrong. She had heard me curse while she was in the living room.

I didn't even attempt to respond to her question. "Come over here and help me count this money," I said excitedly.

"Boo, how much money do you think this is?" she asked.

"I don't know, but whatever it is, it's not bad at all for a few minutes of work."

"You got that right," she replied with cheerful words. We counted the money in complete silence and the only sound that could be heard was the running bathwater Jewel was preparing for me in the bathroom. We had just knocked Franko and his boys off for eighteen grand and a big lump of heroin that gave off a weird odor, like vinegar. Neither Jewel nor I had ever sold heroin, so neither of us could estimate what it was worth. From the sight of it, it looked like hard brown candy.

"I'll be back, I have to make sure your bathwater don't run over," Jewel said leaving the room again. There she goes again telling me what she was about to do, I thought to myself. By the time she returned I had everything put up except the money I had split down the middle and stacked into two piles.

"Pick one, a woman shouldn't never be broke and should know how to manage her own money," I said.

She gave me a look of disapproval but removed one of the stacks from the bed and I did the same with the remaining one, then ambled off to take my bath.

When I walked into the bathroom I noticed Jewel had laid out for me some new underclothes and pajamas on top of the toilet seat and had me a new toothbrush, a bottle of lotion, deodorant and some mint dental floss neatly lined on top of the sink counter. I then realized that I didn't ask her to run me any bath water and thought to myself, What makes her think I was going to stay the night, anyways, to be laying out some pajamas for me? I didn't even wear pajamas and the only reason why I bought them was because Jewel insisted that I get them since everyone else was getting some. But I was tired as hell. I had a long exciting day and a prosperous one at that. So I decided I might as well spend the night and get up in the morning and go visit Big Dee. I soaked in the tub for a few hours. It wasn't intentional but I had fallen asleep. Jewel knocked on the bathroom door and awakened me.

"What are you going to do Boo, sleep in there?" she asked, not knowing that's what I was doing before she knocked on the door.

"I'm on my way out now."

She had already bathed in the master bathroom. I dressed in my two piece pajama set and headed out into the living room where I found jewel sitting on the couch wrapped up in a blanket watching TV with her thumb in her mouth.

What the…! I didn't even bother to roast her about sucking her thumb, but if I hadn't seen it with my own eyes I would have never guessed that she sucked her thumb.

"Come on over here and watch the movie with me."

"Jewel, I'm tired. I don't know if I'll be able to stay up and watch a movie with you and that's real. Ain't you tired? If not, you should be, because I'm beat down. Plus I need to get some rest because I got to go visit Big Dee tomorrow."

"What time are we visiting Big Dee tomorrow?" she asked, inviting herself to go see my home girl.

I hadn't asked her to accompany me to go see Big Dee and I didn't know how Big Dee would react if I brought someone she didn't know with me to invade her privacy. I wasn't about to disrespect my best friend like that, so I told Jewel in the gentlest way I knew that it would be best for me to visit alone. I hadn't had the opportunity to tell Big Dee about Jewel because of what had taken place.

"Well Boo, how bout I just come along with you anyways and just wait in the visiting room until you finish visiting with your friend?" Jewel was insistent. She had thought of a way she could come along and not upset Big Dee.

"No!" I snapped harshly, unintentionally. "I'll just go by myself."

She stared at me with an open mouth with her thumb resting on her bottom lip.

"Okay, gosh, you don't have to be so mean about it. I just wanted to hang out with you, but if you're going to get bent out of shape like that, then I'm cool."

I knew I had hurt Jewel's feelings but I wasn't about to apologize for snapping on her like I did. She would soon learn that when I get tired I become grumpy as hell.

I went and sat down next to her. She unloosened the blanket from around her and opened it wide so I could cover myself. She tucked her legs underneath her and pulled the blanket over her chest and shoulders then glanced over at me and stuck her thumb back into her mouth and continued watching TV. I knew I wasn't going to make it through the movie. I was sound asleep by the time the next commercial came on. I don't know what time Jewel fell asleep, but when I woke I found her snuggled up underneath me on the couch. She had a strawberry body fragrance on and I couldn't help but to inhale the fresh smell of her fragrance. I gazed at her while she slept and admired her beauty, then wrapped my arms around her and fell back asleep.

I heard Jewel's and my name being called one right after the other. Small cold hands slapped at my face with a mild roughness. I could have sworn that I was in a dream.

"Leave Boo and Julia alone, Lisa," Kevin demanded.

"No, you leave me alone. You can't tell me what to do." I heard the same lines being repeated over and over again. I opened my eyes and saw the palm of a small hand coming at me. I wasn't fast enough to avoid being assaulted by the small hand.

"What is it Lisa?" Jewel asked sleepily, intercepting the continuous slaps to my face.

"I'm hungry and no one won't fix me no cereal. Kevin said I had to ask first."

I looked up and saw Lisa standing over us crying with her baby doll clenched to her chest and Tasha leaning over the arm of the couch smiling down at us.

"Good morning Boo," Tasha said and I returned her greeting with a forced smile on my face.

"Kevin, Benny, Jewlean," I called out the names without looking to see who was awake. "Whoever is up, would you please fix your sister a bowl of cereal?" I said before Jewel could demand one of them to do it.

"Now Kevin. Ha-ha, you heard Boo. He said fix me some cereal," Lisa taunted agitatedly. I heard the video game pause.

"Don't touch nothing Benny, not until I come back. There's no bowls to make her any cereal," Kevin announced.

"Well, just clean out one of them McDonalds cups and put it in there," I said.

"There's some plastic bowls in there. I bought them last night. Look in the cabinet," Jewel said.

"Boo, can I read to you?" Tasha asked.

"Yeah, in a minute when I get up, okay?"

Tasha nodded her head.

Jewel turned toward me and said, "Good morning," and kissed me on the lips unexpectedly. "I thought you was going to stay up and watch a movie with me. You was asleep as soon as you laid your head back on the couch."

"I told you I was tired. What you thought, I was playing? And what was that kiss for?" I asked.

"Because this was the first time in a long time that I had slept without having nightmares and waking up in a cold sweat. Being held in your arms, I felt loved and protected without worries so I wanted to give my angel a kiss to thank him. I'm going to get up and get your clothes ready," she said and rose from where we laid.

As soon as Jewel got up Tasha quickly took her place and began reading to me. I just laid there listening until I dozed back off to sleep.

I guess it didn't matter to Tasha if I was awake or asleep; she just wanted to read to me.

Jewel woke me and I went and groomed up, took a shower and got dressed. I stuffed my pockets with money and placed my heat in the small of my back and the other in my waist. Then grabbed my duffle bag and the two books I bought for Big Dee and caught a taxi to the hospital. All the kids stared with sad faces as I was walking out the room with my duffel bag. None of them asked where I was going. Even Jewel stood there with sad eyes like she didn't know where I was heading.

The taxi pulled up in the hospital parking lot. I paid the driver and strolled inside. I was seventeen minutes too early for my visit so I went to the gift shop and bought Big Dee some flowers, balloons and a teddy bear. They didn't have any lemon head candy, which was her favorite. I would have gotten her all she could eat of the sour sweet marble shaped candies.

Seventeen minutes had flown by like the blink of an eye. I was now ten minutes late, so I rushed out of the gift shop to the intensive care unit and signed in to visit. I had no problem getting in because one of the nurses in the front desk remembered who I was from the first time I came in. She smiled at me and asked if the flowers and balloons were for her. I matched her smile and said, "Only if you say yes to marrying me."

She lifted her hand in the air just above the counter so I could see the diamond ring on her finger. "I guess you know the answer to that question with your mannish self."

"So I guess you know the answer about these gifts with your fast self," I shot back. She was at a loss for words and just pointed toward the door, indicating that it was time for me to get pushing along about my business. I didn't take her actions too personally because I've known this was the norm for a sister to be demanding and aggressive and it was all meant in a good and humorous way.

Big Dee didn't notice me when I walked into her room. She laid watching soap operas in her bed that was propped up in a sitting position. She had on a hospital Johnny, open at the back.

"Hellooo, is it me your looking for?" I harmonized. She quickly turned her head when she heard my voice and tears immediately fell from her eyes as she reached out her arm for me to come close so she could hug me. I thought she was never going to turn me loose as she held me in her arms.

"Boy, I was worried sick about you. I love you a whole lot, Boo. I've asked all the nurses if they seen you in the waiting room and they said no. I thought you left me."

"Dee, could you please let me loose?" I said breathlessly. She released me from her tight hug and scooted over so I could sit on the side of the bed next to her. I gave her the gifts I bought her, except for the books. She took them and set them on top of her dresser next to her bed. She seemed not to care about the gifts because she didn't even take the time to admire them. *"Unappreciative heifer"*, I mumbled to myself.

"So are you going to tell me where you have been, or am I going to have to get out this bed and sling these dawgs at you until I get answers?" she asked jokingly.

I could tell that Big Dee was over excited to see me and for that reason she had forgotten about all of her problems and hurt.

"Just hold your horses woman. Can I first give you the gifts I have gotten you and get a kiss before you start acting like you are my momma or something? I'm gonna tell you where I've been."

"Well, I'm waiting," she snapped and then folded her arms over her huge breasts.

"Girl, don't be rushing me," I replied with a frown and then shot her a big smile and added, "First I need to know how you been holding up and feeling?"

"Can't you tell, Boo? I'm fine. I'm alive, aren't I?"

As I looked deep into her eyes, I saw my best friend was hurting deep inside and she was trying her best to hide her pain from me, but I knew her too well to be fooled. It would be foolish of me to think that she was okay, especially after what Jewel told me about the after effects of how the mind replays the attack over and over again. Plus, I had seen what Jewel had done to Fat Clayman for sexually assaulting her. She didn't even flinch when she blew his head off with the twelve gauge shot gun and she wasn't treated nearly as bad as Dee was. Also, I knew how Big Dee felt about someone taking something from her, and Flaco and them took something she could never get back. I knew in my heart she was not going to accept it and that is what I was worried about.

"Woman, I see that you are being difficult. If you have to know, I been out hustling with my new friend Jewel. Her real name is Julia Monevilay Perez."

"Your new friend? Where you meet this new friend at?"

"I met her the day I went job hunting. And why? What difference does it make where and when I met her? The fact is she's my friend and that's where I was last night."

"Boo, you don't have to cop no attitude. All I did was ask you a simple funky question about your little girlfriend you was hanging out with."

"Why is everyone keep saying she's my girlfriend? She's not my girl."

"Who is everyone that saying that, Boo? Has someone else said that to you other than me? Where is she? In the waiting room waiting for you to finish visiting me so y'all can run off together and you leave me here by myself again?" she said.

I realized that Big Dee was jealous of Jewel even though she had never met her. She didn't want to see another girl get my attention. This was the same way she acted when other girls tried to talk to me at the boys and girls club.

"Dee, why is you trying to piss me off? For one, I didn't leave you. They wouldn't allow me to come back here and see you when you got out of surgery. Plus you was heavily drugged and needed rest. So I went back to the house, cleaned it up, then went to Jewel's spot to hustle. We got to eat you know, plus she's in worse shape than we in. She's all alone with five mouths to feed and her mother just up one day and disappeared leaving her to attend to her brothers and sisters. Plus, she was also raped during the course of all this and what's so cold about it is she's only sixteen years old. I know what you thinking Dee, but you can get that thought out your head because she's not coming between our friendship."

"Who said I was thinking that, Boo? I never said nothing like that."

"Whatever Dee, I'm just saying, but check this out. I have something for you that you have been trying to get for the longest," I said and reached in my duffel bag and pulled out the two books and handed them to her. She had forgotten all about our argument when she saw the titles of her favorite books. She thanked me and opened up the "Red Beans and Dirty Rice for the Soul" book and read me one of its poems called "Togetherness." It was a beautiful poem I have to admit.

"Check this out Big Dee," I said reaching into my front pocket and pulling out one of my wads and holding it up so she could see it.

"Where did you get that from?" she asked excitedly in a whisper.

"Hustling, me and Jewel hit a lick and came up proper."

"I can see that," she said.

"This money is on us Dee. We can eat good now and don't have to be eating top ramens and hot dogs all the time. You can cook us some of that real Mexican food now and you know how much I love those homemade tortillas you be hooking up. Plus I'm going to take you shopping, but for right now here is a few dollars so you can buy whatever you want when you get out of here." I peeled off ten big-faced Franklins from my wad and handed them to her. "That's on you," I said.

She neatly folded the money and tucked it under her left bosom. I had always wondered why women with big breasts put their money there because my mother and aunts used to do the same thing.

Big Dee reached out her arms and told me to come and give her a big hug. I had to decline because I didn't feel like having the air squeezed out of me just yet. She didn't know her own strength and I had told her a long time ago that she had to stop hugging me so tightly.

Big Dee mentioned that she was hungry, so I ordered a large cheese pizza and two orders of Buffalo wings with two root beer sodas from Pizza Hut. Big Dee and I took the pizza down. I was too full to do anything else but sit down in a chair and try to get comfortable, which I did and Big Dee and I talked for hours.

The nurses came by and peeked into the room, waved and continued on about their business. Visiting hours had been over three and a half hours ago, but for some reason they weren't sweating me. Big Dee had told me that the police came by snooping around, but she stuck to her story about not being raped. They left a card with a detective's name and phone number and told her to call if she felt like talking.

The doctor told her she would be able to go home in a few days. I asked her if she knew where Flaco and his cousin lived. She said she knew where they all lived and gave me directions. I knew the area she described. I stood up and turned toward her, blocking the view of the entrance just in case someone walked into the room. Then I raised up my shirt and asked, "Is it on?"

She looked down at my waist and saw the handle of the gun I had used to pop Franko with last night. She looked up at me and said, "Most definitely."

I smiled at her response and she returned my smile. I let my shirt fall back down and reclaimed my seat. There wasn't anything else that needed to be said concerning that matter. We both knew what was up.

We watched two movies together that came on BET and by the time the third one came on Big Dee was sound asleep. It was past eleven o'clock and I hadn't noticed that the new shift came on. I thought they were going to tell me I had to leave, but the nurses came in and spoke then ambled onto their next destination.

I wasn't tired so I pulled out the diary from my duffel bag and began reading. It read:

"This is the property of Julia Christina Perez. Target: Story of my life events. Aim: to make a better life for my children. Thoughts: they change by the second. Chapter: this is the eighth diary of my life. The other seven complete diaries were left behind at my mother's home in New York. I hid them in the back of my father's tool shed that he no longer used."

I now had a lead on the whereabouts of Jewel's family on her mother's side plus her mother's full name and the area where she hid the other diaries. All I needed now was an address and a phone number and we would be in business. I continued on reading.

"I've found the willpower to escape from an abusive man who I thought I was in love with. Chad Mason was his name. He used to beat my ass for any little reason he could think of. He hated my kids because they all resembled their biological father, Larry Kevin Ridley, who was my first and only honest true love who treated me like I was the most precious woman on earth.

Chad used to come home drunk and shoot me up with heroin and then rape me continuously. I feared that he would soon do Julia like that because she was beginning to fill out as a little woman and I couldn't allow my daughter to go through that. But I needed Chad mainly for the heroin. I had become addicted within a matter of weeks and didn't even know it. My entire body would ache and I would be in pain and I couldn't get out of bed. Chad had to know what he was doing to me because he no longer had to force the drug into my arm. I did it willingly. He was controlling me with the drug. I even had sex with three of his friends at the same time as he watched them use and abuse me, then right after he beat me viciously. He would say I cheated on him with his friends. Once he got tired of beating me he would toss me a ten dollar bag of heroin so I could shoot up. I would shoot the heroin and it would take away all my pain and worries. I allowed this to go on for several years because I looked forward to getting that heroin sack right after the beatings. I started to care less and less about nothing and no one but the heroin. While Chad would be at work I would go out to turn a trick or two to buy heroin because the amount of heroin he would give me was not doing anything to me to get rid of my sickness."

Damn. I cursed as I thought about how heroin could be so controlling over a person's life. I thought crack was a cold blooded drug, but reading what Jewel's mother had written about heroin had me thinking twice. I began to wonder if I should ever let Jewel read her mother's diary although she was entitled to know about her mother. So who was I to keep her from knowing? I asked myself.

I quickly closed the book and hid it under my right thigh when I heard Big Dee roll over in bed and call my name. She looked over at me and saw that I was still there. Then she smiled at me and rolled over and went back to sleep. I assumed she had awakened from a nightmare. I waited until I heard her light snores before I started reading the diary again. Some of the handwriting was so poor that I wasn't able to make it out but I guessed that she might have written those parts of the diary when she was high, so I skipped to the part that was written neatly.

"Chad came home Friday evening with two friends I had never seen before. They sat at the kitchen table sniffing lines of coke and talking. Chad called Julia to the kitchen and introduced her to the two men and told her to go take a shower and put on some nice clothes. I overheard them talking about who was going to have sex with her first. Chad told them he wanted an ounce of powder and two grams of heroin for him to allow them to have sex with my daughter. I walked into the kitchen and Chad told me to go back into the room and don't come out until he said I could.

"Julia was in the shower, not knowing what was about to happen to her. I went in the room and cried not knowing how I could stop Chad and the two men from hurting my daughter. I knew I had to do something, so I picked up Chad's work axe and entered the kitchen. I had hidden it in the small of my back. Chad jumped up from his chair and slapped me in the face for disobeying him. That's when I hit him in the side of

the neck with the axe, then one of the other men in the back of his neck and before the other guy realized what was going on I caught him in the head with the axe. I don't remember how I had gotten the butcher knife in my hand, but I stabbed all three of the bastards until they were dead.

"It happened so quickly. I couldn't let them hurt my daughter. I don't know where I found the will to do such a thing. I guess it came from my deep Puerto Rican bloodline to protect my family at any means. I removed the drugs and money from all of their pockets and got Julia out of the shower and the rest of my kids and we went out the back door. I didn't want them to see what I had just done. We left everything behind. I couldn't risk being taken away from my kids and going to prison, so we left New York heading for Las Vegas.

"During our travel, I used the heroin I took off the guys to keep the monkey off my back and through the states I sold the coke to get food and pay for motel rooms. We hitchhiked most of the way and then I came across this trick and stole his van and wallet with his credit cards and I drove the rest of the way to Vegas. I figured no one would look for me there. Plus Larry's family stayed in LA, only four hours away from Vegas, so I could take the kids to their grandmother's house if I needed to.

"I hated Larry for leaving me. Ever since he went to prison my life has been shit. If he was to see me now he would be so ashamed of me because he taught me better. I hadn't written or sent him any pictures of the kids since he'd been in prison and I was sure he wouldn't forgive me for that. He loves his kids and me more than anything on this earth and here I ran off with another man when times got tough, a man who didn't care about me, who beat me daily, abused me mentally, kept me confined in a house like I was a prisoner, forced me to sell my body and purposely got me strung out on dope. I couldn't even hold strong for Larry when he needed me the most because I was too damn selfish and blamed him for killing the man who broke into our home and tied us all up and tried to rape me, but Larry somehow freed himself and beat the man to death with his hands.

"I never could understand why my parents hated Larry.

They felt he was going to be the death of me and right after his incarceration for murdering the man in order to protect his family my parents really laid into me about Larry that I'd heard so many times. I didn't bother to stick around and denied them seeing their grandkids. That's when I ended up with Chad, who started off being a complete gentlemen, but Larry always schooled me to watch out for those types of people. He was very street smart and taught me to be the same, but I had become too blind, dumb and hateful to all the things he taught me just because I was hurting so deeply inside that he was no longer in my life and I blamed him for it, because he didn't have to beat that man to death.

"Me and the kids have been living out of motel rooms in Las Vegas. I couldn't shake the monkey off my back and my kids noticed that I was sick all the time. I hustled the streets to support my family, mainly my heroin habit, but I was quickly falling short of being a good mother. I even began taking Julia and Kevin out to hustle with me. I taught them how to steal, sell drugs, rob tricks and when to lure them into an alley behind a building. I even taught them how to fight. I was exceptionally hard on Julia because she was a young lady and needed to know how to protect herself so I taught her how to use a pocket knife the same way her father had shown me.

"We had been in Las Vegas for four years living in and out of motel rooms and I was not getting any better with my drug habit. I stopped the kids from accompanying me with my hustles. All our holidays and birthdays were the same, nothing different than the last but a few used books that I made Julia read to the kids. She made them all read three full pages to everyone each day. That was a rule that she forced on her sibling's.

"Julia became more of a mother figure than I actually was. I wrote Larry for the first time in four years. After the third letter I received from him, I up and moved so he wouldn't send any of his people to Vegas and take our kids. I told him about my habit but didn't say anything about the abuse that Julia and I went through. That would for sure spark his rage of hatred and who knows, he might have had some of his LA gangster friends try and kill me because I allowed his daughter to be abused by another man. I had no

doubts about that's what he would do."

I closed the diary when a funny looking doctor with a long nose and silver clipboard came walking into the room to awaken Big Dee. He hadn't noticed me sitting in the chair and I hadn't noticed that I had been reading so long. The early morning light had pushed the night away. So that's how Jewel learned how to fight and hustle. Her mother taught her the tricks of the trade and that also explained how Tasha knows how to read so well and is so smart, but since I've been around Jewel I never recalled her making any of the other kids read anything to each other. I guessed that was because I hadn't been around them long enough to see that.

My mind wondered off to the letters I found in the dresser. Could they be the letters that Jewel's mother mentioned that she had received from Larry in prison? If so, then I had the letters with me but I decided to wait and check them out when I was alone. I was easing the diary back into my duffel bag when I heard the doctor telling Big Dee that he was going to release her today.

Now that was music to my ears. I hadn't anticipated it being so soon. From what Big Dee said, it was going to be a few days, so I figured that meant about three more days from then, but today was perfectly fine with me. I had no complaints.

I began planning the day out. First I will take her shopping for a couple of outfits and get her hair and nails done. She would like that. Then go and eat at Olive Garden; they had the bomb salad and Italian dishes plus you could get the strawberry daiquiri without the alcohol there. I loved the sweet flavored icy drink; it tasted just like Kool-Aid to me. Then we'll go catch a movie at a cinema in one of the casinos.

Yeah, that's the plan, I assured myself and stood up to stretch out my arms and say good morning to Big Dee. The doctor had given her a small piece of paper with a bunch of scribbling on it. I removed it gently from her hand, glanced at it and noticed that it was only a prescription for medication that he wanted her to take.

I told her I would go get the prescription filled on the second floor and to be dressed by the time I came back. I picked up my duffel bag, put the prescription in my front pocket and headed out the door.

When I came back Big Dee was ready to go. She told me she had called us a taxi. That was fast thinking for the both of us because I had totally forgotten that we didn't have any transportation to get around. We strolled out of the hospital. The taxicab was just pulling up and the driver was looking around for his customers. I waved at him and he stopped.

We got in and Big Dee told him the address. She wanted to go home first and take a bath before going shopping. That was understandable because she did smell like the hospital.

When we got to Big Dee's flat her mother was there. She was in the kitchen cooking and the strong smell of chilies welcomed us as we walked inside. Big Dee's mother rambled off in Spanish to her not knowing that I understood every word she just said. She had never known that Big Dee taught me how to speak Spanish over the years we had been friends. Big Dee turned toward me, smiled, than winked an eye. I knew exactly why she did it; it went back to what she had told me a long time ago; don't let people know that I know Spanish because I could learn a lot about how others really felt or who was trying to talk behind my back. So I played dumb as if I didn't understand any of the words and sat down on the sofa. It was good that I had cleaned the house up because me and Big Dee weren't expecting her mother to show up any time soon being that she had been gone for so long.

She told Dee that she had just returned from Columbia on a business trip for her new job and some sort of rebel group, guerrillas, had kidnapped her and about twenty five others. She only got released when her company had paid the ransom the guerrillas had requested.

Big Dee didn't know anything about her mother having a new job traveling around the world, conducting business for the company, that's why she was gone from home so much. The man who she had seen her mother with was her business partner who traveled with her.

Big Dee had me believing that her mother had abandoned her to live with another man just to get her freak on, but looking at it from Big Dee's point of view, that's how it would also seem to me if my mother never told me anything and was always seen leaving with the same man I had known nothing about. Her mother hadn't asked Big Dee where she had been or if she was okay. So I assumed that she had just come home a few hours ago and no one had contacted her about her daughter being in the hospital and Dee didn't even attempt to let her know.

"Hello Boo," Dee's mother said to me in English. "I see you and Dee been running the streets together. I kinda figured she would be calling you when she hadn't heard from me. So how's your grandmother?" she asked.

Her question caused me to choke up on my words. Dee's mother wasn't aware of my grandmother's death. "She just passed away," I blurted out. She dried her hands on her cooking apron and came over to where I sat and hugged me. She hugged me just like Big Dee would have, clasping me to her soft breasts so strong and tight that it seemed to stop my flow of air. I then knew where Big Dee got all her strength from. She released her back breaking hug and kissed me on the forehead and then stood up and returned to the kitchen.

Big Dee was in the bathroom running some bath water. Her mom brought me a plate of food. She didn't even ask if I was hungry. It was one of my favorite dishes; jalapeño beef fajitas with homemade flour tortillas and baked chili rellenos. The rellenos were large jalapeno peppers sliced in half and seeded with shredded Monterey jack and cheddar cheese. The pepper halves were then baked. It was the bombs with mild salsa.

Big Dee used to hook this dish up for me all the time. I took a bite of the fajita and tears immediately came streaming down my cheeks from the burning heat in my mouth and throat. I felt beads of sweat form on my forehead and chest. My lips and mouth were throbbing like a bad headache. I took another bite because the food was bomb; good taste but hot as hell.

I couldn't take the pain anymore so I dashed for the kitchen sink and stuck my mouth under the faucet and let the cold water run over my tongue and a little down my throat, but the burning didn't stop.

"Momma, you know Boo can't eat hot food like us! Why you didn't make his mild?" Big Dee snapped coldly in disapproval of her mother giving me food that was too hot for the devil himself to be eating. Big Dee had never made my food with so much kick. This stuff made your insides feel like you were on fire.

"Oh, I didn't know honey. I thought that I did make it mild for him."

Thought my ass. I wanted to say to Dee's mother. She damn near killed me with a chili pepper. I learned my lesson not to eat any of her cooking again.

Big Dee stood over me, rubbing my back. She felt the handle of the other gun I had in the small of my back and she made sure my shirt didn't come up to expose it. I wasn't about to eat any more food on my plate so Big Dee asked if she could have it and took the plate with her into the bathroom.

I sat back down on the sofa praying that my mouth would stop burning.

"Boo, where you and Dee heading to?" her mother asked, trying to strike up a conversation.

"We probably go walking around the mall to look at some of the new stuff that's out and check out the arcade games," I said, not really wanting to expose the real. I didn't really want to be bothered, but I'm sure she was going to keep probing.

"So what's the deal with you and my daughter? I know you both are good friends, but good friends turn into other things like boy and girl friends. You two hasn't reached that stage yet, have you?"

I was shocked at her line of questioning. I didn't even know where she was trying to take this, but I was way too sharp to fall victim to old school slickness. If only she had known how fast I could have her head spinning she wouldn't be bothering me with such silly questions, but I figured I'll play her little game.

"Me and Big Dee are best friends. I truly do love your daughter with all my heart like a sister. I'm loyal to her like no other person I know. If I was to become Dee's boyfriend you would be the second person to know after I told God and thanked Him for blessing me with such a beautiful girl who I would cherish, and then we would come to you so you would know our decision was made together and of course you will know that there will come a time we would want to explore each other's anatomy. But the fact is me and your daughter can sleep in the same bed without any type of sexual chemistry. We both were taught by good parents the morals of life and we have chosen to wait until we are married before we venture into sex," I said with convincing words. I saw in her eyes that she bought my drag about choosing to wait to have sex.

"Oh, darling how beautifully put that was. You have my blessings as a son-in-law if you two ever decided to grow up and get married."

"Mom, what? What you just told Boo?" Big Dee asked as she walked into the living room and overheard the conversation. "Why is you trying to marry me off to my best friend? Boo don't like me like that and we don't even talk about anything on that level, mom, okay?"

"I was just telling Boo he was the type of young man that would have my blessings to take my daughter's hand in marriage when you older."

"Mom, you buggin'. Well, my future husband, let's go before my mother run you off with talk of marriage."

"And where are you heading off to young lady?"

I had just told Big Dee's mother that we were going to the mall, but I guess she was asking Big Dee to see if I had told her the truth.

"Mom, me and Boo was going to go to the mall."

Her mother smiled down at me and reached into her bosom and gave Big Dee some money. Although she didn't need it she took it anyways.

"Boo, you take care of her, you hear?" her mother said. I waved and closed the door. We caught the bus to the mall and bought matching outfits, then took pictures. She got her nails done and we ate Chinese food instead of Olive Garden. We went go cart racing and then bowling and hadn't had time to catch a movie. We decided to go see a movie tomorrow.

We took the bus back to her flat. She liked riding the bus over taking a taxi, I didn't ask why. She hadn't taken any of the medication like the doctor prescribed and I had gotten on her case about that, but like always she didn't take me seriously.

The bus dropped us off two blocks from her flat. We strolled down the street with our shopping bags and I had my duffle bag hanging over my shoulder. The streetlights had just come on. The full light of the evening hadn't gone from the sky yet. We saw a group of guys and girls hanging out, smoking weed, drinking and listening to music. Some were playing, running in and out of the apartments laughing and giggling at each other.

We made our way across the deadened grass yards to her apartment. She keyed the lock and we headed to her room. I tossed the bags I was carrying onto the bed and lay down with my left leg resting on the floor. I noticed Big Dee acting skittish.

"Home girl, what's up with you? You're not acting like yourself," I said as she stood fumbling with a plastic bag she had in her hand.

"Boo, they hurt me really bad. They did things to me that I haven't told you about and when I seen them it brought all the bad memories back."

"Seen them?" I replied coldly. "Dee, you seen who? Joker and them? Where and when?"

"Boo, that was all them at that apartment where all those other people was. Joker seen us and ran into the apartment."

Damn, where was I when Dee seen all this, I thought to myself.

I raised up from the bed, locked the bedroom door and told her to put on that new black cotton sweat suit I had bought her at the mall and find a pair of gloves. I quickly undressed and slid into a matching pullover sweat suit. I put on the gloves that Jewel had gotten me, tied a black dew rag around my head then dropped the clips of both .45's to make sure they were fully loaded. I tucked one in the small of my back and handed Big Dee the other. I then removed my H-K (Heckler and Koch, a small sub machine gun) from the duffle bag with two extra clips, laid it on the bed and quickly folded my clothes and stuffed them in the bag.

Big Dee stared at the H-K. She didn't know I had the automatic weapon. "Boo, where you get that from?" she asked.

I didn't reply but I saw it in her face, now she knew why I toted the duffle bag with me everywhere I went.

"You remember how to use one of them, don't you?" I asked pointing at the gun in her hand.

"Come on now Boo, of course I do," she assured me.

"Listen home girl. Whatever happens tonight, we both don't know anything because there ain't no turning back. We going to get everyone who gets in our way; no exceptions, no regrets, no feelings, right?" I asked looking up at her.

"Right," she said.

"Well, let's shake on it, we will take what we about to do to our graves and never tell another soul." She shook my hand in agreement, moved close to me and kissed me deeply. She took me by surprise and I hadn't made any attempt to stop her. I just kissed her back until she pulled away from my lips.

"What was that all about?" I asked.

"I'm just letting my future husband know I've always loved him and had the biggest crush on him from the first time we met," she admitted.

That explained why she didn't want other girls around me, I thought to myself.

"Girl you trippin'. Let's take care of this business so we can come back and you can re-braid my hair for me. You know it's looking messed up," I said trying to think of something to say to avoid confronting the kiss she had just laid on me. I emptied one of the shopping bags and put the H-K inside, then told Dee to hurry up and tuck her hair under the beanie cap and let's go.

We swiftly cut through the yards of the flats and made it to where we saw the people standing outside. The car we saw in front of the flat was no longer there and everyone was either inside the flat or gone. I told Big Dee the plan, that I will be crouched down under the picture window next to the door, but she would have to knock on the door and as soon as it opens, step out the way and I would rush in first with the H-K.

I pulled the H-K from the bag and tossed it to the ground and we made our moves. As soon as the door opened I had the barrel of the H-K embedded into the woman's right eye forcing her back into the flat. Big Dee followed with her weapon drawn and closed the door behind us. She was a gansta deep inside if I ever saw one. I didn't even have to tell her what to do; we were in sequence with each other.

Joker, Flaco and his cousin were all in the apartment, high as hell. They were taken off guard when they realized what was going down and saw Big Dee with the gun pointed at them. They didn't bother to move from the sofa when we barged in and interrupted their little party.

There was another girl in the flat sitting on Flaco's lap. Dee demanded everyone lie on the ground. While I escorted the girl I had to check the two bedrooms to make sure there wasn't anyone else inside. I saw a roll of gray duct tape lying on the floor by the folded up cardboard box in the room. I swooped it up and headed back in the living room. I made the women lie down, gave Big Dee the H-K and began duct tapping everyone's hands, feet and mouths, then did my usual pat down and came up on two small caliber handguns off of Flaco and Joker and tucked them in my waist.

I swiftly made my way to the front door to secure the chain and bolt locks, then took my H-K from Dee and told her to punish those fools but save Flaco for me. She took the roll of duct tape and wrapped it around Flaco's cousin's mouth and nose to stop his airflow. His screams were muffled by the tape. He was panicking and not able to breathe. He shook his head furiously, but all that did was take up the rest of the air he had in his lungs. His eyes bulged as if they were about to pop out of his head and his cheeks were puffed out as if they were going to explode at any moment. He passed gas uncontrollably and then began to jerk, twist and wrench all at the same time. I squatted down in front of him and smiled as we stared in each other's eyes. I wanted my face to be the last he would ever see while he was on his way to hell. I stayed crouched in front of him until his body stopped moving, then stood up and turned toward Dee and said, "Next."

She dragged Joker by his shirt into the kitchen. He tried to put up a fight as much as he could. She let him loose and kicked him in the stomach. I watched from the living room to see what she was about to do. I was wondering why she removed a plastic bowl from the dish rack and filled it with water and cooking oil and placed it in the microwave. She lifted his shirt, exposing his bare skin and then pulled down his pants to his ankles where the tape bound his legs together.

The microwave beeped and she carefully removed the bowl of boiling water mixed with cooking oil and began pouring the scorching hot liquid between his legs and chest. He helplessly twisted and turned frantically as the liquid continued to cover his body.

I had to turn my head from the gross sight when I saw Joker's skin melting away from his body and red blisters formed where his skin used to be. His screams of pain could be heard in the living room where I stood, but they weren't loud enough to be heard through the brick walls that confined us. I never would have thought that Big Dee could be so cold blooded, heartless, ruthless, brutal and inhumane to a person if I weren't witnessing her acts with my very own eyes. She was torturing Joker for the pain and suffering he inflicted on her, but that still didn't explain how she came up with such psychopathic acts.

Big Dee walked back into the living room, kissed me on the cheek and said, "It's your turn Boo."

I turned toward the kitchen to get one last look at Joker and noticed that his penis had been removed and placed on top of his chest and his throat had been cut. The sight of that gave me the jitters and I clenched my hand around my own manhood to feel myself before moving to punish Flaco.

"Dee, I think you should do the pleasures," I told her. I was feeling sick in the stomach at the thought of having my penis cut off and cooked alive.

Big Dee walked into the back room and came out with some electric curling irons. She plugged them up in a socket next to the TV. The red light popped on, indicating they were on. She pulled down Flaco's pants the same way she did Joker's and dragged him next to where the curling irons were plugged up. She rested her left knee on his back to keep him steady and opened the crack of his butt cheeks and grabbed the curling iron and slowly inserted it into his anus. She brought it in and out slowly several times and started speeding up with deep thrusts and then left it inlaid inside of him.

Tears rolled down Flaco's eyes. Big Dee asked me to hold him steady until she came back so I placed my foot on his neck to keep him lying on his stomach. I wondered what she was up to now. She returned with a cup of water and a bowl and set them on the floor and reclaimed her spot. I stared in curiosity at what she was doing when she partially removed the duct tape from his mouth. He immediately pleaded for his life and said he was sorry.

"I know you are sorry, you son of a bitch," Dee snapped cold-bloodedly. "You will never get the chance to hurt any other girls like y'all did me." She wrapped one hand around his throat and squeezed hard. He gagged and she stuffed what she had in the bowl into his mouth and quickly resealed the tape. I didn't want to believe what I just saw. She stuffed Joker's cut off penis into Flaco's mouth. She raised up and stood on his back. Flaco's legs started moving like he was swimming. I was wondering what the hell was wrong with him because Dee wasn't doing anything to him now but standing on his back until I remembered the curling iron that was heating up embedded into his anus. She let it heat up inside him for five minutes. You could smell the stench of cooked flesh. She stepped off his back and immediately turned to his side trying to get the hot curling iron out of him. Big Dee tossed the cup of water onto him. The electric shock shot through his body and straightened him out. The charge of electricity only sent him jerking and cooking from the inside out and in seconds his body stopped moving completely.

Big Dee kicked the plug out of the socket. I covered my nose to avoid the odor.

"What are we going to do about these two?" I said, pointing down at the two girls on the floor.

"What do you mean, what are we going to do with them? One of them is Flaco's sister who knocked on my door when they came to rape me and the other one is just a hood rat, but we can't leave any witnesses, can we?" Dee whispered irritably.

"No we can't."

"Well then, I guess you know," she stated before turning to a coffee table and grabbing up a steak knife they all had been using to cut open cigars to make blunts. She then cut the girls' throats.

I kept my shirt pulled up over my face as we walked out of the apartment. Big Dee pulled her shirt over her nose as well.

We made our way back to her flat. I stayed outside just in case her mother was awake. I didn't want to walk in with the H-K in my hand. Dee opened her bedroom window and I passed her the gun and ambled into her flat. We quickly undressed, stuffed the clothes inside a plastic garbage bag, poured bleach over the clothes went outside and tossed them in the dumpster.

Big Dee took a shower first and by the time I got out of the shower the police were at her door. My heart dropped. I was about to start shooting my way out of the flat until I heard Dee exclaim to her mother that no one had raped her.

Man, I felt a big load had been lifted of my heart. I eased my way into her room, packed my belongings into the duffel bag and waited in the room until I heard the police leave.

Big Dee and her mother were now arguing. Dee was caught up between a rock and a hard spot because she had to tell the police she wasn't raped and that she had had consensual sex and her mother heard it for the first time. And here I was in her room. Just earlier I had been telling her mother about how Dee wasn't thinking about having sex, she was saving herself for marriage. Now her mother's finding out her daughter has had sex.

The room door came flying open. "You get your little lying ass out of my house and I don't want to see you around my daughter again or I will call the police."

"Momma, he didn't do nothing. Why is you jumping down on him like that? Boo don't know nothing about this."

"Yeah, he know y'all two share everything, even each other. I want you out of here now."

I stood up and tossed my duffel bag on my shoulder. I didn't even say one word in trying to defend myself from the accusations. My loyalty and friendship with Dee were more important than telling her mother she had been raped, which would have hurt Dee so I tucked my tongue. When Dee was ready to tell her mother the truth, she would, I was sure of it, but I knew just as well as Big Dee knew her mother couldn't keep us away from each other. I walked outside and Big Dee ran out and hugged me. I smiled up at her and told her to keep the gun for her protection and said in a whisper, "She has to go to work soon, I'll see you then."

"Love you, Boo," I heard her say in a low voice but I acted as if I hadn't heard her and kept walking.

CHAPTER 6

As I approached the motel room where Jewel and her brothers and sisters were living, I could hear the video game action song clearly outside the door. The drapes were pulled, so I couldn't view inside. I knocked on the door firmly a lot harder than I normally would have if the volume of the TV wasn't so high. My knocks robbed the late afternoon of its peacefulness. I had forgotten that I had the room key in my duffle bag. Jewel insisted that I take it with me. I had begun to scramble in the bag in search of the key. When the door opened I was beset with hugs from everyone. It was only obvious that they weren't expecting my return, but they were happy I had proved them wrong. I struggled to get my balance from the tugs, hugs and pulls and trying to hold up the bodies who had clenched onto me.

Jewel was in my arms with her legs around my waist and her arms clenched around my neck with her head tucked into the side of my face. Tasha had somehow climbed onto my back and Lisa was scaling the duffle bag that was hanging over my right shoulder.

"Everybody hold up," I said, using my right arm to lift Lisa off the bag and then pulling Tasha from my back. I tapped Jewel on her butt with my left hand to indicate for her to get off me. She released her hold and I guided her down to the floor. She looked up at me wide eyed with excitement. I saw the remains of falling tears where she had been crying.

"What's all that?" I asked, touching her left cheek.

"It's nothing," she told me, wiping underneath both eyes with her hand.

Everyone asked questions at the same time. The kids wanted to know if I would take them swimming tomorrow. Tasha wanted to know if she could read to me and Jewel asked me how Big Dee was doing. I looked at everyone with a big smile on my face. I felt the warm feeling of love and the sense of being needed from them. It felt like I was around family members who I hadn't seen in years.

"Yes, if everyone is good tomorrow we all will go swimming in the pool," I announced. The kids went wild in excitement. "Jewel and I will take y'all to get some swim suits tomorrow."

"Okay. Now everyone calm down. Jewlean, shut the door for me please. Kevin, run your sisters some bath water and when they through, y'all take a bath and get dressed for bed. And turn that video game off," Jewel dictated.

Jewel told me she had something she wanted to tell me and asked if I would come in her room for privacy. I followed her into the room and set my bag down on the side of the bed. She locked the door and walked toward me and paused to collect her thoughts, looking down at my shirt, fumbling with a loose thread and then looked up at me.

"Boo, I would like to be your girlfriend," she began, staring me in my eyes, ready to defend this last statement if necessary. But she saw that I had made no attempt to reject her. "I want to spend the rest of my life with you. I know that we haven't known each other for a long time, but I know God has sent you to me and my heart, mind and the feelings inside tell me you are the one for me. I feel so at peace, safe and loved when I'm around you and you treat me like I'm special. Plus, my sisters and brothers love when you are around. I talked to them last night concerning you and when you didn't come back they bugged me to go find you. Plus, I haven't slept at all since you been gone to visit your friend. I honestly thought that you had abandoned us, especially when you didn't come back. I couldn't stop crying. I even prayed to God that He bring you back to me. I even promised Him if He does, I would cherish His gift and forgive Him for the hard life He gave me. Boo, you don't have to answer me right now, but I do want you to know this and this is a promise from my soul. If you choose to accept me as your girl, I will always be loyal and love you till the day I die. I will do my best to make you happy and be on your side no matter what you choose to do. And I wouldn't let anything or no one come between us. I don't care if we were living in cardboard boxes, as long as I was with you I would be happy and content."

Jewel's emotional words penetrated the core of my heart. She had exposed her true feelings about me and it bounced around in my mind like a ping-pong ball. I was astonished and overwhelmed at what my ears had witnessed. My thoughts were digressing back and forth, thinking about what Big Dee had said about me being her future husband one day. I was wondering was she really anticipating and assuming such a future?

I was now in a cross with two beautiful girls who had strong feelings for me. I loved Big Dee wholeheartedly, and being that she was my best friend and loved me as much as I did her, she seemed to be a more likely choice of who I would pick to be intimate with, but I didn't look at Big Dee any other way than what she was, my best friend. But Jewel was different. I was building up love for her and making her my girlfriend had crossed my mind. Both Big Dee and Jewel had shown me all the qualities I expected from a girl. Jewel's beauty made my heart skip a beat and I was leaning toward her for the simple fact that I could see myself with her intimately.

Jewel saw that I was deep in thought. She hugged me around my waist and laid her head up against my chest and I hugged her back. "Julia Monevilay Perez", I began reciting Jewel's name. she looked up at me in shock that I had remembered her full name.

"You are so gorgeous and I have felt that way from the very first time I saw you. I can't honestly say that I'm in love with you but I can say that I have love for you and each day it's growing stronger and someday I will be in love with you, I'm sure, but I just want to make sure it's all for the right reasons and not for selfish motives."

"So, Boo, is that a 'yes' to my question?" Jewel asked excitedly.

I hadn't made a decision, but I was surprised at myself when I carelessly blurted out the word "Yes."

Jewel hugged me even tighter, as if she were trying to join our souls together, then released her grip and pulled my head down gently so she could introduce her lips to mine, and softly kissed me. Her lips tasted like the natural sweetness of an exotic fruit, and the longer I kissed her, the flavor seemed to change from peach to cherry, and then strawberry. I started to wonder, was I just imagining the flavors, but I remembered the first time she kissed me with her tongue, and when she caught mine, she trapped it and sucked it deeply into her mouth, massaging it with her tongue. I didn't attempt to stop her and I had forgotten about what I wanted to say, but she had already heard what she wanted to hear.

We stood kissing for what seemed like hours, but was actually only a little over thirty minutes. I pulled away because if I hadn't, she would have kissed me as long as I let it go on. She hugged me again and said, "I will always make you happy and proud of me. You are the best thing that ever happened in my life."

I thought those were some powerful statements to make, and it had to be influenced by her hormones racing wildly. But she was a virgin, so then I asked myself, what does being a virgin have to do with hormones flaring up?

"Jewel, I'm already proud of you, and every time I look into your pretty face, that makes me happy." She blushed and turned from me so I wouldn't see the tears of joy that were falling from her eyes. "Baby girl, how about you, me and the kids make some popcorn balls and watch a movie on cable together?"

"Boo, what are popcorn balls?" she asked.

"Girl, you telling me you don't know what a popcorn ball is? Well, y'all going to like them and I'm going to teach you how to make them. The kids didn't eat up all the marshmallows we bought, did they?" I asked.

"No, I really doubt it. They don't know what marshmallows are, so it's very unlikely that they would eat something that was strange to them," she said. I found it odd for Jewel's brothers and sisters not to know what a marshmallow was, but I had let it slip my mind that they had always survived on the bare minimum necessities.

Jewel and I walked out of the room and into the kitchen. The TV was off and the girls were already in bed. The boys were in the bathroom finishing up their bath, which I assumed was really a group shower because it was too quick to be baths. I wasn't tripping. As long as they hit that water every night, I was cool with that. Jewel was the one who was pushing a line about baths every night and showers in the morning, and I wasn't about to tell her to ease up on them because I admired a woman who understood the importance of cleanliness.

I asked Jewel to go get the girls up and have them come into the kitchen. I washed my hands and took the bag of uncooked popcorn from the cabinet, got a big mixing bowl, the marshmallows and then quickly grabbed everything else needed to prepare the sweet treats.

"Yes, Boo, did you want us?" Tasha was standing there holding Lisa's hand. They were wearing identical pink and blue nightgowns and looked really cute.

"You guys want to help me make popcorn balls and then eat them all up?" I asked.

"Sure! But we don't know, what's a popcorn ball?" Tasha asked shyly.

"Never mind that; I'm going to show you, so go wash your hands and come on back."

When all the kids were gathered in the kitchen with Jewel leaning against the counter, I began. "Everyone listen carefully. I'm about to teach you how to make popcorn balls. First, we have to pop the popcorn, then put some butter in the pan and melt all the marshmallows very slowly. Once the marshmallows are melted, you pour it over the popcorn and mix it all together very carefully with a big wooden spoon. Then you rub a little cooking oil on your hands and take a handful of the popcorn mix and gently squeeze it into a ball. Then you let them sit for a bit while they harden, and you can eat them up!"

"Boo, can I make a giant one?" Benny asked.

"Yeah, Little Playa, you can make it as big as you like, because I'ma make mine as big as Jewel's head." They all burst into laughter at my joke while Jewel smiled and gave me her middle finger.

Everyone had a good time making their popcorn balls about the size of coconuts. I spread out a blanket on the living room floor in front of the TV. Everybody claimed a spot and we watched a movie, ate popcorn balls and drank grape Kool-Aid that Benny had made. Benny sure knew how to make good Kool-Aid. He became our official Kool-Aid maker. I heard no talking from anyone, only the sounds of popcorn being demolished by small mouths. I couldn't eat all of mine, so I gave it to Lisa, who was the first one finished eating hers and didn't waste any time polishing off the rest of mine.

After the movie, the kids gave Jewel and me hugs, washed their hands and faces, brushed their teeth and went to bed. Jewel got up and began cleaning the kitchen. I surfed TV channels for another movie, but found nothing that interested me. I pressed the power button and tossed the remote onto the couch, stood and began folding the blanket. I wasn't tired even though I hadn't had any sleep for two days now. I wanted to read some more of Jewel's mother's diary and go through those letters, but Jewel being up was keeping me from doing so. I slipped on my black leather gloves and pulled out the two guns I had taken off Joker and Flaco to check them out. One was a .22 and the other was a .25 caliber.

"Man, these little things would only make someone mad if they were shot with one," I said out loud and pocketed the two baby pistols.

"Poppy, would you like to go take a walk?" Jewel asked. She had called me Poppy and she sounded so sexy saying it with her slight accent.

"Yeah, Baby, let's do that. I could use the fresh air. I was just trying to think of something to do, plus we need to talk anyways, about us and your family."

Jewel dried her hands, went to her room and came out with her gloves and jacket. We locked the door on our way out and noticed the motel security was roaming the complex. The security guard waved at us from afar. We waved back and he continued on with whatever he was doing. I noticed the pool was lit with soft underwater lights and there were two couples enjoying a late night swim. I would have loved to take me a swim if I had some swim trunks. Tomorrow we would all go to Wal-Mart and buy some. I hugged Jewel as we strolled down the street. I asked her if she knew her father.

"Yes, I knew my dad. He was good to us and my mother. Something happened between them and he ended up leaving the house one day, never to come back. The last time I saw him was the night he kissed me good night and tucked me into bed. A man had broken into our home and tied me and my brothers and sisters up, and after that day my father never came back home. We ended up moving in with my grandmother, but that didn't work out because my mother and her would always argue. That's when we moved in with my mother's boyfriend, Chad. I hated him. He never treated us good. When I used to ask my mom about my dad, she would always say negative things about him and say he didn't love us, because if he did, he wouldn't have left us. She told me never to mention his name again around her. I don't know what my dad could have done that was so bad, Boo, for my mother to stop loving him and start hating him like she does. I know in my heart that my father loves us, and for him to leave us like that, there had to be a good reason for it. One day I hope to find him. I know his family stay in Los Angeles, California somewhere. My mother knew the address, but she wouldn't tell me. She felt that I would run away to Los Angeles to find my dad, and she was right, I would have. But now that I have you in my life, Boo, I don't care about any of that anymore, but my brothers and sisters might," she said.

I could feel that Jewel was hurting inside. I wanted to tell her so badly about her mother's diary and the truth about her father, but I wanted to do some more investigation first and have strong leads into finding her family. I figured by the time our rental agreement came around, I should have some type of address to somebody in her family. If the letters that I had were from her father in prison, it would be smooth sailing, because all I had to do was contact him and wait for a response.

I promised Jewel that I would help her find her family and be right in her corner all the way. I told her Big Dee might be coming along with us also, but first I would have to talk it over with her to see if she wanted to go. Jewel seemed not to have any objections about Big Dee accompanying us and I didn't attempt to inquire into her personal thoughts.

We had walked a long distance from our motel room without even realizing it. Between the serious dialog, personal thoughts and opinions, we had lost track of time and our sense of awareness as we ambled unconsciously down the street. We turned and headed back for the motel. The night air had become nippy and my nose began to run. Jewel had given me some toilet paper she had folded in her jacket pocket to clean my nose. The stroll had sapped the energy I had when we first left the room and now my body and eyes were feeling the deprivation of two days' sleep.

Jewel had noticed the change in my walk from a stroll to a drag. My attentiveness was dwindling and I had a hard time concentrating on what she was saying. Soon all conversation ceased. She just continued walking to keep me entertained, which I was glad because I was practically sleepwalking by then. She came to a sudden halt at a corner, causing me to bump into her.

"Girl, whatcha stopping for?" I said sharply with a frown. When I'm sleepy I get easily irritated by the smallest of things.

"Poppy, look at that," she said in a whisper, pointing across the street at the same time tapping her other hand on my chest. I looked at what she was directing my attention to, and suddenly felt reenergized.

"Jewel, is they tripping and slipping or what? That there is easy pickings. They just asking to be knocked off. Do you feel like getting down and dirty and having a little fun?" I asked.

"Most definitely, Poppy, you know that!"

I couldn't help but smile at her answer. She was my type of girl, down to put in work with her man under any circumstances. She had pointed out to me an armored truck with its back doors open, being loaded on the side of a bank. We could view the inside of the truck. There were three armed guards, but only one held post with an assault rifle hanging from his shoulder and a .357 magnum in his right hand that was held down at his side. The other two guards were busy loading the truck, but I noticed their gun straps were loose, just in case they needed to make a quick move for their guns.

I gazed at the building to see if the bank had outside security cameras. It didn't. I asked myself, *Is everyone who works at this bank stupid, or did they believe that someone would not attempt to rob them because they were near a police station? What careless thinking. Me and my girl are going to clip these fools on a street level and teach them not to disrespect the criminal mind.* I looked at Jewel and asked, "Are you ready to do this?"

She replied, "Ain't nothing to it but to do it."

I gave her the low down on how we were going to execute the robbery. She ambled across the street as I cut to the left in a different direction. I crossed the street. Once I passed in front of the armored truck without either one of the guards noticing me, I pushed down the street right across from them. The guard who held post lifted his left hand up in a stop motion at Jewel and said she was not allowed to walk their way while they were loading their vehicle. She stopped in her tracks and began walking back across the street in the direction she came from. She had noticed me creeping up behind the guard and I was not able to see the other two who were behind the truck, loading it.

I placed the barrel of my gun to the back of the guard's head and in a whisper said, "You move, you dead." I removed his pistol from his hand and tucked it in my waistband, then eased the assault rifle from his shoulder, swiftly placing my gun in the small of my back, pulled the level on the AK-47 assault rifle to inject a round into its chamber, just to realize that it was already set for action because the previous shell had propelled out.

I walked the guard to the back of the truck. When Jewel saw that I had secured him, she pulled out her .38 and headed toward the truck, but I swiftly took full control and had the drop on them. Before they realized what was going down, the barrel of the AK-47 was pointing directly in their direction.

"Ah-ah, I wouldn't try that if I was you. Don't be no damn fool and get yourself killed over somebody else's money," I said. "Just come on down from there and lay down on the ground."

The two men followed my orders and lay face-down on the asphalt. I directed the other man to do the same.

Jewel knew the protocol. She removed the handcuffs from their leather utility belts and secured their hands behind their backs, then removed their guns from the holsters and secured them in the front of her waistband. I gave her the AK-47 to keep watch as I got up in the truck to get the money. I rambled through the bags, the ones that didn't have locks on them, and came across five long duffel bags filled with stacks of money wrapped in plastic.

"Damn," I exclaimed with excitement. I lifted one of the bags and tossed it out onto the ground. I knew Jewel and I wouldn't be able to carry all five bags because they were just too heavy. I figured Jewel would be struggling with lugging just one of them, but I was for sure I could manage carrying two myself. I really didn't want to leave behind all this money, but there wasn't any way we could take it. Damn, and this is a proper ass come up, too. I noticed two AK-47s lying on the truck's floor. I picked them up and removed the banana clips and forced them into the bag with the money, then began tossing the bags out onto the ground. I decided we were going to take four bags. We would just have to manage some type of way to get them back to the spot. I just didn't feel comfortable leaving all this loot behind.

I jumped down from the truck and snatched two of the men to their feet and said, "Today is y'all lucky day. You get the back seat. Now get up in there and lay down."

The men climbed into the back of the truck and flopped down, still in handcuffs.

I told Jewel to give me the AK-47 and to pick up one of the bags to see if she could tote it. She squatted down and placed the bag's strap over her shoulder and stood up with ease and nodded. I knew we could take the fourth one for sure now. She was stronger than I thought.

I snatched the other guard to his feet and faced him toward the back of the truck.

"Baby, give me some cover while I unhandcuff this fool," I instructed.

Jewel held the .38 to the man's head as I freed his right hand from the cuff and cuffed his left hand to his leather belt. I put the man in a choke hold with my left arm and placed the AK-47 in his right hand and told him to aim it inside the truck and pull the trigger and I would let him live. He did as I asked and the weapon fired off with a kick, many rounds flying out in rapid succession. I supported his arm as he unloaded the full clip. I released him from my hold and released his other hand from the cuff and told him he was free to go. He dropped the empty smoking gun and turned toward me to thank me for sparing his life. Before he could get all the words out of his mouth, Jewel domed him, sending his brains out the back of his head. His lifeless body fell crashing to the cold asphalt in front of me.

"Poppy, did the dumb ass really think we was going to let him go?"

"I don't know Baby Girl, I believe so," I said and smiled up at her before lifting a bag onto each shoulder and grabbing the end of the third one. I told her to grab the other end and leave the gun she just smoked the guard with. We carried the bags down the streets until we came to an alley where we saw a shopping cart with cans, bottles and other garbage in it. We gave the bum a Franklin for his cart, dumped its contents and placed the big duffel bags into the basket and pushed it toward the motel. We dumped the basket on the side of the motel dumpster and lugged the bags into our room after looking around to see if the motel security were in the area. The couples who had been in the pool when we left were no longer there and the coast was clear.

I was sweating and out of breath by the time we got inside the room. "Baby, I'm getting out of shape," I said, flopping down on the bed and inhaling deeply.

Jewel laid on me smiling, then kissed me and said, "I love you, Boo."

Even though I couldn't breathe, it felt nice with her laying on me, so I didn't say anything. I knew we had to lay low for a minute and couldn't be spending any of the money freely. We got up and I took a shower while Jewel bathed in the other bathroom. I knew I wasn't going to get a chance to read any part of the diary, not today anyways. We pulled out all the money from the bags and checked the stacks to make sure there weren't any dye packs or tracers hidden anywhere.

Jewel couldn't believe her eyes at how much money we had now. She had never seen so much money in her entire life. Neither had I, come to think of it, but I kept cool while I watched her cry in joy and play with all those bills. I grabbed a blanket and two pillows from the bed and said, "Whenever you get tired of staring at that money, then you can put it all back in the bags."

"Poppy, where are you going?" she asked.

"Where does it look like I'm going? To the couch so I can go to sleep."

"Huh-uh, you are sleeping in here with me tonight," she said, rushing toward me. She closed the bedroom door, then went in the bathroom and washed her hands and got into bed. Big as the bed was, she had to crawl right up under me. I was dead to the world in a matter of seconds.

I awakened to find Jewel cuddled up in my arms, staring into my face. I wondered how long she had been awake, watching me sleep.

"Good morning, Sleepy Bug," she said, touching the top of my nose lightly with her forefinger.

I didn't want to speak because of my morning breath. She must have been anxious because she slid me some tongue despite my breath, and she didn't stop until I tried to pull away. We laid there exploring each other's mouths with our tongues. I felt nature rising, poking at her leg. She had finally allowed me to have my tongue back. I crawled over her and got out of bed. She slapped my left butt cheek.

"Okay, now keep it up," I warned. "I'ma hold you down over my lap and bite you on your butt hard until you start crying."

"So come do it," she snapped. "Get up out of bed with your lazy self so we can take the kids to eat breakfast at the Casino Buffet, and from there we'll go to the mall and do some shopping. We need to get a few things anyway."

By the time Jewel and I got dressed and walked into the living room, all the kids were up and dressed.

We took a cab to Sam's Town and ate at the buffet. It was the first time Jewel and the kids had been to a place where you could eat all you wanted and had such a variety of food and drinks to choose from. From there we caught a cab and headed to the mall on the strip. The kids ran wild. We spent most of the day shopping, going in and out of stores, playing video games, eating junk food and taking pictures with a disposable camera. I thought that I might have to stop at the pet shop and buy three dog leashes and collars for Jewel, Jewlean and Lisa to keep them from getting lost. They didn't seem to know how to stop running off in their own directions. By the time we returned from our shopping spree, everyone was too tired to go swimming.

The kids had walked into the motel room and dropped all the bags in the middle of the floor. I flopped down on the couch. Jewel came moping over and sat on my lap, trying to get me to go lay down with her. She acted like she was afraid to go in the bedroom and go to sleep by herself. She was like a leech. Wherever I went, she had to follow. It became so bad that she even wanted to be in the bathroom with me. It seemed as though she cared about nothing except being with me. I had gotten tired of her whimpering about us taking a nap, so I gave in just to shut her up. She snuggled up under me like usual, stuck her thumb in her mouth and was sound asleep in minutes.

I waited long enough to hear her light snores and eased myself out of bed. I removed the letters and diary from my duffel bag and advanced toward the door, but was stopped in my tracks by the sound of Jewel's voice.

"Boo, where you going?" she asked, now rising up from the bed to follow me.

"I'll be back to lay with you in a minute," I said

"Why? What's up?"

"I'm going to the bathroom. Go on and lay back down," I said, trying to convince her to lay down before she got all the way up and saw the diary and letters in my hand that I was now hiding in front of me.

"There's a bathroom in here. Why can't you use this one?"

I couldn't win for losing. I had no excuse for why I couldn't use the bathroom in the bedroom. I tried to play it off. "Yeah, huh," and locked the door behind me. I didn't have to use the facilities, but I pulled down my pants anyway and squatted on the toilet and set the diary between my legs on the floor and the letters on the edge of the counter next to me. I glanced at the outside of the letters and noticed that the sender's name and address had been torn from the envelopes. I opened the letter with the most recent postmark and began reading its contents.

> *Dear Julian, my love;*
>
> *I pray and hope by the time your soft and lovely hands caress my written words, that they would have found you and my kids in the best of health and high spirits, with the thought of me in your hearts. There is not one minute that passes me by that I don't have you all in my thoughts and heart, for my world consists of you all and without my family, there is no reason for me to exist on this earth. When I received your second letter telling me you have been shooting heroin, it brought me to my knees. I schooled you better than that, but I was glad to hear you were trying to shake that bad habit.*
>
> *Did you give my daughter Julia the letter I wrote to her and the others? The reason I ask is because I haven't heard from her and I have really been anticipating a letter from my kids. I am not going to make this letter long. I just wanted to write you back and let you know how much I love you and to give you mom's address and phone number just in case you had forgotten it. I had a talk with moms the other day and I told her you had contacted me and were living in Vegas.*

*She told me to have you call her if you need anything
and she would like to see her grandbabies.*

*You take care and give all my kids hugs and kisses
for me, and tell Julia I said to write. Love y'all.*

p.s. here's mom's hookup: Barbara Will...

Jewel's mother had scribbled out the address and part of the last name with a black ink pen. I stood up off the toilet with my pants down around my ankles and held the letter up to the light, trying to make out the address underneath the scribbles. I flipped the paper over, upside down and back up, trying every angle in hope that I could get the address, but it was impossible to read. It was really shaded in dark.

I set the letter down when I realized there was no possible way to get the address off of it. I picked up the next letter and scanned through it. There was nothing useful to help me find Jewel's family, so I folded the letters back up and stuffed them back into their original envelopes, then reached down to pick up the diary and unfasten its leather latch to begin reading where I had left off:

I'm losing my damn mind! Today the thought crossed my mind to have Julia sell her body so I could get high. The dope man, Clayman, said he would hook me up with three grams if I allowed him to have sex with her. The fat bastard knew I was sick and needed a fix badly, and figured I would jump on the offer. I'd rather die in pain before having my baby do something like that. It's bad enough that I had already stooped so low, prostituting just to get high. Nothin' has changed but the days of the weeks and names of the months. My kids are getting restless, being confined inside the room without nothing to do but read books and play on a typewriter that don't even work. I'm a poor excuse for a mother. They don't even say much to me anymore when I stumble in after staying gone for two and three days at a time. I told Julia and Kevin about the leftover food Burger King tossed out after closing and to go there and get food every night, but that only lasted for four good months before the Burger King manager realized that people was stealing the food out of the garbage dumpster, so he had a lock put on it to keep people from taking the food that was trashed.

I had to put the diary down for a second. My stomach had knotted up from the thought of having to eat food that had been in the filthy garbage. I found myself becoming angry and Jewel's mother was the reason. Growing up in the ghetto, I have seen a lot of cold things, but one thing I was sure of was no one around there was eating out of garbage dumpsters, regardless of how bad they were doing, because you could believe that someone around there would have fed them kids. I picked up the diary to continue, but decided I should just glance through its pages to see if she had written down any addresses or phone numbers of anyone who could assist me with finding Jewel's family. I eyeballed the pages quickly, until I came across one with the title "My Last Entry" in bold letters. This sparked my interest and I started reading.

> This is my last entry into this diary and my last day of shooting dope. I'm going to kill this demon who I have become. I can't stand the thought of how my kids see me. They don't deserve such a mother like me. I'm sure one of them will find this diary, probably Benny because he's the one who likes to snoop around in my belongings and report what he finds to my daughter Julia. So kids, you have found mother's diary. I want to say I love you all, but your...

There was a knock on the bathroom door, interrupting my serious intimacy with the words I was reading. I knew it could only be Jewel even before she called my name.

"What?" I said harshly. "Leave me alone. Damn."

She ignored my hostile reply and asked what I was doing in there and could she come in.

"No, Miss Julia Monevilay Perez. No, you can't come in here now. Please leave me alone. I'll be there in a minute."

She knew that I only use her full name when I was very serious about what I was saying and there was no chance of changing my mind, so she didn't continue to push the issue, she just let me be. I continued where I'd left off:

> ...but your mother is very ill and has to leave. I'm sorry, but this is the only way I seen fit. I have faith in your big sister. She will make sure you all are taken care of. Don't give her a hard time and do as she says, especially you, Kevin.
>
> Julia, I'm so sorry for everything that I put you through. I know you probably won't ever forgive me in

this lifetime, but I want you to know that I love you dearly. I left to go get some help from a rehab drug center. I'm trying to clean up so I could be a better mother than I have been. Please try to understand. Also, your father wrote you and the kids a letter, but I never gave it to you because I was still mad at him and didn't want you to know he was in prison. He never abandoned us, he got locked up for trying to protect us, but I blamed him for that. All those bad things I said about him were out of spite from my own hurt and pain. Write to your father at this address:

CDC #T-40463
Salinas Valley State Prison
PO Box 1040
Soledad, California 93960

I would have left you your grandmother's address and number, but I had forgotten it. Your father will send it to you when he writes you back. Please do me a big favor, please don't tell him about Chad hitting on you. That would do nothing but upset him more than he is.

"Yes," I said excitedly in a whisper, standing to pull up my pants. I had her father's hookup and all I had to do is ask Jewel his real name and write him a letter myself.

I closed the diary and laid it on the counter and began washing my hands, a habit I had since I was a kid, even though I didn't use the toilet. I ambled out of the bathroom, returned the letters and diary back into my duffel bag and laid back down with Jewel, who was staring at the bathroom door when I came out. She was now watching every move I made. She pulled back the sheets, indicating to crawl in next to her. I glanced down and had to take another look. She was dressed in a light purple and white silk lace matching panties and bra. I hadn't ever noticed that she was so thick and shapely. She was a brick house, fine as hell. I saw why fat Clayman wanted to holla at this and why Jewel chose to wear big clothes. She had the whole package, a beauty that was beyond belief and a body any woman would die for, without one blemish on her smooth skin. I just stood there scoping her sexy everything. She looked up at me with her innocent stare, which I knew was nothing but a camouflage and said, "Come on, Poppy, take your clothes off and get in here, because I'm getting cold."

I stripped down to my black No Question boxers and allowed the clothes and guns to fall right where I stood, which I had tucked into the small of my back and waistband. Then I made my way underneath the sheets. She swung the sheets over my body and laid on top of me with her arms underneath my arm pits and head on my chest. For some reason, she found lying on me more comfortable than lying on the mattress next to me. I rested my hand on her round butt cheeks and couldn't refrain myself from squeezing them. She purred with pleasure as I gripped and rubbed up and down her back. She raised up and kissed me aggressively, with light moans of pleasure, trying to swallow my tongue as she straddled herself on top of me.

There was no turning back for either of us. It was going down in a major way. We stripped away each other's underwear. I felt like a starving infant and began nursing on her breasts. We made more than love. We had mind blowing sex, exploring the realm of our souls that left the bed sheets drenched in our perspiration and the walls sweating from the high temperature that our bodies made when connecting together. We enjoyed the sensation of our arousing passion for each other. We laid in our essence tightly cuddled up, staring in fascination at one another and pondering the sensational bonding of our souls. I found myself totally drained from the activity. Jewel's eyelids had closed. She was now in a deep sleep. I called out her name twice, but she didn't budge to the sound of my voice. I just lay there in silence, thinking about how her soft cries of pleasure excited me, until I became seduced by the darkness of sleep.

CHAPTER 7

Someone was banging on the front door. At first I thought I was dreaming, before I opened my eyes. I held my breath and remained motionless, listening, until I heard the loud banging again. I swiftly leaped out of bed, snatching up the .357 magnum and my pants from the floor. A rapid light knocking sounded off at the bedroom door. I quickly unlocked it and opened it to find Benny and Tasha standing there. "Someone's at the front door," they both said at once.

I lifted my forefinger to my lips and gave a hand signal to come in the room and go wake Jewel up. I hurried to the front door and stood off to the side before asking, "Who is it?" I looked over toward my bedroom and saw Jewel in a t-shirt with an AK-47 pointed directly at the door, so I unsecured the locks and slightly cracked open the door with my weapon aimed at the waist.

"Hi. I'm a rep for a new company called Pure And Fresh Waters," the man said with a smile. "I would like to..."

Before he could finish his sentence I slammed the door in his face. He was lucky that I didn't pop a cap in his ass for waking me up. I locked the door and glanced at the clock to realize that it was 11:00 o'clock in the morning and everyone was just now getting up.

Jewel cooked a huge breakfast of eggs, hash browns, grits, sausage and biscuits. I had always thought only black folks hooked up the bomb breakfasts like this. I wondered, did Puerto Ricans burn the same way we do in the kitchen? I loved a woman who could cook.

After we ate, Jewel and I began slap-boxing. She could sling them pretty well for a girl. Within a matter of seconds the whole house was in an uproar. It was the boys against the girls. It went from slap-boxing to pillow fighting. Tasha had one of the coldest fighting styles I've ever seen and was fast with her punches. My crew gave up because they were winded and gasping for air. I had everyone to line up next to each other and began teaching them how to throw a correct punch with their body weight behind it with combination.

We practiced and played around in the house for hours. We all were hungry again, so we ate rocky road ice cream and baked pecan cookies.

"Boo, man, I wish you could stay with us forever," said Kevin.

"Yeah," Lisa shouted.

"He is, so don't worry about that, because we going to get married and have kids," Jewel said.

"Are you for real, Julia," Jewlean asked with wide eyes.

"Yeah, I'm for real," she said with confidence.

I sat there listening to all this and ain't no one asked me nothing. From what I had just heard, Jewel had already decided my fate. We both were too young, but living an adult life and taking care of a family.

Someone mentioned swimming and everyone broke wide to their rooms to put on suits. We headed for the pool. To my surprise the only one who could swim was Lisa and myself. I spent the rest of the day teaching everyone how to swim. Jewel was so fine she made the two-piece suit stand out. That girl had junk in the trunk and you could see the six-pack in her stomach. Aw, I tell you she was beyond a dime piece. I was sure she could make a blind man turn his head and lift up his shades just to get a glimpse of that ass.

We had Chinese take-out for dinner, then Kevin and Tasha strolled with me to the gas station so I could buy some writing materials and postage stamps. Then I stopped at a pay phone to call Big Dee's house. Her mother picked up, so I hung up in her face. I figured that I'll just bring Jewel with me the next time and have her to ask for Big Dee. I peeled off two franklins from my wad and gave one to Kevin and the other to Tasha.

"Thanks, Boo, man, you the best. No one has never gave me a hundred dollars before. Man. I'm going to share this with Jewlean, Benny and Lisa," he said.

"You don't have to do that, young playa. I got one for each of them also."

Tasha thanked me and pocketed her money with the rest of the money I had given her. We headed back to the room after stopping at a newspaper stand to pick up a copy of the free neighborhood paper. I wanted to look through it because they always had used cars advertised for sale. When we made it back to the room, everyone was occupied with a chore. Tasha stayed clinched to me to avoid being ordered to help with the domestic work and I played right along with her little scheme, handing her the newspaper so she could read the car ads to me while I shuffled through my wad just to give myself something to do. Once the other kids were finished with their assigned chores I gave each one of them a big faced Franklin. I reached over and kissed Tasha on the cheek and departed from her company with the quickness when I saw Jewel standing in front of our bedroom door, motioning her finger to come into the room. She wasted no time pulling away my clothes for a little quicky, we thought, but it turned into two hours of pure pleasure. We bathed and lotioned each other and I brushed her long hair, then got dressed. I asked questions about her father and then asked, "What was his real name?" She told me freely, not expecting anything. I now knew his real name. She wanted me to lay down with her, but I wasn't tired, plus I really wasn't about to go for any of her pouting and I guess she saw it in my face, because she didn't try to pressure me.

"Kevin, Tasha, come here for a minute," I yelled out the door to the living room. They broke and dropped whatever they were doing and were in my room in a matter of seconds.

"Yes, Boo, you wanted us?" Tasha asked politely. All the kids had exceptionally good manners, but Tasha was another Jewel who had this totally innocent look, sweet, and spoke softly with her words.

"Y'all want to roll with me and get the pictures developed?"

"Yeah," they both said.

"I want to go," said Jewel.

"If you go, who's going to stay here with the kids?"

"Boo, we can all just go, then."

"Not. We're just going to go get the pictures developed and maybe a book or two for Tasha. Just stay here. Do you want anything while we're out?" I asked.

Jewel rolled her eyes and didn't answer my question. She was upset because I wouldn't allow her to follow up behind me, but I wasn't tripping. Kevin and Tasha and I just shook the spot. I had gotten double prints of the pictures so I could send Jewel's father some pictures of the kids. I had gotten the pictures developed at the One-Hour Photo in Wal-Mart and picked up two books for Tasha and Benny on criminal law and computer science. Computers were what sparked Benny's interest. The criminal law books were for Tasha. She liked to read stuff that was a challenge, so I figured law would do the trick. I got us some jump ropes, hand wraps, mouthpieces and two pairs of 16 ounce and 8 ounce boxing gloves, leather catching mitts, head gear, a medicine ball and a stopwatch from the sports' department. On our way out we stopped at the concession stand and got cherry slurpies and sour licorice candies. Before we entered our motel room we got rid of any evidence having to do with sweets, but I allowed them to eat what they wanted when they were around me. I was greeted at the door with a kiss.

"Huh, huh. Y'all been eating candy?" Jewel asked. We all shook our heads No at the same time. "Don't be lying. I can taste it when I kiss Boo, and if he ate some, then you both also had some. Stick out your tongues and let me see." No one revealed their tongues. Tasha crept off to the side to avoid Jewel's interrogation. "Okay, Boo. When one of these kids get a toothache because you letting them eat a bunch of candy, you going be the one staying up with them all night, not me," she said, sounding like someone's mother.

"Whatever," I said, and walked past her and began emptying the bags. It was time for another boxing lesson. I taught everyone how to wrap their hands. We trained and sparred. They took turns trying to punch me. It was late at night and we were making a lot of noise. By the time we settled down it was well into the early morning. We all took baths and went to bed. I couldn't sleep, so I sat at the table and wrote Jewel's father a letter.

"Dear Sir, How are you doing up under such extreme situations? I do hope when you get this letter that it would find you well. I know it may seem strange to be receiving a letter from someone you don't personally know, but I can assure you by the time you finish reading this letter you will understand why I wrote and will learn who I am. So let me introduce myself. My name is Leonard James Weems, but my family and friends call me Boo. I'm your daughter Julia's boyfriend. I'm fifteen years old. However, out of respect of you being my girl's father, I felt you needed to know how your kids are doing and where they are. It's a long story to how I came about finding out that you existed, where you were located, and that you didn't know where your kids were. Your daughter, Julia, who I call Jewel, she don't know that I'm writing to you, let alone she don't even know that you are locked up, because her mother never gave her the letter you wrote to her. I figured

I'll write to you first to make sure you are still locked up and give you a heads up about everything. I hope you understand that I have to take this course of action to protect her from any more pain than she's already been through. Just to let you know, all your kids are doing well and they love you.

Now what I need for you to do is send me your mother's address and phone number, because your daughter has been trying to find you, not knowing that you are locked up. So I am not going to be the one to tell her, you need to talk to her yourself. Once I hear back from you with the information I requested, then I will take your kids to your mother's house and from there your contact starts with your family. Enclosed with this letter are pictures of me and your kids. Also I'm sending you a few chips just in case you need it. It's not much, only five hundred. Maybe next time I could do a little better. You take care and write me soon as possible.

Respectfully, Your daughter's boyfriend, Boo.

I folded the letter and stuck it in the envelope with twenty pictures. I hadn't addressed the front or sealed the letter yet because I hadn't purchased the money order or gotten the post office box yet. I hid the letter in the bottom of my duffel bag. I figured I'll send Jewel's father five hundred just in case he was doing bad and now he could at least get himself some new shoes and whatever else he needed, because I was sure he wanted to take a picture and send it to his kids and I didn't want them to see their father looking all tore up. Plus, five hundred wasn't nothing compared to what we had now in the room. I stayed up the entire morning and headed out alone, rented a post office box for a year, purchased a postal money order and mailed the letter off certified mail. Now all I had to do was wait for a reply.

I called Big Dee's house. Her mother answered. I decided that I was going to ask for Big Dee. "May I speak to Dee?"

"May I ask who's calling?"

I paused for a few seconds to find my voice before responding. "This is Boo."

"Boo, didn't I tell you not to be calling my home. You can't speak to my daughter," she shouted.

"Momma, who is that on the phone?" I heard Big Dee asking in the background.

"Nobody. Now shut my damn door and mind your own business," her mother said harshly before slamming down the phone.

Aw, she's tripping big time, I said to myself, replacing my cell phone back into my pocket before strolling off. I was only a few blocks away from the motel room when I saw Jewel heading my way.

"Girl, where you headed?" I yelled out.

"To find you."

"To find me? Why you hunting me down?"

"Boo, you know why? Because you didn't leave me a note or tell anyone you were leaving the house. I don't know if you was running away or in some trouble, so I was coming to find my man, and I found him."

"Where is he?" I asked.

"Boo, you'd better stop playing with me," she said, hugging and kissing me.

"Jewel, while we're out I need for you to ask for Big Dee for me. Her punk ass momma is tripping big time on me. She just hung up in my face when I called, but whatever you do, don't say my name. Just ask Dee when she will be able to go to the movies. She'll understand what you mean, and when you talk to her, act like you two are friends, because her mother will be eavesdropping on y'all conversation for sure."

I removed my cell phone from my pocket and dialed the number and gave Jewel the phone.

"Hello?"

"Hi. May I speak to Dee? This is her friend, Jewel." Big Dee's mother handed her the phone. " Hello, Big Dee, what's up girl? This is Jewel. I was just calling to see when are you going to be able to go to the movies with us?" She paused to listen to Big Dee's reply. "Okay, then, I'll holla at you next week sometime. Bye bye."

Jewel hung up the phone and relayed what Dee had said. Next week was when her mother would be gone again out of town for work. I hugged Jewel with one arm around the neck and strolled off. I told Jewel, let's go dump the work we still had. We didn't need the money, but I wanted to get the drugs up out of the room. We walked back to the room, grabbed the work and a fresh pair of gloves. I brought Tasha along. We took the bus to my old neck of the woods where I knew I could get off the crack cocaine for sure. The heroin would be a different story, but I'm sure someone on the west side would know where I could dump the heroin for a good price. I was now on familiar turf in my neighborhood. On the west side of Las Vegas were the best of the best hustlers, pimps, gangstas, thugs, drug dealers, hoes, jackers and smokers mingled. Although the west side was known for having the most ruthless and grimmest people roaming its blocks, it was a hustler's paradise with endless paper to be made and never-ending excitement.

I stepped off the bus and inhaled the aroma of soul food. We were right across the street from Hamburger Heaven, a fast food eatery that had some of the best food on the west side. I figured I'll take Jewel and Tasha there to eat. We walked inside and I saw a bunch of familiar faces smile up at me. I ordered my usual, a catfish dinner with chili cheese fries, a slice of carmel cake and a fruit punch. Jewel asked me if they had value meals. I laughed in her face at what I assumed to be a joke, but she looked up at me with a serious expression.

"Baby, this is not Mickey D's. This is the real deal here. You order what you want. Just check out the menu and see what you want," I said, then turned toward Tasha and asked her what she wanted to eat. I already knew the answer—a hamburger and French fries, so I ordered her the biggest hamburger they sold, the Big Wheel, and I did it on purpose. It was made with real beef and come with French fries.

Jewel ordered two tacos, fries and a fruit punch. I knew that wasn't going to be enough for her, but I didn't bother to say anything because I already knew what she had in mind eating some of my food. That's why I ordered the catfish dinner instead of the catfish sandwich. I paid for our food and went and sat down at one of the booths. I wasted no time digging in, then looked up at Tasha, who was staring at the Big Hamburger in amazement. I smiled with a full mouth.

"Boo, why you buy her all that food? You know she will never be able to eat it all." Just as I figured, Jewel had her hands in my plate and so did Tasha. They ate until they were stuffed. We got up and headed out. The owner waved good-bye. Jewel had left a twenty-dollar tip on the table, not knowing that was the wrong thing to do, because soon as we left out the door one of the customers was going to snatch that dub up and pocket it. It seemed like eyes were watching us when we ambled down the street. I already knew what the hounds were peeping out and drooling at the mouth over, but I couldn't even get mad, because Jewel was that bad, a head turner and I sported her like a new mink coat at a big music award show. A pimp named Break-a-Hoe, who I had known was hanging out checking traps, saw me with my girl.

"Say, young playa. What's been going on with you? I haven't seen you around in a minute. I see you went cop you some dynamite that's pure explosive, baby. So what is she, your moneymaker or you just being a caretaker?" he asked.

"Break-a-Hoe, folks. I'm just simping, because pimping women is not my line of business. Plus my girl ain't that type of broad. She's a diamond, sure enough, but also an undercover time bomb without a timer, you feel me?"

"Ha. Ha. I like it in you, young playa. The truth is in ya, and if you ever start pimping you going to be a bad cat to reckon with. So you finally found you a ride-or-die, huh? That fits a young playa like a glove. Pimpulations, then," he said.

I thanked him for the congratulations and said, "I have some work that I'm trying to get off of." He asked me what type of work I was trying to sell. I said heroin, and showed him what I had.

"Say, young playa. What you asking for this? You know this a lot of black girl you got here," he said, eyeballing the amount.

"Folks, what do you think it's worth?" I asked, knowing that he was going to keep it real with me and then shoot some game, but I really didn't care about the dope, I just wanted to at least get a couple grand for it, because I couldn't see myself just giving it away for free. "Well, young playa, it depends on how good it is, I would say it's worth about nineteen grand, give or take, but I'll hit you on the hip with ten grand right now for it," he said.

"Break it off, then, folks, and you have a deal." I said.

He gave me the ten thousand dollars in small denominations. After I counted it, I put it back inside the Crown Royal bag and stuck it in my sweatshirt pocket. We both had known that he got over big time, but that was the game of wheeling and dealing and I wasn't even tripping. I had made five times what I would have asked for. We pointed our fingers at each other in a players' manner that indicated to stay up and I ambled off with my girl and Tasha, heading for the West Coast apartments so I could dump the crack.

We were now entering the belly of one of the biggest, most notorious and treacherous Blood gang hoods in Vegas, known as the West Coast Bloods, but I had no fear whatsoever. I was raised up on the west side and knew just about everyone who roamed the west as their stomping grounds. I saw some of the fellows hanging out shooting dice, blowing indo and downing 40s, but they had also noticed us before we pushed up. Fifteen dudes and twenty- two females stood hanging out in one area. I didn't recognize every one.

"B-Mack, Blaze, look who's out roaming the streets, and look at baby! Who he got with him. Damn, she's out of line for being so fine," D-Rick said, stretching out his hand that was made into a B symbol to shake mine.

I formed my hand into a lower case B symbol as well and we connected our hands to make a capital B, then released our connection and snapped our fingers. I repeated the same formal greeting with about nine others. "So, Blood, you're not going to introduce us to your girl?" D-Rick asked me, not waiting for my reply, introducing himself. He held out his hand toward Jewel, but she didn't speak or shake his hand.

"Damn Blood, you got her fine ass trained, don't you?"

"Why you say that, D-Rick? Because she won't acknowledge you? No, I don't got her trained. She got herself trained, respecting her man, not talking to anyone without my approval. And before you get to going on one, don't say nothing out of line to my girl. Yeah, I'm tripping over that one," I warned him.

"Blood, I'm not going to disrespect your girl."

"Alright then, that's all I'm saying folks. Just leave her out of your mouth."

The home girls gave me a hug and kissed me on the cheek. Jewel couldn't stand the sight of them kissing my face. She rushed over to where I stood and licked the tip of her forefinger, then rubbed the spot on my face where they had kissed me at.

"Damn Boo, you got her sprung like that? If I knew that the "D" would have women tripping like that, I would have been done holla at that," Shawonda said. Jewel shot a harsh evil look her way.

"Boo, you better check that hoe of yours before she get her ass beat down out here," Shawonda said cold bloodedly. I seen it coming, Shawonda's bad mouth was going to incite the other home girls and they all would end up jumping on Jewel, but I wasn't going to let them all jump on my girl like that. Plus, I was positive that Jewel would have plugged a lot of them before that happened.

"Well what's wrong with your beating?" Jewel asked. "And the tramp that had your ugly ass is the hoe!"

I would never have thought that Jewel had such a bad mouth. This was the first time I ever heard her trip out like this, but I had forgotten just that fast that Puerto Rican's does have aggressive ways and foul mouths.

"Aw hoe, we going to beat your pretty ass now," someone in the crowed said.

111

My anger immediately flared. I felt my face twisted up in a frown. "Y'all ain't gonna do shit to my girl, so you can get that out cha mind now! If Shawonda gots a beef with her, they can go head up and after that either one of y'all can do the same."

I pulled Tasha close to me and told Jewel to handle up. She walked in the middle of the street and quickly slipped on her gloves. Everyone had stopped shooting dice to watch the cat fight.

"I got a B-note on the home girl Shawonda," someone said.

"Dawg, I'll take that bet. Matter of fact, I'm covering all bets that's against my girl, no matter what the amount is," I said. I knew the home girl Shawonda had major scraps, and I've seen her knock out dudes in the past, but I've also slap boxed with Jewel and taught her how to put her power into every punch. Plus, I figured she was going to fight harder than ever in order not to disappoint me. One fool who I didn't know tossed down a thousand. I pulled out one of my wads and matched his. Before I knew it, I had seven grand laying on the ground on Jewel. Shawonda ran out in the street on Jewel and released a pretty one-two combination which didn't hit nothing and caused her to step off balance. Jewel released a hard left hook that collided with Shawonda's jaw. That was the end of the fight. Shawonda hit the concrete with exceptional force.

"Money gone!" I yelled out loud and told Tasha to pick up all the money that was in piles on the ground. I kept an eye on the fools I didn't know just in case they tried something so I could down them fast.

"Next runner up, who feels they can get with my girl," I announced. I was talking major shit now. The fool who I won the grand off of ran around the corner and returned with his sister that was two sizes bigger than Jewel and she looked like a man by the face with a shadow mustache. The hair on her head had barely came together in a pony tail.

"Why you go get him for, to fight me?" I asked.

Everyone burst out in laughter at what they thought was a joke, but I was serious.

"Blood, that's my sister if you feel that your girl is all that, then let's see if she could fade her since you doin' all that hootin' and hollerin'. Let me get action back at my bread."

"Hold up home boy. Say baby, you feel like knocking out that man, monster, ii mean woman or whatever the hell it is?" I asked Jewel.

She nodded her head yes. I turned toward ole boy and asked what was he betting. That fool went for broke. He put up eight hundred and the car title to his red Cadillac Coupe that set on chrome Daltons up against my three grand.

"Well, drop the keys on top of the money and let the fight begin," I said. There was no other bets made. I had broken all the others with the first fight. Jewel squared off with the giant. I yelled out, "Work the body, baby, and then the head."

Jewel wasted no time. She rushed in with an overhand right that sent tears falling from the monster's face and then a left body shot up underneath her heart. The monster grabbed hold of Jewel, but that was a big mistake. Jewel squatted down and came up with an explosive right upper cut underneath the monster's chin. She staggered backwards and then Jewel released two heavy blows to both sides of her head sending her to get acquainted with the concrete. She was knocked out cold. The spectators were amazed by my girl's performance. I was also, but I played it cool like it wasn't nothing, but in the back of my mind I knew if that monster would have hurt my girl, I told myself that I was going to fill her and her brother up with some hot slug's regardless if it was a head up fade or not. I make up my own rules to how I seen fit when it came to me and mine, and Jewel was mine and I was going to protect her at all cost. Tasha swooped up my winnings with the keys to my new ride.

I told her to pocket the money and pass me the car key and title. I checked to make sure the fool had scribbled his signature on the back and that it matched the name on the front of the title. I seen in his face that he was burning up inside. If I didn't know any better, I would have swore that I seen wisps of steam curling upwards from the top of his head. So to avoid any problems, I pulled out my strap and held it to my side to let him know that I was heated.

I opened the passenger door for Tasha and Jewel, then made my way to the driver's side and started the engine. It roared aggressively when I pressed on the gas pedal. I knew then that I knocked him off big time for his ride. The inside was immaculate with custom white leather interior and a Pioneer deck with a voice command navigation system with a touch screen. That alone was worth the three grand I put up against the car.

"*Dumb ass chump,*" I said to myself and drove off. I pulled up in front of my female cousin Shell's house and parked. She and seven of her male friends was hanging out in the front yard playing dominoes on a fold out table and drinking like usual. Shell was a straight tomboy who could ball her ass off. We was real tight but I hadn't seen her in a minute. We exited the ride and I went and gave Shell a hug, then introduced her to Jewel and Tasha. Her male friends undressed my girl with their eyes and a few made sexual comments to each other. They all was twice my age for sure because my cousin Shell was thirty-two herself. I had seen a few of the dudes numerous times at my cousin's house and had been introduced once before, but I was bad with remembering names. They remembered me, though.

"Boo, what's up dawg? You and your girl want to hit this blunt?" one of the dudes asked. I declined for the both of us since we didn't smoke. Jewel stayed clinched to me. I walked over to the table and introduced myself to the fellas that I didn't know and asked for next on the dominoes. The guy that I was standing next to asked what I knew about the bones. I told him enough to place my money on my game.

He looked up at me when he heard the sound of money as if he had an easy mark and quickly returned his eyes back to his hand and said, "So young buck, you think you got game? I'm telling you now I'm a dominoligst. I'm the one who put the dots on these bones, so if you still want to gamble, just put your money where your mouth is."

I laughed coldly, then reached in my pocket and pulled out my other wad and dropped it in the middle of the table egotistically to allow all the hundreds to fall freely so they could be viewed. I wasn't worried about no one trying to pull a jack move because I was sure they felt I was heated, just as well, as I was pretty sure they were packing. From their style of dress and cars parked in front of the house and across the street, they looked like dope boys. I wasn't sweating nothing. I was in my back yard now and they was just visitors.

"Man, youngsta, that's a proper knot you got there. I see you about your paper, but I'm going to pass on your challenge. It's not like I can't match you." He reached between his lap and held up two big bundles of money with a big rubber band wrapped around each stack. "I just respect a young hustler who's at his paper. I wouldn't feel right taking your money, but if you trying to get into something, them cats next door got a dice game going over there."

I looked over to where he was pointing and seen a small group of dudes crouched in a circle in the driveway shooting dice. I hadn't noticed them when I pulled up. I cursed myself for slipping and not paying more attention to my surroundings, but I assured myself the reason why I hadn't seen them was because of the truck that was half way parked in the driveway. I knew that wasn't the reason. The real was I just wasn't paying any attention. Shell reached out a soda toward Tasha, she looked up at me for my approval before she accepted.

I picked my money up off the table and told Jewel to kick it with my cousin while I go next door to shoot some dice. Me and Tasha headed to the game.

"Say folks, can a real shooter get in the game?" I asked.

They all turned their heads toward me and then back to the game. Someone out in the crowd said, "We shooting a hundred a hand."

"Is that it?" I said and walked up. They opened a hole so I could get a spot. Tasha stood over me watching the game. I quickly lost thirty-five hundred on other peoples' come out numbers.

"Damn!" I shouted in frustration. They all laughed at me, but I didn't find nothing to be funny.

"Man, if you can't stand the loss, you don't need to be gambling," one of them said.

I wasn't tripping on the loss, but more on my roll because I realized I was in the company of professional die hard gamblers who knew all the tricks of the trade. The dice was passed to me. On my first come out I hit the snake eyes and lost that quickly. I lost forty-five hundred because I was taking bets from everyone.

"Damn, dawg, pass me a new pair of dice," I said visibly irritated. I gave the dice a good shake and sent them spinning. They stopped on a five and a six, an automatic winner on the first come out. I came out again, but this time they stopped on a six.

"I bet you seven or eleven before you six or eight," three of the guys said at the same time.

"I'm betting nothing but a grand at a time," I announced harshly. All of them didn't hesitate to drop a grand down. I had bets all around the board. I yelled out, "Waitress, I need them tres," and sent the dice spinning again and what do you know, there they was, threes on both dice. I aggressively grabbed my winnings with a frown on my face. The next four rolls knocked a hole into everybody's pockets except for one cat who was smart enough to quit before he lost all of his bread. My A-game was on and by the time they realized it, I was scooping up all the money.

"Ha, ha, game over," I said, pocketing and gripping some of the money in my left hand while Tasha scooped up the rest. "Thanks for the payday dawgs," I said. Then me and Tasha made our way back into my cousin's yard.

"How you do, youngsta?" one of the dudes asked.

"I bust that shit up," I said harshly holding out the money in my hand and stepping aside so they could see the rest in Tasha's hands and pockets, they were stuffed full.

"That's right youngsta, stay down," he said.

I gave Jewel some of the money to pocket and told Tasha to do the same. I pulled out the big sandwich bag full of crack and held it in my hand.

"Say youngsta, what's all that you got there?" Eastwood asked. "What you trying to do with it?"

He knew exactly what it was, just like everyone else did who seen it.

"Why what's up, you trying to get something?" I asked.

"Nah youngsta, I'm holding also, getting at my money, you know both of us can't be working the same block," he said.

At first what he said didn't register, but then I thought about what he was trying to tell me and became hot.

"Well bro, then I guess you better go find you another spot to hustle at because I'm going to kick it right here and do what I want to do. I don't know who you think you talking to about trying to tell me I can't hustle in my hood. You got me fucked up with somebody else. Matter of fact, who gave you permission to be over here hustling since you want to push up on me?" I replied coldly.

"Say little dude, you better watch that mouth how you talking to me before I close it up for you."

"Punk, you ain't going to do shit to my man. If anything you will be the one with a closed mouth!" Jewel said.

"What you say you little..."

"Eastwood, you need to calm that down with tripping on my little cousin. I can't let you do nothing to him, he has every right to be here," Shell said.

"Yeah dawg, put that shit on ice, this is his hood and his relatives spot and you know the home girl Shell is not about to let you jump on her cousin. All that's going to do is start up a lot of unnecessary bullshit you don't need. Let the nigga make his money," one of the dudes said to Eastwood.

"Yeah whatever, I ain't never let no little punk talk to me any type of way, so what makes him any different? What you need to do, Shell, is check your relly!" Eastwood replied sharply.

"Punk bastard, how about you check me and Ms. Magnum!" I

exclaimed angrily drawing down on him with the .357 magnum.

Everyone pushed away from the table trying to duck out the way when I displayed the gun.

"Break yourself punk, since you don't know how to leave well enough alone. And I want it all, money, jewelry, dope and car keys!"

"Is it like that, youngsta?"

"Damn right, it's like that and I thought 'cha knew. So stop frontin' and break mine off, then strip down to your boxers and hurry that shit up before the temptation of watching your head explode get the best of me and I pull this trigger!"

Eastwood stripped down to his boxers and placed everything else on the table. I told him to get to stepping. The guys next door was laughing hard at the show. Eastwood made tracks up the street. I gave Shell the gun, money and sack of rocks he had placed on the table. Trashed his clothes, kept the jewelry and made my way for his car. I pressed the button on the key chain and the lights blinked and a horn beeped twice, then fell back silent. I knew then which car belonged to him. The black Lincoln.

I searched the inside of the car and came up on a 9mm Uzi with three clips. I popped the trunk and seen that he had been shopping, or a booster musta hooked him up. There was a box of all types of name brand men's and women's perfumes. I spotted my favorite kind, No Question, and dropped it in my pocket. There were a bunch of new video games and movies and a new laptop computer. I pulled it all out and checked around the trunk and came across a pound of indo. I loaded my ride with the items and asked the fellows next door who wanted to buy the rims and sound system. There was only one with any bread in his pocket. I told him to give me what he had and he could take the whole car and take what he wanted off it. He gave me what he had in his pocket and I tossed him the keys. He and two of his boys jetted out in the car. I was sure that Eastwood would be popping back up with a few of his boys tripping about his car and the rest of his belongings that I jacked him for, but he didn't.

All the other cats had shook the spot right after the incident. Me, Jewel and Tasha hung out the rest of the night with Shell while I hustled the crack off to the smokers, and when word got out about the love I was giving up, the street stayed with traffic coming and going to purchase or trade merchandise. I had a trunk and back seat full of new stolen merchandise and Shell had a grip of different items she wanted. Shell fired up the grill and barbequed us some chicken, steak, beef hot links and corn on the cob. I closed the shop down around four o'clock in the morning when Shell announced she was sleepy. I had two ounces left, so I gave them to the three smokers that were working for me, plus a Franklin each for their assistance.

They acted like that was the best day of their life and asked if I would be back later on, so we could get it back cracking. I told them, nah, that was it for me. We said our good-byes to Shell and drove off.

"Little mamma, you ain't sleepy yet?" I asked Tasha.

She said "No."

"Well, do you know how to drive?"

"Boo, I'm too young to drive. I don't know how to drive a car yet, but when I get older I'm going to learn."

"Nonsense, I'll teach you now, come on over here and get in my lap and drive this caddie," I said. Tasha crawled into my lap excitedly and placed her small hands on the wheel next to mine and we cruised down the street. The streets were light with traffic. I looked over at Jewel and seen she had stuck her thumb in her mouth, I knew exactly what that meant. So I got onto the 115 freeway to shorten our drive to our motel room and exited on Las Vegas Boulevard.

I noticed we needed gas so I pulled into the gas station to fill the tank. I stood next to Tasha inhaling the fresh morning air and enjoying the view of the sun rising over the Vegas desert while I let her pump the gas. I couldn't help but notice a stocky built, clean shaved, nicely dressed white man getting out of a gray Carrera turbo Porsche with a chrome briefcase handcuffed to his right wrist. I watched him closely, how he held the handle tightly as he walked into the station. All type of thoughts ran through my mind. Was it money inside or important secret documents, or could it be a bomb I wondered. Whatever it was inside, I assumed it must be important.

The gas pump jolted, that let me know that the tank couldn't hold no more gas. I took control of it from Tasha and removed it from the tank, then placed it back into its cradle, secured the gas cap and opened the car door for Tasha to crawl in and I followed. From the corner of my left eye I seen the white man exit back out the station with the briefcase and a cup of coffee in his other hand. I wanted to know what was inside that briefcase. Curiosity was haunting me with great torment. The man walked to the side of the station to his Porsche and set the cup of coffee on top of its roof and began keying the door. I made my move swiftly toward the car. I had no time to alert Jewel that I was making a move on a mark. I didn't want him to make it inside the car before I got up on him. I had no time to creep up on him. I had the .357 magnum aimed in plain view at the man's face. He felt my presence because he looked up slowly and froze in his tracks.

"You choose," I said aggressively.

He understood exactly what I meant and without any hesitation he keyed the cuff from his wrist and set the briefcase on the hood with the keys to the Porsche and laid face down on the ground. It scared me how easy he was giving up the briefcase and his car. I was for sure now there was a bomb in the briefcase and wondered if I should even take it, because you couldn't never tell about the white boys these days. They was known for blowing up things and dealing in explosives. But I snatched up the briefcase anyways and made tracks to my ride and pulled off.

I didn't care who might have seen the license plates on the car because the car wasn't registered to me or Jewel anyway, and plus the used to be owner didn't know my real name, so it didn't matter. I pulled into our motel parking lot and parked in one of its empty spaces in the far back. We unloaded the car of all the merchandise. Then I wiped it clean of any possible finger prints or anything that could lead back to Jewel or I.

Everyone in the house was asleep, Kevin had everything under control just like it would have been if Jewel had been there. I sat at the dinner table for over an hour and a half trying to pick open the locks of the briefcase while Jewel slept in my arms. Trying to balance her and take care of business wasn't panning out like I wanted it too. Tasha sat quietly leaning on the table with her hands underneath her chin observing me trying to open the briefcase until she got tired. She realized that I didn't know what I was doing and asked me if I would like her to go get Kevin to open it for me.

"Can Kevin open one of these?" I asked her.

She shook her head yes, so I told her to go wake him and tell him to get in here on the double. She wasted no time doing what I asked. Kevin ambled up to where I sat, rubbing the sleep out of his eyes.

"Yeah Boo?" He asked sleepily.

"I need for you to open this for me and then you could go back to sleep," I said.

He turned and ambled back into his room.

"Where are you going?" I asked, but he didn't respond. He slowly returned with two paper clips in hand, pulled the briefcase in front of him, giggled at the locks and they snapped unfastened and he headed back to bed. I eased the briefcase back in front of me and then shot Tasha an evil frown because she was breathing down my neck being nosey, but I noticed she didn't take my frown personally when she didn't budge from being all up on me. I slowly eased the briefcase open.

"Wow," Tasha said as we both stared at the jewelry and loose diamonds. I woke Jewel up to look at what I just stung for.

"Oh Poppy, I want this," she said picking up a sapphire and diamond gold necklace. Her eyes sparkled at its beauty. I didn't deny her because in my heart nothing was too good for my girl. I placed it around her neck. The necklace was beautiful, but it didn't come close to watching the beauty of my girl's looks and I told her so. She blushed and told me I was so romantic. I wasn't trying to be romantic. I was just telling the truth. I shut the case and told Tasha to hit the tub and then to bed.

She asked me if I wanted the money she had that belonged to me. I had forgotten all about the money. I insisted that she hold on to it for me. Me and Jewel took a shower. She couldn't stop touching her neck to make sure the necklace was still there. I stood thinking that we would have to find us a different place to live other than a motel room. We were accumulating too much stuff too fast and the room was starting to feel cluttered to me. We finished our shower and headed for bed leaving everything right where it laid.

Jewel couldn't sleep, she was too excited about her new necklace. So she massaged my back, legs, feet, and kissed up and down my body until I had fallen sleep and then she just laid on my back thinking about her past life to what it now had become until tiredness overcame her. Her life was just beginning and mine was moving in the opposite direction in destruction of a once innocent soul that now was becoming cold-hearted, ruthless and insensitive to human life other than those who I loved: Big Dee, Shell, Jewel and the kids. Everyone else had no significance in my life other than being a pawn, to be used for the furtherance of my financial gain and personal interests I knew all too well I was losing myself to the mentality and ways of the street life.

CHAPTER 8

The commotion that was taking place in the front room awakened me. I leaped out of bed to see what all the racket and rumbling was about. I yanked open the bedroom door and saw a full scale squabble going down, the kids were going at each other with boxing gloves. I stood in the middle of the doorway enjoying the brawl. It seemed like the girls were a lot tougher than the boys and fought a lot harder. I wanted to believe that was because the boys didn't want to hurt their sisters so they withheld their full range of abilities and strength. But from what I was seeing, they were giving it all they had because the girls were kicking ass and not easing up.

Jewel was in the bathroom staring through the mirror at the necklace. I don't know how long she had been stuck there, but however long it was I began to regret that I gave it to her because she hadn't made an attempt to cook breakfast or tell the kids to keep it down when I was asleep. I told myself if that necklace continued to be a distraction that I was going to make sure it disappeared.

As soon as the kids finished boxing with each other, I had them go put on their workout clothes and we all headed out to the clubhouse that had an inside gym with punching bags. I trained them the way I was taught to train in kick boxing; sit-ups, squats, lunges, calf raises, pushups, pull-ups, shadow boxing, punching and kicking the bag, footwork and running. Every day we spent two hours training. The kids loved it because now they were learning how to fight with their hands, knees and legs.

A full week passed and there was no letter from Jewel's father when I went to check the post office box. I also found a jeweler to melt some of the jewelry down to customize necklaces and bracelets for me, Jewel and the kids. I gave him a few diamonds for payment and he changed the numbers on all the signature watches. I immediately strapped on my wrist a Emporio Armani platinum watch that had 22.5 carats Belfian cut diamonds on the dial, bezel case and the strap keeper and a 30 carat platinum bracelet. I made sure Jewel had a nice size personal jewelry collection. The kids loved their red ruby and diamond jewelry. Each necklace was customized with a locket that featured Jewel's and my facial silhouette. On the inside was a picture of us all. I also had the girls matching ankle bracelets made. I set aside a vintage Cartier diamond necklace, watch, bracelet and ankle bracelet for Big Dee. I figured she would look nice in the pieces I'd chosen for her.

Benny didn't care much about anything else but the computer that I had taken out of Eastwood's car. Jewel practically had to threaten him from using the computer in order to get him to eat. He didn't want to do anything but sit in front of the computer screen. He stayed on it so much that none of the other kids had even got a chance to use it. He didn't have to worry about me wanting to use it because I had no use for it.

I had Jewel call Big Dee and this time her mother didn't answer the phone. She told Jewel to put me on the phone. She was so excited to hear my voice, she told me that her mother was out of town for six weeks. Then she insisted that Jewel and I come hang out with her. That was right up my alley, I figured Big Dee's spot would be the perfect place to parley.

So I asked, "Say home girl, do you mind if we all come and spend a few weeks with you? Your boy is on fire out this way," I told her.

"Boo, you already know that answer, so I don't know why you would ask that crazy question. I'm wondering what's taking you so long to get here. You and Jewel can have my room and I'll sleep on the couch," she said.

"What about the kids, Dee?" I asked.

"They can sleep in the living room with me or in the room with you and Jewel. Don't worry about that, just bring your tail on. I'm also going to cook your favorite meal for you."

"Now girl, that's what I'm talking about there, you sho' do know the right thing to say in order to get me motivated," I said and laughed, then continued. "Oh, by the way, I got something for you. It's a gift from me and Jewel."

"What is it?" she asked.

"Girl, I'm not going to tell you. You just gonna have to wait and see. Now let me get off this phone so I can go pack up," I said and blew her a kiss through the phone and hung up. Jewel was standing there listening to the conversation. She heard me making plans for us to move with Big Dee for a few weeks. She didn't like the idea because she didn't know how her and Dee would get along. She didn't express it to me, but I seen the look in her eyes. We went back to the motel room and I announced to everyone that we were moving and to go pack their belongings. Everyone packed their clothes in the Gucci luggage I bought from the fashion show mall. Benny packed the computer and announced that he had all he was taking.

"Boy, if you don't get your butt in that room and get the rest of your stuff, I'm going to break you and that computer," I warned him with a frown on my face. I went and pulled the car up into a parking space that was closer to the room and we packed the trunk, made sure the motel room was clean and hadn't forgotten anything. We had to leave the food behind because there was no room left in the car to bring it. I tossed the motel room keys to a homeless couple, greased their palms with five franklins and told them the room was good for a few more weeks. I ambled to the car when they tried to thank me and pulled off. It was the first time that the other kids had seen the car other than Tasha who was sitting in my lap driving the car with me and smiling back at everyone.

"Man, this is a tight car you have Boo," Kevin said admiring the inside. "Boo, you know what type of car stereo you have here?" Benny asked, excitedly reaching over the seat touching the screen in different places, lighting it up. He didn't wait for a response before saying, "That's the Pioneer AVIC-NI, it can play DVD's, CD's, CDR's and MP3's and you can enhance the screen. It is a touch screen on top of that."

"Benny, how do you know so much about this radio?" I asked. He told me to watch him turn on the music. He moved his finger over the screen and a CD title came across it in red lettering. "Lil Wayne, The Block is Hot," and the music came bumping through the speakers. He quickly flipped to another CD, Rihanna, Unapologetic. I wondered what he knew about Rihanna. I come to find out that Benny was a genius when it came to computers and electronics.

I blew the horn and I backed up to park in Big Dee's driveway. She opened the door with the chain lock still fastened, peeking out to see who it was parking in her driveway. When I got out she had the gun I'd given her in hand.

"Hold up woman before you shoot somebody," I said, trying to duck out the way of the barrel when she moved to give me a hug. She secured the gun in her waistband and like usual, she hugged me tight and kissed my face. I introduced her to Jewel and the kids and we all walked into the house. I smelled the well seasoned beef and strong jalapeño peppers.

"Girl, I'm ready to eat," I said walking toward the kitchen. Big Dee made me a plate of food with four beef fajitas, two corn tortillas and some homemade salsa that was not too hot with chilies. She tossed me a family size bag of Nacho Cheese Doritos and I sat on the couch and dug in.

Jewel helped Dee fix the kids plates and to her surprise Big Dee and her had hit it off. They pranced around me in conversation like they had known each other all their lives and paid me no attention. So after I finished eating, I stepped out to the back yard where I had buried Squeegee to visit his grave site.

"You thought that I had forgotten about you, huh old buddy? Never that, you will always have a place in my heart and thoughts. I don't know if Dee told you or not, but we got all them fools who hurt y'all and we got them good too. By the way, I got a girl, and no it's not Dee. Her name is Julia Monevilay Perez. She's Puerto Rican, but I think she has some black in her blood line somewhere because she has all the features like a sista, cook like a sista, got junk in the trunk like a sista, sweet as an angel. I call her Jewel. You gonna have to meet her, she's beautiful Squeegee. She's in the spot now, but first I wanted to tell you about her before pushing her on you. Oh yeah! I'm not struggling anymore. I've been hustling and now got long bread to buy whatever I want. I wish you were still here so I could buy your favorite ferret snacks. Man I'm full. Dee just hook me up some of those bomb fajitas and I tell you, they was screamin'. Did I tell you that Jewel has little brothers and sisters? Well, there's five total. Well Squeegee, I'm going to get back inside before Jewel realizes I'm gone and get to looking for me. She's one of those overprotective types. I don't know who's worse, her or Big Dee. Tell my grandmother I said hello and I love her and I love you too little fellow. Talk to you soon, one love," I said placing my right hand on my heart and ambled back inside the house.

Big Dee and Jewel was in her room looking at photo albums while everyone else was still eating except Benny who stood leaning up against the wall with his arms folded. When he seen me come in he pushed off the wall and followed me into Dee's room.

"Boo, can I get the computer out the car?" he asked.

"Benny, didn't I just tell you not to be bugging Boo about that computer?" Jewel said coldly looking up at him with stone eyes.

"Let us get settled in first and we'll get the computer," I told him.

"So I guess somebody don't want this gift I got for them?" I said, knowing it would get Dee's attention.

"Yeah, I want my gift boy," she replied quickly and stood up and followed me to the car with Jewel and Benny in tow. I gave her the jewelry box. She opened it and her eyes widened at the sight of the expensive jewelry.

"Aw shit," I exclaimed and walked around the car when I saw her about to cry from excitement. Jewel and Benny hadn't realized why I had moved away from them, but Benny followed my lead. When Big Dee thanked Jewel with a hug, she understood. I wasn't about to have Big Dee squeeze the air out of me again, especially when she was excited as she was. I burst out in laughter at the sight of Jewel's face when a tear escaped from her right eye when Big Dee released the massive hug. Man that was funny.

Dee didn't waste any time putting on her jewelry. Me and Benny shot back inside the spot. For the rest of the day we all enjoyed each other's company, listening to music, dancing and telling jokes. Everyone slept in the living room, we made pallets on the floor. Me, Jewel and Dee stayed up talking. Dee asked me about the car, so I filled her in on everything and we laughed.

I felt something run across my face and then my arm. I sprung up to my feet and cut the kitchen light on. Roaches broke wide for cover.

"Aw, hell naw Dee, we can't be living like this. Jewel, help me take the kids into the bedroom and put them in the bed," I said.

I went and washed my face and Dee gave me and Jewel the couch. She went to sleep in her mom's bed. I couldn't wait until the morning came. I got up and found the number to an exterminator and called them to spray the flat. I wasn't about to have roaches crawling all over my face at night. The exterminator told us that once he sprayed we couldn't return into the apartment for three hours.

So we all went to the city park and grilled some hot links and hamburgers. We played around in the park for a few hours and then went to Walker's furniture store. We shopped around while I listened to Jewel and watched her point out all the things she talked about getting whenever we decided to buy a home. She really had in her mind that we were going to be together for the rest of our lives. I wasn't that vain to believe such a thing, but I didn't crush her dreams. If God wish it to be, then that's what it will be and that's how I looked at it. Big Dee picked out some things and I took down the item numbers and purchased them without her ever knowing.

We stopped at a grocery store to buy cleaning supplies before heading back to the flat. When we walked inside dead roaches were everywhere. We spent four hours sanitizing the place. Me and the boys removed all the furniture in the house and threw it in the garbage dumpster. When we finished there was nothing in the apartment except the clothes that were hanging in the closets and sitting in plastic garbage bags on the floor. The furniture trucks had pulled up. When Big Dee saw them lugging the furniture inside, she was overwhelmed. I had refurnished the entire apartment, even her mother's room. I had called myself getting the 60-inch screen TV with the X-box so I could kick back and play video games on it, but Jewel and Dee had brought them plans to a quick end. They stayed watching BET all day and night. I was downgraded to the 32-inch color TV in the room just that fast, and I was the one who bought the 60-inch flat screen TV. I knew there was no winning with both of them against me, so I forced myself to be content with the 32-inch. Dee didn't ask where I had gotten the money to buy all the stuff. I put the receipts in the dresser drawer.

The next day we went out and bought all new pots, pans, silverware, dishes, bathroom articles and bed linen. Everything in the flat was new, even the refrigerator which was now packed with food. Dee let Benny set up the computer in her mother's room and he hung out in there all day and most of the night playing on it. Within three days we was all comfortably settled in. No more roaches and no more second hand furniture. I had bought Squeegee a big bag of his ferret snacks and set it by his grave site. I visited him every day and finally introduced him to Jewel and the kids. Lisa was too young to understand why she couldn't see him and the more I explained the more questions she asked, so I gave up trying to explain. Every day after dinner we had movie night. We ordered two new movies from Netflix and watched them together.

Movie night was Dee's idea and when the kids went to sleep we would stay up watching the Platinum Comedy Series. Big Dee had bought me the DVDs of my favorite comedians. Bernie Mac, Cedric the Entertainer, Bruce Bruce, Adele Givens, Dave Chappelle, Steve Harvey, D.L. Hughley and the Torry Brother's, but she didn't get Chris Tucker. I guess they didn't have his DVD in stock or I'm sure she would have gotten that one too.

Jewel spoke in Spanish to Big Dee when she didn't want me to know what she was saying. Dee played along with her idea knowing that I understood everything that was being said. She wanted to see how honest, loyal and trustworthy Jewel was to me. So she nonchalantly asked questions about other guys, how she felt about me, how good I was in bed and did I have a big one. I shot Dee the look not to be inquiring about how I get down in the bed and about the size of my manhood, but she continued to do it anyway. Jewel told her in detail and I had to sit there and listen to all this being told about my sex life to my best friend, acting like I couldn't understand their conversation in Spanish. I had learned a lot of things about Jewel through her girl to girl talk with Dee in Spanish. Jewel was really in love with me. When Jewel took her baths, Dee and I would have our private talks. She would tease me about having Jewel so sprung over me. Then let me know she was happy that I had a girlfriend who cared about me as much as she does. She also told me how jealous she was and if Jewel ever broke my heart, what she would do to her. I took Dee's words seriously but figured Jewel wouldn't do nothing to hurt me on purpose, so there was no need for her having to harm Jewel.

Big Dee asked me, "How does it feel to have two women madly in love with you, and how I was going to handle that?"

I told her, "Just like I've been doing. Keeping you as my best friend and Jewel as my woman and when I get tired of Jewel, I'll switch the titles around and Jewel would become my best friend and you'll become my woman." Big Dee looked up at me as if I was insane. I knew my answer would knock her off guard, but the truth of the matter is I was really thinking that at the time.

"No you not Boo," she said snobbishly. "You not going to be playing musical chairs with us. It has to be one or the other."

"Dee, what is you talking about? Why is we even on such a subject like this anyway? If I wanted to be with both of y'all, why couldn't I be? What would stop me from doing so if I chose to? This is my life. If I want two women as girlfriends, then that's what it would be. No one could have nothing to say about it because I'm going to run my life the way I want it, you understand?" I replied sharply.

Jewel walked in on the last of the conversation. She asked Dee what it was all about in Spanish and Dee told her it was nothing. Jewel came and sat next to me and stared in my face. I didn't even attempt to look toward her. I kept my gaze on the TV screen. Big Dee kissed me on the side of my lips and said, "He will be okay," and ambled off to take her bath. When she had finished she crawled up under my free arm and we watched a movie. There I was with two fine girls lying in my arms smelling good, and thicker than a six dollar hamburger.

Three weeks passed and there was still no letter from Jewel's father at the post office box. What's up with this chump? I figured I'll give him one more week before I go hire a private investigator to find Jewel's family, which I should have done from the very beginning. Jewel and Big Dee had found some business credit cards in the women's bathroom at the mall and went on a shopping spree. They purchased everyone a laptop and a bunch of nice clothes and body wash gels and lotions. They came pushing through the door with all the bags, having to make several trips back to the cab to retrieve the rest of their purchases. I sat on the couch staring at the two chit chatting, giggling and laughing with each other when they came in with their last load. I didn't bother to get up or attempt to help and they didn't seem to care. I was hot as hell at both of them because they neglected to tell me they were going out to the mall. I woke up and they were nowhere to be found, so I became worried and figured the worst. Both of them knew better than to run off without informing someone in the house where they were going. Big Dee set down right next to me reaching inside one of the bags pulling out a Montblanc Boheme fountain pen, an iPhone, a pair of Giorgio Armani monk-strap shoes and set the items on my lap. I shoved the items onto the floor then looked toward where Jewel stood.

"Where you two heifers been?"

"What you call me Boo?" Dee asked in surprise.

"Heifer, you heard me." I said, "Where you two heifers been? Are we just running off now and not telling anyone where we going?"

"Boo you was asleep and Jewel and I wanted to go hang out at the mall. We left you a note on the dresser mirror."

"For one Dee, how was I supposed to see a note on the mirror in your room? Do you really think I was going to find it? Another thing, what's all this I want to hang out at the mall shit? Neither one of y'all never told me y'all like to hang out at no malls. When y'all start liking to do that? I see what's going on here, you two hot heifer's want to chase dudes, huh?"

"Nobody wasn't even studding any boys, Boo," Jewel snapped angrily. "We just went to hang out."

"Well y'all can keep on hanging out and not telling nobody where y'all hopping off to. When something happens to y'all asses then y'all going to wish that you told somebody something. Now what is all this you two went and spent money on?" I asked.

They told me how they found the two business credit cards and went shopping with them. I gave them both a tongue lashing about how careless and dumb they were for using the credit cards in stores that had video cameras. Now the stores had their pictures, and when the police come and take them to juvenile hall I wasn't going to be able to help them, because they were going to be locked up for a long time and I would have to go find me another girl to hang with.

Jewel broke down in tears and ran into my arms, crying and saying she never wants to leave me and she would never leave or do nothing without telling me again. Big Dee held her composure. She wasn't worried about me not being there for her. She knew I said that out of anger and it was directed toward Jewel so she would act right. From that day forward, I never had to worry about Jewel going off without personally informing me where she was going. She was through with any hanging out if it wasn't with me.

Dee gave everyone their gifts. Dee had styled Jewel's hair and they dressed up to model some of their new outfits for me. I never imagined seeing either one of them in a dress. The different No Question and Gucci gowns they modeled fit their bodies so firmly and displayed their shapely figures, it excited me deeply. They both were drop dead gorgeous, but I wouldn't allow my eyes to gaze at nothing higher than the waist and nothing lower than the knees. I was stuck watching booty and thighs being twisted at the hips provocatively.

They both decided it was now my turn to model for them. I agreed and gave them a shocking surprise when I came walking out baby oiled up in white No Question boxer briefs and black loafers with no socks. Big Dee screamed and waved money in her hand as if I was a male stripper. Jewel held her hands over her mouth in disbelief and immediately announced that was the end of my modeling career. Her and Dee took it upon themselves to dress me to their liking in a white cotton No Question tank top, Python jacket, shredded jeans, studded belt and lizard boots with a small splash of Gucci Rush on my chest, inner arms and behind the ear. I was the man of their fantasy and when I took a glance through the mirror at their finished creation, I even had to admire my looks and their choice of clothes. I was real stylish with a sophisticated, elegant appearance that still gave off a touch of the bad boy look. I put on my wraparound sunglasses and was ready to hit the town.

I decided to take Jewel and Dee out to the Blue Man Show at the Luxor Hotel and Casino. I really just wanted to be seen with two fine women on each arm. I secured the .45 in the small of my back and stuck the 9mm Uzi underneath my car seat, then hurried around to the passenger side to open the door for Jewel and Dee. They both sat in the front seat and I ambled back to the driver's side and pulled out of the driveway. I pulled up into the Luxor parking lot where a valet attendant immediately escorted us from the car and through the double door of the casino. He gave me a ticket with a number on it so I could retrieve my car when I was ready and I greased his palm with a dub. He thanked me for the twenty and rushed off to park my ride.

I strolled with Jewel and Dee holding onto each one of my arms through the casino and then purchased the tickets for the next Blue Man Show. I felt all eyes on us as we walked, enjoying each other's company. We went and seen the show and it was off the hook. I told myself that we would have to come back and see it again with the kids. The $100 admission charge was worth the show. We took pictures and had a romantic dinner in front of a burning fireplace with a glass of Perrier jouet at Mr. Chow. Jewel asked if she could get a tattoo on the small of her back. I frowned up at the idea because I didn't believe in marking up my body, but I figured one wouldn't hurt so I told her she could. If I had known she was going to get a picture of my face and my name tattooed on her, I would have told her no. Big Dee also got a tattoo but it was with hers and my full name creating a heart on the upper left side of her chest. Something told me to stay in the tattoo parlor to see what kind of tats they were going to get, but I had gone to gamble at the black jack table.

To my surprise no one questioned my age. I guess they figured from all the expensive clothes and jewelry I had on that I had to be over 21 years old. I won eleven grand just that fast playing thousand dollar hands. Big Dee went wild when she saw Omar Epps hanging out at the casino. I couldn't see why women went so crazy over him with his peanut head self. I was way flyer than he was and women wasn't falling all down at my feet as they were for him. I figured it had to be because he was a movie star. I was just waiting for Jewel to go wild trying to get his autograph and a hug like Dee was doing, and then I was going to see if I could snatch all the Puerto Rican blood line out of her body, but she didn't seem to care who he was and stayed clenched to my arm. Dee had already cramped my playa style when she ran off to go meet him. I wasn't feeling that. I glanced around to make sure there was no real playas peeping me out or it would have messed up my level of respect with them. But it really didn't matter if they respected it or not, because if push come to shove and they ever stepped out of line with my girl, Ms. .45 would suck the life out of them.

After Dee got her hug and autograph, we headed for the car. I hadn't cashed in the chips I won, but I know they would always be good as long as the casino was in business. I gave the valet my ticket and he quickly returned with my car. I flicked a $100 casino chip at him, got in the car and pulled out into the street and headed back to Dee's spot. Big Dee couldn't stop talking about how cute Omar Epps was.

"He don't look better than my poppy," Jewel said and laid her head on my shoulder.

"You got that right my precious gem," I agreed with her.

"You just saying that because that's your man, Jewel. If Boo was my man I would say the same thing," Big Dee said. Dee was really jealous of Jewel. Deep down inside she felt I should have been with her. She wanted to see me happy with her, and being that Jewel was my girl, she was starting to feel that all my time was being focused on Jewel, which it was, and that was the way I wanted it.

It had been a total of four weeks now that we been living with Big Dee. There was nothing but fun, fun, fun, going to the movies, go-cart racing, skate rink, bowling, plays, paint ball fighting and having water balloon fights and cook outs. The kids loved being at Dee's and they thought she was the coolest person in the world besides me.

I went to check the post office box and found what I've been waiting for, a letter from Jewel's father. I wasted no time opening it to read its contents. It was only one paper which read:

"Dear Boo, thank you very, very much young man for contacting me concerning my family. There's no written words to express my gratitude and appreciation for what you have done for me by bringing me the most joy that anything on this earth could possibly give to a person, my kids. Also thanks for the money, it was much needed. This letter is short only because I wanted to send you the address and phone number to my mothers' house as soon as possible. It took these people here fifteen days to give me your letter so that's why it took me so long to respond back, if you were

wondering.   My mother's name is Barbra Williams Ridley, 1717 West 107 Street, Los Angeles, California 90007.   The phone number (213) 237-0012.

P.S. I got the pictures and you seem like the type of young man who would make a good son-in-law, you have my blessings. Sincerely, Larry Ridley, write soon."

Bingo, I have Jewel's grandmother's address and phone number. Now she can go see her family. I told everyone to pack up because we was moving out of town. The kids didn't like the sound of that, they all wanted to stay at Dee's. They begged, cried and pleaded with Jewel and Dee to stay. Jewel herself didn't want to leave and tried to get me to change my mind as well. I never told her that we was going to go see her grandmother, but I don't think that would have made any difference. Benny gave me the most problems about not wanting to go. He made up every excuse he could think of to stay with Dee. He even tried to play sick. I told Dee why I was bouncing out of town and not to mention it to Jewel. I asked her was she coming along and she said, no. I could tell she had an attitude with me about jumping up and leaving, but the truth of the matter was, Big Dee had gotten attached to us being there. She had someone else other than me to play mom to, like the kids, who she spoiled and Benny was the main one. I told everyone to pack light and leave the rest. I said my good-bye's to Squeegee before packing the trunk with our belongings. Dee made us steak and cheese burritos to take on the trip. I emptied out my old backpack that had Squeegee and my stuff in it and filled it with money along with the casino chips. I removed the dresser drawer from the side of Dee's new bed and stuffed the backpack deep in the back and replaced the drawer. Everyone gave Dee a hug and slowly took their time getting in the car. I walked back in the flat to make sure I hadn't forgotten anything. Dee came trailing behind me giving me orders to be careful and not to get into any shit out there in L.A. She insisted that I call as soon as I get there to let her know we made it safely and to call once a week thereafter.

"Yes mom," I said looking up at her smiling, reaching in my pants pocket pulling out a huge wad and handling it to her.

"Boo, what's this for?" she asked.

"It's for you, what you think it's for?"

"Boo, I can't take all of this, you going to need it on your trip."

"Dee, take this money and stop worrying about us, we all to the good. Do you really think I'd be giving you my last?" I asked with a smile, then winked. "Now come and put me in your bear hug so I can get up out of here."

She shut the door, hugged me and then kissed me deeply with her tongue and I didn't stop her. When we pulled away there was no need to question what that was about. Her desire for me was now beyond a best friend relationship. I hurried to the car and pulled out of the driveway. Big Dee now stood in the middle of the doorway waving, and just as we were leaving her mother was pulling up and she looked at me dead in my eyes as we drove past each other. I told Jewel, "God sure do work in mysterious ways because that is Dee's mother who just passed us."

Jewel turned around in her seat to look back toward Dee's apartment and seen Dee's mother step out of the car arguing with Dee. I got on the freeway and stretched the Cadillac out heading for the big city known as Los Angeles. "Killa Cali, here we come."

CHAPTER 9

It had taken me four hours to drive from Las Vegas to Los Angeles. The atmosphere appeared to have been foggy, but I assumed it was my eyes that needed a rest from the constant stare of the road. Everyone breathed a sigh of relief from the relentless drive when I pulled up into the parking lot of the Marriott Hotel. We got out and headed inside while a bellboy escorted us with our luggage. Benny decided to carry his own to avoid any possible unfortunate accident by the bellboy that could cause any damage to the laptops that were inside his luggage. I paid for a luxury suite for one week, even though the suite wasn't supplied with all the luxuries I anticipated for the price.

There were two separate bedrooms with full size canopy beds, matching night stands and dressers. The bathrooms had standard double sinks with marble counter tops, wall sized mirrors, toilets, showers and Jacuzzi tubs. The living room was spacious with wall–to-wall carpets, furnished in a style to give an antique appearance with cream colored patterned drapes covering the entire wall of the windows. The eight-seater, polished ebony wood dinner table sat in an area of its own in the living room under a chandelier. There was a wall unit with a 32-inch color TV, stereo system, and a computer positioned on the interior, which was the first thing Benny noticed. He immediately began tapping on its keys to figure out the range of its capabilities. When he realized that it was hooked up to the internet, in a matter of minutes he had four laptops connected up to the main frame. His fingers swiftly moved over the keyboard at high speed, never once glancing down at his hands, but stayed watching the computer screens.

I was too tired to even care what he was up to on the computer. Lisa was squatted down observing him. I figured Benny had to be doing something outrageous and exciting in order to hold her attention.

Kevin and Jewlean had found an area in the living room where they could practice their kickboxing skills. Jewel was cleaning the bathrooms, even though they were already cleaned to perfection. She wanted to make sure they were disinfected to her liking. That was one thing about her, she was an extraordinarily clean conscious person. I tried to call the phone number Jewel's father sent me, but the line stayed busy. I tried several more times, but I got a busy signal. I assumed that someone must have knocked it off the hook by accident. So I figured I'll try to call back in the morning. I crashed out on the bed and felt my shoes being removed from my feet. It was Jewel I assured myself. I wasn't planning on going to sleep so early, I just wanted to rest my eyes. But I had fallen asleep and when I awoke I was underneath the covers with Jewel snuggled up under me as usual and Tasha lying wildly on the other side of me with her left arm across my neck. I hadn't remembered undressing or getting into bed, I guess I was extremely tired after all.

I glanced at my watch to notice it was a new day, then crawled out of bed and ambled out to the balcony. The early morning sunlight caused me to squint my eyes and shade them with my hands until they adjusted to the light. The birds were out chirping and I inhaled the morning air as its coolness caressed my body. I leaned onto the balcony railing to enjoy the view down below. I stood in thought, focusing on nothing in particular, just allowing my mind to roam freely like the birds that were playing in the air.

I walked inside and liberated a bottle of water from its plastic noose, unscrewed the cap and took a sip. I frowned at the taste, bottled water was never one of my preferences. I preferred regular tap water any day.

I took a seat on the sofa. I set the bottle of water on the end table, picked up the phone and dialed the number to Jewel's grandmother's house. The line was still busy and I was now sure that it was off the hook. I returned the phone back to its cradle, stood back up and made my way toward the room. I awakened Jewel and Tasha and requested they get up and go wake everyone else and then made my way to the shower.

Once everyone had bathed and gotten dressed, I took them to Roscoe's Chicken & Waffles for breakfast. From there I figured we would just drop in on their grandmother's, Mrs. Barbra's house, unannounced since I couldn't ever seem to reach anyone by phone. Jewel knew that we were in L.A. to look for her family, but she had no idea that I had the address to her father's mother's house. I pulled up on 107th Street in my red Cadillac Coupe cruising at a slow speed so I could glance at the house numbers in order to locate Mrs. Barbra's home.

I was wondering why the dudes on the corner yards and sidewalks stared at my car so hard when I turned down the street. It never crossed my mind that I was in a gang neighborhood that hated the color red with a passion.

"Hoooover," I heard someone yell out. That word had no meaning to me, so I didn't pay it any attention. I spotted the number I was looking for on a small house that seemed like it had seen better days. The paint was pealing from its walls, the roof wood trimming was missing in different places, the front yard was dried dirt packed down hard from the constant trampling back and forth and there was no life of Mother Nature.

When I pulled up to the curb, two men and a woman stood on the sidewalk in front of the house, drinking tall cans. I pressed the button on the side of my door to roll down the passenger side window where Jewel was sitting, then leaned over toward it so I could look out up at the people.

"Say folks, is this Mrs. Barbra Williams Ridley's house?" I asked, not directing the question to any particular person but just shooting it out there. The women bent down to look into the car to see who I was before considering answering the question. I noticed one of the men was now peeking inside the car through the front window. I gripped the butt of the .45 in the small of my back because I had now become nervous and fidgety. From the rear view mirror I saw two men who were watching the car walking toward us. They were dressed like gang members with blue rags on their head.

"Julia, is that you?" the woman said excitedly in surprise.

"Excuse me, but do I know you?" Jewel asked, as her mind raced in wonder how the woman knew her name. I saw her reach for her gun, but I grabbed her hand to assure her not to trip, that I had her back already.

"Young lady, if you don't get your tail out of that car and give your aunty a big hug, you better, your daddy wrote and told mama y'all was coming to see us," the woman said.

I was now the one in shock. If this black lady was Jewel's aunt, then that meant that Jewel's father was black also and that would explain where Jewel gets the big booty, shapely body, pretty big almond eyes and full sexy, juicy lips from. That also meant she was half black. "Aw shhh, I exclaimed just below a whisper to myself. Why hadn't I figured that out a long time ago?

Jewel got out of the car and gave her aunt a hug and told the kids to do the same, then I exited the car. Tasha stayed clinched to me. She didn't know the lady and didn't care to get to know her. She asked me if she had to hug a stranger and I told her no.

"Brenda, what's up cuzz? You know cuzz?" one of the dudes asked as they approached.

"Yeah, with this loud-ass red car," his friend added.

I knew right then I was in the wrong neighborhood to be driving a red car and I might have some funk over it, being that I was in a Crip hood.

"C-Crazy and Baby-C, everything is cool. This is my brotha Larry's kids. Y'all remember Larry, don't y'all?" she asked.

"Yeah, we remember that slob brotha of yours. Where's his crazy ass at anyway?" C-Crazy asked.

I thought about tripping with the two fools, because I didn't like the words that were coming from their mouths, but I kept my anger contained because I was there to bring Jewel back together with some of her family, not to be tripping with idiots.

Brenda overlooked C-Crazy's question concerning where her brother Larry was. She introduced him and his friend to Jewel and that's where I drew the line. Their frowns turned to smiles, their eyes sparked with lust and their words became gentle. I was ready to dome both of them fools just because the thought of them trying to get to my girl with that fakeness. I already knew Jewel wasn't going to speak to them at all or give them any type of rhythm.

I strolled around the car and hugged my girl around the shoulder and we made our way to the front of the house. Brenda left C-Crazy and Baby-C standing on the sidewalk and the other two men came strolling behind us.

Brenda let us in. There was an elderly woman who sat at the kitchen table sipping some coffee from a white mug. I could see the wisps of steam curling upwards. I was sure the woman was Mrs. Barbra. She was short and skinny, wearing a flower patterned terry cloth bathrobe. She clutched it tightly around the bosom area noticing us coming toward her with Brenda.

"Mama, look who came to see you?" said Brenda, gesturing toward us.

"Lord have mercy. God is good," Mrs. Barbra said, putting down the cup of coffee and raising up from the chair to hug everyone.

"Y'all's daddy told me sho's his name is Larry Ridley that my grand babies was going to come see me real soon. Y'all just don't know how long I waited for this day. I prayed every night to the good Lord that y'all was safe and would come stay with me. Y'all have gotten so big since the last time I saw you. I don't know why that mother of yours was being so stubborn and wouldn't bring y'all to me. She knows exactly where I stay. She seems to have lost her cotton-picking mind since y'all daddy got into that trouble," she said.

Jewel and the kids didn't know what she meant about that, but I understood clearly because I knew about what happened, plus they didn't know anything about their father being in prison. I could see the hurt in Mrs. Barbra's eyes. Living in the ghetto I had a good idea of what categories of people it contained and who might have put some of that decades of hurt there.

"Julia, who is this handsome man you have with you?" she asked.

"That's my boyfriend, grandma. His name is Boo," Jewel said, wiping away the tears that were falling from her eyes. It was an emotional moment for the older kids to be reunited with their loved ones.

"So you the one my son told me about. He mentioned you in his letter. God bless your soul, baby. You such a wonderful kid and I thank you so much for looking after my grand babies. Now come and give me a hug and some sugar," Mrs. Barbra said.

I gave Jewel's grandmother a hug and she kissed me on the cheek. Jewel looked up at me with eyes wanting to know what she was talking about. She was now fitting the pieces of the puzzle together herself, but I knew soon I would be forced to explain everything in detail.

We walked into the living room and I sat down on the old, light brown couch complete with cigarette burns. The living room was now filled with strange faces and the two men who were outside when we pulled up turned out to be Jewel's uncles. A smooth brown complexioned and attractive woman appeared from the back room. She appeared to be in her early twenties and when she smiled it highlighted her high cheekbones. The black No-Question t-shirt that she was wearing stopped slightly above her naval. Her tight No-Question jeans gave me a view of her voluptuous figure. I noticed she was scoping me out, she decided to try to get at me. Her slender face was only inches from mine and her big dark brown eyes penetrated my comfort zone.

Jewel hadn't noticed the woman who was sitting next to me because her family members had her occupied with questions, but Tasha did.

"What's your name, sexy?" the woman asked me, freely touching the diamond chain I had on my neck, admiring its beauty.

"Check this out, baby. You need to back up off me so close before my girl get to tripping," I said.

Tasha ambled her way over to where I was and forced her body between us to create a space so I could breathe without the woman looking all down my throat. Tasha was super smart. She recognized what the woman was trying to do, and knew if Jewel had seen what was going on, that woman would have had a fight on her hands. A fight she really didn't want, and who knows, she might end up getting smoked.

The woman tried to start up a conversation with Tasha, but Tasha ignored her questions, lying her head against my left arm and announcing that she was ready to go. I glanced around the living room and noticed all the furniture was outdated and worn down. Up against the wall was a floor model TV with a built-in record player, radio and an eight-track cassette player on top. Now if that wasn't outdated, then I don't know what is. The ceiling slumped downward as if it would cave in any moment. A big cooking pot sat on the floor to catch the falling water that leaked through the roof into the house from the swamp cooler. The once green carpet was nothing more than part of the concrete it laid on. Old yellowing family pictures decorated the dingy walls and cabinets.

The kitchen was in no better shape. The metal cabinets were rusting at the edges and the wallpaper they were covered in had peeled back. The kitchen ceiling was black with soot from the smoke of food being cooked and the dinner table was missing one of its legs. It had been pushed up against the corner of a wall to keep it from falling. The grunge filled kitchen floor was missing tiles. It looked like a dirty, unfinished puzzle.

I spent all day and some of the night at the house getting acquainted with Jewel's family. The woman who sat by me and Tasha turned out to be one of their aunts. I spent most of my time sitting right on the couch enjoying the strong blow of cold air from the swamp cooler, its humming sound relaxed me. I laid back and enjoyed the moment as I would do at my own house before my grandmother passed away.

Mrs. Barbra insisted that we stay the night. I had no problem with that because I had already claimed my resting ground, but the kids didn't want to. Plus from what it seemed like, she already had too many people living there. So we said our good-bye's and promised to return tomorrow. I also wanted to eat some of the gumbo she mentioned she would cook tomorrow. I asked if I could help out with buying the ingredients.

"Oh, no baby, bless your heart. You have done too much already. The least I can do is feed you," she said.

I insisted that I give her some money to buy some of the items because the ingredients for some real good Down South gumbo could cost anywhere between two to three hundred dollars. I was assuming that there would be a lot more people at her house tomorrow coming by to see Jewel and the kids, and once they smelled that gumbo they were going to want to eat. One thing I was sure about, black folks loves gumbo, barbeque and chicken. I gave Mrs. Barbara $300 before we left her house. When we made it back to our rooms everyone was too tired to do anything but hit the sack.

The morning came quickly. We started off at Roscoe's Chicken & Waffles which had become our favorite place for breakfast. I had written Jewel's father Larry a quick note and mailed it off from the hotel. I asked him to call home soon as possible so he could speak to his kids. Jewel questioned me about what her grandmother had said and how I knew where she lived, I figured she would. I couldn't shine her question off because she waited for the right time to ask me, when I had finished eating breakfast.

I told her it would be best if she spoke with her father first and then I promised to explain everything to her. She didn't press the issue, the subject was dropped and we discussed her uncles and aunts she had forgotten on her father's side.

"Jewel, why you never told me that your father was black?" I asked.

"Boo, you never asked."

I left that subject alone because she was right, I had never asked. I paid the tab and left a dub on the table for the waitress and headed for Mrs. Barbra's house. When we got there, new faces were seated inside visiting, waiting for us to arrive. More people flowed in as the evening began to creep in. This family was big. Mrs. Barbra had thirteen kids, eight girls and five boys, and eleven of them had kids of their own. She had a lot of grand kids, Jewel's cousins, and they were of every age, and some had kids of their own. It looked like a family reunion.

I would have given Mrs. Barbra a grand if I would have known her whole family was coming over. Jewel had this aunt who was in her early thirties. She was super cool, I immediately took a liking to her. She kept me laughing with her jokes, talking about everyone who was there at the house. Her name was Diana. She had jet black hair that fell to her shoulders, pretty face, with unblemished caramel skin. She had a big gap in her front teeth. You wouldn't ever known that she smoked crack by just looking at her. I was shocked when she told me she did. She was outspoken and straight forward about herself, I respected her. She kept herself clean, looking nice and wasn't into running the streets like most smokers I've known.

Jewel and the rest of the kids, except Tasha, were enjoying their family company. Tasha stayed glued to me. Diana, Tasha, Brenda and eight more relatives and I hung outside on the front porch kicking it. I saw a big barbeque grill on the side of the house and asked Diana if she wanted to fire it up. Brenda jumped in on our conversation and agreed to help cook as long as I got her a tall can. I noticed Brenda liked to drink beer. I told Diana if she cooked, I'd buy the food. She agreed.

Diana, Tasha, Brenda and I shot to the grocery store and bought charcoal, lighter fluid, barbeque sauce, six cases of beef ribs, ten whole chickens, ten boxes of Farmer John beef hot links, twenty t-bone steaks, a half case of hot dog buns, a loaf of wheat bread, paper plates, spoons, forks, napkins, two big plastic garbage cans and ten cases of sodas. I gave Brenda the money to go purchase the liquor and ice since I was underage to buy liquor. She got a case of Armadale, four cases each of the fridge pack Old English 800 and Miller Genuine Draft, and four bottles of Bacardi.

We packed up the car and headed back to the house. The barbeque grill had been cleaned and stood next to its twin grill. Someone figured that one grill was not enough and they were right. The men that were outside unloaded the car and filled the new garbage cans with the sodas and ice in one and the other with adult drinks, then sat them on the side of the house. Diana was inside cleaning and preparing the meats while one of her brothers fired up the big grills. Jewel came out and introduced all her female cousins to me and I couldn't help but notice all of them had big round firm booties. One of her cousins had a video and digital camera. We took pictures and kicked it outside listening to music. I watched them all dance, staring at all that rump and voluptuous breast bounce around. Diana had the grills now smoking, sending the aroma off into the air through the neighborhood.

There were now people who lived in the neighborhood coming

around. Most were gang members, wondering what was going on, and saw all the girls hanging out dancing. There were well over fifty family members here at the house. Those who weren't family, Diana made them stay on the other side of the fence. She noticed that I was now becoming uncomfortable. I strolled to my car reached under the seat, grabbed the Uzi and extra clips, jacked it off and walked back into the front yard with it in my hand, freely exposed to all watching eyes to let it be known that I was heated with something to spray a group of fools at one time if I had to. Jewel looked at me as if something was wrong. I read her eyes and shook my head in her direction and took up a seat on the porch by Brenda.

"What's up nephew?" Diana asked, already claiming me as a family member. That was common among black folks when a person was dating someone in their family.

"It's nothing, Diana. I like to always stay ready so I don't have to get ready. I know them fools peeped those Nevada plates on my ride, plus it's the wrong color and I'm not feeling their style of approach, that's all." I hadn't told her the main reason, that I just didn't like Crip gang members. They made me sick at the pit of my stomach at their sight, the way they wear their clothes, pants hanging all the way down off their stanky, narrow asses, they looked like they can't be trusted or had any morals and seemed to have a natural foul order about themselves. The way they talk sounded ignorant, cuzz this, cuzz that, starting every sentence with that word. I just didn't feel them in no type of way.

I stepped inside the house after tucking the Uzi underneath my shirt and began talking to Mrs. Barbra as I watched her prepare gumbo. She told me all about Jewel's mother and father. I was surprised to find out they were both gangsters back in the days. She said, "When she looks at me and Jewel, she sees her son and Jewel's mother." I asked her when Larry normally called the house.

"He can't call, baby. My phone has one of those blocks on it because the bill is too high from collect calls. I can't never seem to catch up on my bills being that I only get a social security check once a month and these darn lazy kids of mine around here don't want to help out. I know he's probably been having it rough up in there because I hadn't sent him no change in a long while," she said.

"How much is your phone bill, Mrs. Barbra?"

"Oh no baby, don't even think about trying to help me pay it. You have done plenty already."

"Mrs. Barbra, listen. It's very important for Jewel and them kids to speak to their father and have an open relationship with him. If that means that a bill or two have to be paid for them to do that, then that's what I will do. Jewel is my girlfriend and I love her. More importantly, she's a friend and I will not allow something such as an unpaid phone bill be the reason why she can't speak to her father. So I'm asking you respectfully, let me pay the bill and get the block taken off so her father can call home and speak with his kids," I said.

She thought about it while she diced up okra in a pot. "Baby, I only wish my kids were so thoughtful. I see why my granddaughter so crazy over you because you are a respectful, thoughtful young gentleman."

"Don't forget Mrs. Barbra, and handsome as well," I added.

We both shared a laugh. She pulled open a corroded cabinet drawer and shuffled through the small stack of mail and handed me the phone bill. I looked at its total and knew the $252.87 bill wouldn't be a problem to pay. I peeled three crisp Franklins off my wad and returned the bill with the money to her. She thanked me.

I started on my way back outside until I remembered what I wanted to tell her. "Mrs. Barbra, one more thing. Can you call up to the prison and have them notify Larry to call home? Just tell the officials that it is an emergency, that way they will give him the message."

"I sure will baby. I'll take care of everything tomorrow as soon as I pay the bill," she assured me.

I stepped outside and the atmosphere felt like I was at a park. The little kids were running around playing freeze tag. The boys were in the middle of the street playing football and the older girls stood around dancing and trying to look pretty. Jewel looked like she was in deep conversation with a group of cousins. Tasha was sitting in the same place I left her watching the action. Diana was at the grills flipping over the ribs. I had gotten hungry and was ready to get my grub on. Brenda was standing at the fence talking to some guys and pointing toward me. I wondered what that was all about and kept my focus in their direction. She walked over to where I was to tell me, "Those dudes want to know if they could get a plate of barbeque when it is done."

I told her to tell them, "Nope, and they can't buy one either."

She went and told them and they shot me a cold stare and I matched theirs with an even colder one until they walked off. Diana walked over to me with the long fork in her hand she used to turn over the meat with. She stood next to me commenting on the football game that was going on with the kids in the street. A lot of the kids stayed in the neighborhood. She made jokes about every play and I couldn't help but laugh at them. She only clowned loud enough that it could be heard among those who were on the porch.

Kevin had major speed. Every time he got the ball he made a touchdown, and Jewlean was the team quarterback, a real tomboy at heart. An argument had begun with one of the members on the opposite team who said he had tagged Kevin before he made it to the goal. Kevin disputed it and the boy pushed him hard in the chest, sending him to his back on the ground. Jewlean took his place before he could make it back to his feet and shot a straight, hard right to the boy's nose, dropping him to his knees. The boy, crying, jumped up and took off running down the street. Jewlean looked over in my direction. I flared my nose and shot a frown her way displaying my disapproval of her performance. I've trained them to fight until their opponent was out and she only knocked him down and didn't finish him off.

Jewel didn't see what had happened, but someone in the crowd had informed her and when she turned around in Kevin's direction, the action was over. When she looked at me, I shook my head to leave them alone. The boy was on his way back with a group of adults in tow. I didn't move, but Diana walked out into the streets where Kevin was.

"Which one of y'all little bastards hit my boy?" the woman yelled.

"Lady, you better get away from in front of my house with that nonsense and let these kids be kids," Diana said. "Y'all get back up in that yard," she demanded, shouting at the kids.

Kevin or Jewlean didn't budge from her side. The other kids had done what she told them to do and slowly ambled back into the yard and watched from the side line. Jewel and her cousins walked out of the yard, over to where Diana was. That's when me and Tasha made our presence known.

"What the problem here, black?" I asked the man out of the bunch, seemed as though he was the boy's father.

"Cuzz, what you mean what's the problem? There's going to be a big problem in a minute if my son can't get no head-up fade, that's the problem," he snapped harshly.

I was now on fire inside. Here was an old nigga coming down here gang banging, trying to make a big deal out of a kid fight.

"Say, bruh, I don't care about none of all that problem shit you stressing because I'm going to deal with whatever come my way. Now if your boy want to get his fade on with my folks, then that's really not a problem. Ask him which one he wants to scrap, the one he pushed or the girl who hit him in the nose that sent him home crying like a little bitch?"

"Boy, you let a girl beat you up?" his mother snapped. "Boy, you better get over there and kick that girl ass or I'ma beat your ass until I get tired," she said angrily, pushing him toward us.

"Jewlean, I'll fight him for you," Tasha said.

"Yeah, Jewlean, let your little sister take care of your lightweight. He's not in your league. You already sent him home crying to his mammy. Maybe the little sissy could beat up a little seven year old," I said.

"Little punk, my husband will kick your ass," the woman said.

"I doubt that seriously," I replied.

"Tramp, I'll beat your ass now," Jewel threatened her. "We can all get it cracking out here!"

"You got that right, baby," I added. "Tasha, go on and knock that chump out so we can go and eat," I demanded.

Diana asked me not to let Tasha fight the boy. I told her "Don't worry, I taught her well. She's a real rider, and to just kick back and watch the show." The boy's family laughed at Tasha when they saw her size compared to their son. When I let Tasha loose, she was on him like an enraged pit bull. She split his lip with the first blow. That was followed by a roundhouse to the side of his right leg that brought him down to her height, then a flying right knee to his face and a left and right hook to the jaw before his body fell to the ground. She stomped on his head a few times before Jewel pulled her off of him. If she hadn't, I wasn't. I would have let her stomp the life out of that little punk. No one could believe that Tasha had demolished the boy with such ease and grace.

"Caveman, I know you ain't going to stand there and let them hurt Junior like that!" the woman cried out to her husband.

"Cuzz, now you got to give me a fade," he said.

"First, I ain't no crab, and secondly, I really don't have a problem knocking your old ass out since y'all want to come down here and pick on some kids," I said, and pulled the Uzi and extra clips from underneath my shirt and handed them to Jewel. I saw the fear in their eyes when they saw the weapon. They hadn't anticipated the gun. The three guys who were with them had backed up as if they were about to make a break for it at any minute. I quickly put on my black leather gloves and squared off with the man they called Caveman. He did look like a real caveman.

"Boo, beat him up real good," Tasha said.

A left, right, left hook to the body, left uppercut. I dipped to the right with a right hook to the body, a straight left jab and a spinning roundhouse that landed to the side of his head ending the fight before it even started for him. I kicked him in the ribs while he laid knocked out cold on the ground and stomped on the back of his head trying to make his face a part of the street pavement.

His wife screamed and begged for me to stop, but I continued to punish the fool. She didn't make no physical attempts to try to stop me because she knew Jewel had the Uzi in her hand. She cried for the other men to help him, but they paid her no attention. They weren't stupid. Ignorant yes, but not stupid.

Mrs. Barbra must have heard all the commotion because she came outside and saw me putting my feet on the fool real tough.

"Baby cut that out, you hear? Before you kill that man!" she yelled.

Mrs. Barbra saved him from what I had in mind, but I kicked him in the side of the face one last time for good measure. I giggled, staring up at his wife with a smile and said, "Man he's sorry, and you see what ya done got him into because of your big mouth?"

She didn't attempt to say anything, her tough talk was now silent. I motioned for Jewel to give me my Uzi back, tucking it back underneath my shirt. With a blink of the eye Jewel took flight on the woman. The woman had chunkums, but she was still no match for my girl.

I pulled Jewel off her after the woman was on her back going into convulsions.

"Everybody, let's go. I thought we were going to see a fight, not people sleeping," Diana joked and we all laughed.

We all had big plates of barbeque, potato salad and a soda to wash it down with. We stood in front of the house getting our grub on. The dudes that came with Caveman and his wife and son helped them get back to where they came from. We enjoyed the rest of the day. Everyone was too full to eat any of Mrs. Barbra's gumbo, so we took some back with us to the hotel. I woke up in the middle of the night and ate a bowl. Jewlean had beat me to it. She sat at the table with a big bowl in front of her sucking the meat out a crab leg. We both sat there eating.

That morning our day started off with the usual. We decided before we go visit their family, we would spend some quality time together as a family and go sightseeing and do a little shopping for a few short sets in Hollywood. Maybe we would get lucky and see a few stars in the process. There was all types of weird looking people roaming the Hollywood streets. It looked like a circus to me. We walked in a few stores and right back out. The clothes they were selling had outrageous price tags. I could get the exact same items at a mall in Las Vegas for a lot less.

My girl seen a white eyelet shirt she wanted me to have, so she picked it up for me at an outrageous price, I was sure. The shirt looked like something Prince had worn in Purple Rain. I seen a couple of gold color women's purses that I thought would look sexy with Jewel's gowns, but I couldn't decide on which one to get, so I bough both.

We stopped in a jewelry store to browse for women's rings. None of the employees made an attempt to assist us. They catered to the white customers who were dressed in minks and holding small dogs. I glanced around the spacious elegant jewelry store to notice that Jewel, the kids and I were the only people in there that weren't white. The employees who weren't catering to a customer made themselves look busy. Jewel had also noticed the favoritism among the employees by their frowns, evidently assumed we couldn't even afford to buy a pair of gold earrings. Jewel ambled off toward one of the employees who was just standing behind one of the jewelry cases.

"Excuse me, ma'am, I would like to try on a ring I like. Could you please assist me?" she asked.

The woman gave off a feeble smile before responding. "Sure, in which case is the ring you admire?"

Jewel pointed toward the case and moved toward it. The woman followed. Jewel pointed out the ring she liked.

"Now that's a very, very expensive piece, miss, I don't believe that you are able to afford such a piece, I'm sure our prices are beyond your bracket. There's nothing in this store under thirty grand and the diamond rings in this case, especially the one you pointed at, start at one point one million and up. So I am going to have to ask you and your friends to leave our store now," the old woman said as gentle as her feelings would allow her.

"How do you know what I can afford or not afford?" Jewel began.

I grabbed her by the waist and moved toward the exit before she could start arguing with the lady. I felt the hurt in Jewel's voice and I didn't like no one degrading my girl as if she was some type of piece of shit, but I kept my cool and thanked the woman for her assistance. They watched as we exited the store.

"But Boo, that lady!"

"I know, I know exactly what you about to say, but don't trip. One day they will get theirs, believe me, they will get theirs. So don't get all worked up over that. She's right, we don't have millions to be buying diamonds. One day I'll be able to buy you something like that. I don't think they seen your necklace you got around your neck either. If they had, they probably thought it was fake. Like I said, don't trip. Let's go get a bite to eat then go hang out at your grandma's pad."

Jewel didn't want to eat out, she wanted to just go to her grandmother's house and eat some leftovers. She asked me if we could get her grandmother's roof repaired. I told her it was fine by me, that half of the money was hers anyway.

She didn't like when I said what's hers and what's mine. She felt that I should look at it like it's ours together as one. I told her she needed to have the entire house remodeled. We decided to do just that. When I pulled up at her grandmother's house Diana was outside watering the hard dirt.

"What up Diana, what's cracking with you?" I asked.

"Crack, nephew, I'm on one right now I'm off that shit. But I was tweaking so tough, I had to do something, so I'm watering the yard," she said with all honesty and I burst into laughter. "Nephew let me borrow a few ends so I can go get me a hit to calm my nerves. Well I don't know why I said borrow because I really don't have no intentions of paying you back. So let me just have a few dollars because I don't need Uzi's being pulled on me if I can't pay you back."

"Diana you should have been a comedian because you're funny. Yeah I got you, so don't trip. Just let me go up in here and say hello to your mother and I'll be back to hit you on the hip with something," I said and made my way into the house. I didn't feel comfortable about giving her money to go buy drugs and get high with, but I'd rather give her the money than see her in the streets hustling for it. Plus I respected her honesty about what she wanted it for. I went and hugged Mrs. Barbra, she told me that everything was taken care of. I went outside and gave Diana a Franklin. She told me after today it would be her last time smoking crack, she was going to go check into a rehab to clean up. I made her promise me that she would keep her word, then I peeled off four more big face Franklins and handed them to her.

"You might as well do it big since it's going to be your last time," I said.

She looked up at me as if I was crazy and said, "Nephew, you are so different from anyone else I know, are all the men in Vegas like you?"

"Diana, I don't know what you mean about that, but I'm one of a kind."

"I can see that, you got me not wanting to go blow this money on drugs. I'm thinking about giving mama two hundred of it and then go get my hair and nails done," she admitted.

"Well, it's yours to do what you want with it as long as you keep that promise to go get help. I'll tell you what I'll do for you. I'll make sure you have all the things you need in there. I'll personally go buy it and send it to you," I said before Mrs. Barbra stuck her head out the door and told me Larry was on the phone and wanted to speak to me.

"Mama, what Larry? My brotha Larry?" Diana asked.

"Yeah gal, who else you think I'm talking about?"

Diana shot into the house to speak to her brother. When I walked in Jewel was sitting on the couch crying with the phone to her ear. Kevin was on the kitchen phone, and Jewlean, Benny and Lisa shared the cordless. I motioned for Jewel to scoot over so I could sit in my spot where the air from the swamp cooler could blow on me. She passed me the phone.

"Hello?"

"Hey young man, how are you?"

"All's well, and yourself?" I asked.

"Man, I'm one of the happiest men in the world right now and it's all because of you. Boo, I'm telling you man, I promise I'm going to repay you whenever I get out, I promise you that on my life."

"Well, don't trip on that, dawg, you just take care of yourself in there. Hold on one minute folks, let me make these shorties hang up the rest of the phones so we can talk in private," I said, then yelled for Kevin and Jewlean to hang up the phones.

"I'm back dawg, sorry about that."

"Boo, do you gangbang? The reason I'm asking is I've noted you always use the word dawg or folks. Those words are normally used by blood gang bangers," he said.

I told him that I wasn't no gang banger but nothing less than a gangsta who's part of the blood family.

"So am I, dawg," he said excitedly. "I known it was something unique about you from the first time I got your letter and read your words. I should have figured it out myself. When you wrote the letter in red ink and from the pictures you sent me, you always was flamed up, man that's a beautiful thing. Not only that, I got a righteous son-in-law, but he's also a Damu. Mom's always said God is good and you living proof of that. And man, I would really appreciate it if you call me Pops, dad or something else since I am going to be your father-in-law when you and Julia get married. I want a lot of grand babies too," he said.

"Aight then, pops, who's going to be watching all these grand babies you want? Not me, and I don't think Jewel is either because she's always too busy watching me." We both laughed and I continued. I asked him when he was getting out, he didn't say, just said he needed some assistance on his appeal because as of now he had no date. I knew what he meant, he had a life sentence but just couldn't fix his mouth to say it. I told him I knew a top notch lawyer by the name of David Lee Phillips in Las Vegas. He travels all over the state representing clients in high profile cases. I assured him he would be one of the best lawyers to assist him with his appeal.

"Son, I don't have a pot to piss in and a window to throw it out of, yet alone money to pay for a lawyer."

"Pops, why is you tripping? Me and Jewel going to take care of the finances, I just want to know if you wanted me to send him your way?"

"Yeah, do that man, man please do that as soon as possible."

"Don't worry, it's done. Also, can you receive care packages or do you have to buy it from one of those vendors?" I asked.

He told me he could get food and clothes packages, but it had to be purchased from an approved vendor. So I told him to send me the information and to get about seven others who I could send him a package in their name for him while the getting is good. He told me that everything would be in the mail by tomorrow. I said my good-bye's and passed Jewel back the phone. Her and the kids talked for a long time. I dozed off to sleep until the hot air came blowing down on my face and awakened me. I felt sweat rolling down my chest.

"What the hell?" I said, wiping the sweat from my forehead. The front and back door was open to let fresh air flow through the house. The water pump had gone out. Somebody really had to do something about that. I couldn't be hanging out at no hot house, it was time to go. Mrs. Barbra told me that someone was on their way to put in a new water pump.

Jewel told me her dad said he would be home soon. I didn't appreciate him lying to my girl, but I totally understood why he said that. He didn't want to tell her he had a life sentence, which would have broken her heart, so I left her believing that. She also told me about a private contractor who said he could remodel the house for forty three grand and he would be able to start today if we wanted. Whoever was supposed to come and fix the cooler was taking too long, so I told the kids to pack it up and let's go. Jewel also got her grandmother, Mrs. Barbra, to come along with us.

We returned to our hotel room. Mrs. Barbra admired the place and couldn't stop talking about how beautiful it was. Jewel counted out the money for the contractor and called him to pick it up so he could get started. She figured she could get her grandmother to stay at the hotel with us until the house was ready. She hadn't told her about the house being remodeled. It was going to be a surprise and I was wondering how she was going to get her grandmother to stay with us a few weeks without wanting to go home. That was something I did not want to get in the middle of.

Four days passed by and Jewel was on a roll keeping Mrs. Barbra busy. I paid for three more weeks for the hotel room.

Diana kept her promise and checked in a drug rehab. She did give Mrs. Barbra two hundred dollars like she said, and after getting her hair and nails and toes done she smoked the rest. I hired the lawyer David Lee Phillips to do Larry's appeal. He tapped my pockets for forty seven grand, but he was well worth it. If Larry had a chance to get out, David Lee Phillips would be the one to spring him, I was sure.

I stopped by Mrs. Barbra's house every day to see the progress the contractor was making on the house. Plus I wanted to catch Larry's phone calls. There were twenty workers doing different tasks and they were all Mexicans. I admired their work performance, they were hard workers. I treated them all to lunch when I was there and made sure they had a constant supply of cold bottled water and Nectar fruit juices.

I had gotten Larry's letter with the vendor package list of the items and names to send the packages to. Everything was already written out with the price. So I went and bought eight money orders, made them out to Golden State Care Packages, placed them in individual envelopes with the order form and sent them out. I paid for the 21-hour turn around service so soon as they received the orders they would be filled and sent out.

I picked up a magazine with my girl Jennifer Lopez from American Idol on the front cover. Now that's what I call super thick and fine. I kissed the front page before I paid for it. The store cashier shot me a strange look until he saw who was on the front cover, then smiled up at me and announced, "She is fine ain't she!" I gave him a wink in agreement to his analysis, then stormed out the door. I hadn't been able to spend quality time with Jewel, she's been babysitting her grandmother until the house was ready. It was now going on two weeks and not once had Mrs. Barbra inquired about going home. She had met some new friends in the lobby who were also staying at the hotel during their vacation.

Jewel had taken her shopping, got her hair and nails done and she pranced around the hotel like she was twenty-one all over again flirting with the young bellboys and pool attendants. Mrs. Barbra was enjoying herself, her eyes gleamed with a brighter spark than they had before.

I took advantage of the situation to spend some one-on-one time with Jewel. We decided to dress up and step out on the town for the evening. We were back in Hollywood, but now on Sunset where prostitutes were working. Some seemed to be no older than I was, but turning tricks like true professionals. I saw men standing out watching their girls. I never seen a pimp in a jean outfit and tennis shoes communicating to someone over a two way radio They sure didn't look like no pimps to me as rough as they was looking.

I then thought about Break-a-Hoe, how he would have a field day out here styling and profiling, copping and locking and scooping up all the chips just by popping his whip.

"Hey young pimp," a man that stood up against a wall said, interrupting my thoughts.

"You must be new on the land being I haven't seen you around. They call me Pimping Ray money," reaching out his hand as he continued. "I see you trying to get you and your lady knocked off dressed like that, pimp. The one times will swoop on you so fast and put you under the jail, and fine as your work is, what you got standing next to you, I know you don't want to chance that getting knocked off?"

"Say playa, I'm not no pimp and my girl is not a hoe. We just out kicking it," I corrected him.

153

"Oh, my bad baby boy, excuse me. I thought you was in the game, but just a little word of advice. You shouldn't be over here, this is the hoe stroll where the girls work, and you being dressed like you are will bring attention to you that you don't want," he told me. I thanked him for the heads up and walked off. He watched me and Jewel until we was out of his sight. We stopped at the corner where a Mexican man had a pushcart selling snow cones, we purchased two rainbow flavors.

Just then I noticed we was three buildings down from the jewelry store we had prior been kicked out of after being disrespected. I said to Jewel, "Let's go inside and see how they treat us now that we are dressed in the best designer clothes and expensive jewelry." She frowned up at my idea, but she went along with it anyway. We tossed the snow cones and walked inside. There weren't as many workers or customers inside like when we first went there.

I pulled out one of my wads and held it in my hand so the employee at the jewelry case I approached could see all the crisp bills folded over each other.

"May I help you sir with a specific piece?" she asked.

I anticipated such a reaction and I was going to take full advantage of the moment.

"Yes, I have a hundred grand on me," I said pulling out my other wad from my front pocket and added, "I'm looking to spend no more than two million on a wedding ring and there's a ring my soon to be wife liked and I believe it is this one." I pointed at the ring that Jewel told me she liked.

Jewel was at another case browsing around and this time we had no problem getting any assistance. The lady freely opened the case, removed the ring, then handed it to me so I could examine it more closely. The ring was gorgeous and I could envision my girl with it on her finger. So I asked the sales woman if I could place a down payment on it until tomorrow. She didn't hesitate to oblige me. I peeled off ten grand from my wad and she took the ring to the back office and returned with some forms to fill out.

I asked her if they had a restroom I could use and she escorted me to the back to use the employees restroom. I placed on my leather gloves and strode out, passing the door that led to the office. I stopped to turn the knob and the door opened. I saw the woman manager who had kicked us out and two men sitting down watching the store security monitors. I pulled my .357 and rushed in, letting the door close behind me. Before they could realize what was happening, I was on them.

They didn't attempt to move.

I laid them all down on the floor and quickly tied their hands and feet with a phone cord and plastic bags. I watched the security screens as I swiftly emptied the jewelry from the safes and removed the disks from the DVD recorders.

I almost overlooked the safe that was in the floor underneath a desk. When I motioned toward it I seen disappointment in the manger's face. I knew then I had struck a gold mine and what a gold mine it was. Stacks of money and raw diamonds of different colors. I packed everything in one of the jewelry briefcases, untied my three victims and escorted them to the front. I made them lay down in the middle of the floor. When Jewel saw what I was doing, she followed suit with her Glock trained on one of the store employees. Once we had all the employees laying face down, I snatched the manger up and escorted her to the cases until every single piece of jewelry was removed and in my possession. I smiled up in her face and said, "I guess we can't afford to buy anything in your store, so you can see we decided to take what we want from it." The woman looked confused until she remembered who I was.

I asked Jewel if she touched any of the glass cases with her hands and she assured me she had not. I kicked the manger to the floor, aimed my weapon directly at her face. She displayed an expression pleading for her life, but her words were hindered from fear. I squeezed the trigger, her face was instantly mutilated by the .357 hollow point. I then domed the rest of the employees because they could identify us, but it was mainly out of spite for how they treated me and my girl when we first visited the store. I had shown no mercy to anyone who belittled my precious Jewel, especially those who displayed racism. I felt no sympathy for a human life and unsympathetic to whoever I had to walk over to keep those I loved from having to struggle and feel hunger pains ever again.

Jewel and I exited the store calmly with our increased wealth in hand and took our time making our way back to my ride. There was no rush because no one had heard the gun shots or expected any foul play to have taken place. We went unnoticed, at least that's what I assumed.

The hotel room was empty of life when we returned. Mrs. Barbra had left a note for us taped on our bedroom door, stating that she and the kids went to see a movie and for us to enjoy the free time. That was nice of her to recognize that Jewel and I needed some quality time together, but I wasn't comfortable with her just running off with the kids without asking one of us first. It didn't matter to me if she was their grandmother or not. I didn't know much about her or how she may be thinking. It hadn't once crossed my mind that she would harm them, but what did bother me was she might try to hide them out so she can keep them with her.

After I pondered on the possibilities, I quickly shook that thought out of my mind because I known black women way too well to be trying to kidnap some kids. I smiled to myself at the thought knowing that no one wanted to kidnap no black kids because they are bad as hell, at least these ones I know.

I followed Jewel into the room and secured the door behind me. I found the ring that Jewel had wanted and took a hold of her hand and gently slid it onto her finger. She smiled at the sight then looked up at me to capture my eyes with her own, probing my mind and soul with her burning desire.

We stood in silence for a few minutes then she murmured. "Thank you poppy, I never...no one has!" Tears formed in her eyes and her voice shook when she spoke before I interrupted.

"Baby girl, I know...I know what you're trying to say, don't trip. You are my life and you are entitled to the best of everything."

She raised her arms to me and I wrapped my arms around her. She began to melt in my embrace. She tilted her head back and opened her lips inviting my tongue inside to explore the moist sweetness of her kiss. She moaned softly. We undressed each other with gentle hands. Her nipples hardened from the cool breeze from the ceiling fan that windmilled at a medium speed and I leaned forward taking one of them in my mouth. Our hunger for each other was evident. We made love with the most intimate strokes and caresses until our sexual cravings was sufficiently satisfied. We laid on the bed exhausted from deliberately prolonging the pleasures we exchanged. I put my arms around her waist and she turned in my arms to face me with a smile before closing her eyes. I laid in silence with her in my arms admiring her beauty before I joined her in the dream world.

CHAPTER 10

Mrs. Barbra announced she was ready to return home. "My stay here has been wonderful, but it's time to return back to my reality," she offered as a demand rather than a request.

Jewel sat up slowly rubbing the sleep from her eyes as Mrs. Barbra vanished into the silence of the hotel room. Her soft leather sandaled feet left a mere whisper of her passing somewhere in the distance. I stood quietly, staring at Jewel for a few minutes, wondering if she planned on keeping her grandmother here at the hotel. I could see clearly in her face that she was in deep thought of how she could prolong her grandmother's stay. She looked up at me with eyes pleading for a suggestion, but I was not about to offer one by any means. Honestly, I was ready for Mrs. Barbra to get back home with the quickness so she could cook some soul food and I could get my eat on. Yes, it may seem selfish and immature of me, but I had to keep it real with myself.

After we finished dressing, we took Mrs. Barbra home. There was no sight of the construction workers I assumed would be there working. Only the traces of their professional skills remained. But they had made the house beautiful and it was nearly unrecognizable. I parked and we got out. The contractor had done a fine job on the place. There was now nature around the house, grass, trees and rose bushes that lined the front windows of the house. I entered the house first and everyone followed me carefully. The house was completed and the new furniture I had brought for Ms. Barbra had been delivered and nicely placed in the house. Mrs. Barbra was overwhelmed as she toured the house to find that it was fully furnished and it had been remodeled. She just assumed I was the caper behind all this new excitement her eyes and heart were experiencing.

157

"Baby, you shouldn't have," she said looking directly at me. "Where you get the money to do all of this?"

I arched one eyebrow, rubbed the right side of my cheek and calmly pointed a finger at Jewel and said, "Mrs. Barbra, I didn't have anything to do with this, that's all her doing."

Jewel looked up at me with a wide mouth as if she was going to defend herself from my accusation, but decided not to. She bit her bottom lip in frustration rolling her eyes at me. I shot a cunning smile, then a wink her way and made my way back into the living room.

"Thank you, baby," Mrs. Barbra said to Jewel and pulled her into her arms. "That's a fine young man you have there, you take good care of him, you hear?" I heard her say as I was leaving from where they stood in the hallway.

A week passed and I hadn't yet called Big Dee. I spent most of my time up under the new swamp cooler, resting and being pampered by Mrs. Barbra with soul food. She sure did know how to burn in the kitchen and one of my favorite dishes she cooked was mustard greens, hot water corn bread and neck bones and gravy with rice. Jewel and the kids had the pleasure of spending a lot of time with their father over the phone. Tasha stayed under me reading from the dictionary I had gotten her. Benny and those damn laptops kept him out of the picture. Jewlean, Kevin and Lisa did whatever made them happy and Jewel lounged around me gossiping on the phone with her female relatives when she wasn't speaking to her father.

Larry told me all about himself and Jewel's mother and where I could find Jewel's other family on her mother's side. He sent me two addresses that were located in New York, one in Rochester and the other in Auburn. He said I could locate her other family at either address, but Rochester was where her grandparents resided. That was where I decided we would go.

I told Jewel and the kids we would be leaving for New York in a few days, so we must start preparing now for the trip. I made reservations with American Airlines for first class seats to New York. I rented a storage room to park my ride and trunk the stuff that we were not taking with us. I packaged up the rest of the stolen jewelry into five pound cans that I had cushioned with money and sealed them with a can sealer. Then I mailed to Big Dee with a typed letter concerning my position and what I wanted her to do with the cans. I was sure the package would be in her hands within twenty-four hours because I mailed it from the post office with their overnight delivery service. I packed the heat as well, I wasn't about to risk trying to carry them on the plane. I just figured I'll hook up with someone out in New York who has a gun connection and cop out that way.

Jewel had stuffed two huge teddy bears with money to bring along with us, wrapped up like gifts. There was a law about how much money each person could travel with on the airplanes. Nothing over ten grand was allowable without the approval of the Airport Federal Security who needed to see all legal records where the money came from. Nothing we had was actually legal, depending on whose point of view you accept. We all pocketed ten grand on our person. We exited the taxi in the Los Angeles LAX parking lot and headed inside with our luggage. I walked up to the service counter and gave the clerk my name so I could pay for our tickets. She punched my name in the computer and smiled up at me.

"Freeze! Put your hands in the air so I can see them, now, do it now!" someone shouted. I turned to my right to see what was going on and found barrels of pistols, MP-5's, and 12-guage shotguns pointed directly at me.

"What the hell?" I dropped the money I had in my hand onto the counter and raised my hands into the air. Tasha stood next to me looking directly at the uniformed officers who had their weapons trained on me and were shouting demands all at once. I nudged Tasha with my leg, directing her to get away from me, but she didn't move.

"Tasha, walk over there where Jewel at," I said gently in a whisper, trying not to sound nervous, but she didn't budge from my side as if she stood a chance of protecting me from being shot.

"I want you to walk backwards slowly away from the little girl, sir, keeping your hands where I can see them. Do as I say, place your hands on your head. Now with your left arm bring it behind you. Now do the same with the right hand." I complied with the instructions.

Tasha followed me as I was backing up.

"Little girl, I need for you to move away from that man," the officer snapped. It was more with caution for her safety than anger. His words had fallen on deaf ears because she wasn't complying.

"Tasha, get your ass over there where Jewel at now!" I said harshly with a voice deeper than usual. I had frightened her with my words, being that I never once snapped at her. She turned toward me and looked up in my face. Tears were now rolling down her cheeks. She hugged me at the waist and that quickly I had almost forgotten that I had been ordered to put my hands behind my back. As badly as I wanted to hug her back, I wasn't going to risk being shot. She released me from her hug and walked over to where Jewel and the other children were standing. When I looked toward their direction I seen tears in all their eyes. I forced a smile to my face and winked at them all to reassure them that everything would be okay.

"Now sir, get on your knees and cross your legs," the officer ordered.

As soon as I crossed my legs, I was rushed to the ground, causing me to strike my chin on the tile floor. I felt knees pinning me down on different parts of my body as they struggled to handcuff me. I made no attempt to resist, but they were so anxious to secure my hands.

"Sir, I am placing you under arrest for murder and robbery of a Wells Fargo Bank," the officer announced breathing rapidly.

My mind swiftly thought back to the jewelry store that Jewel and I had knocked off. That was the only thing I could think of he could be talking about. If so, they had nothing on me because the bank wasn't robbed, the jewelry store was.

"Officer, you have the wrong man, I ain't done nothing like that," I said.

"Yeah, well you will have your chance in court to prove it. But right now you are going straight to jail," one of the officers said sarcastically, and then laughed.

I didn't find nothing to be funny, but I forced a smile his way as if he was amusing. I knew if we was on even ground, Jewel or I would have turned that smile into a terrifying expression and that laugh into a cry of pure desperation for his life. Two of the officers helped me to my feet and began conducting a body search.

"Well, well, what do we have here?" one of the officers said, removing the money from my front pockets. "I wonder where you get this type of dough from, maybe a bank? Is this yours son?" the officer asked me, showing me the money that he just removed from my pockets.

"Hell yeah, that's my money, why? Whose else do you think it is?"

"Well son, I'm assuming it's some of the money from the bank you robbed," he said.

I made no attempt to respond. I knew he was just fishing and hoping that I'd say something out of anger to give him something to go on. I glanced in the area where Jewel and them was standing and noticed they were gone. I was sure she and the kids made tracks out of the airport when they saw me being handcuffed.

I was hauled out of the airport and placed into the back of an unmarked patrol car. Then taken to the Los Angeles County jail and booked on two counts of murder, two counts of second degree robbery, possession of a firearm by a felon, and resisting and obstruction of a peace officer. Them bastards hit me with a resisting charge when I hadn't done nothing and a firearm charge by a felony charge on top of that when I am not even a felon.

Dirty cock suckers, I thought coldly. I strolled inside the holding cell, mad doggin everyone that attempted to glance up at me. Basically asking for unnecessary trouble by doing so, but I was angry and frustrated from the whole ordeal, being busted and away from my family, but I kept assuring myself that Jewel will keep things in order.

The foul orders of urine, feces and funk caused me to grimace much more with an unkind expression. I noticed that there was a long line of inmates waiting to use the phone which only added to my frustration. I claimed a spot up against the far back wall so I could view the movement and action of the inmates. I stood there leaning against the wall with my arms folded, listening to two fools gossip about which dope man on the streets had the most bread and pushed the most weight. Things they shouldn't be speaking on.

The tank was filled with mostly gang members and it was obvious they was Crips from all the cuzzing they was doing.

"Say homie, where you from loc?" a light complected frail man asked walking toward me. I made no attempt to respond but just stared him down with an expression of disgust. He stopped five feet in front of me and said, "Loc, you didn't hear me? You can't talk or something? Where you from?"

"Tiny Loc leave that nigga alone and come over here and finish putting me up on that hood rat Erica," one of his home boys said.

"Yeah Tiny Location, do as your boy say and leave me the hell alone before I twist your frail ass up for fucking with me."

Tiny Loc stared me down trying to make up his mind if he should take off on me or let me be. He made the right decision by turning around and walking off. He must of seen death in my eyes because normally if a person stare down a gang member or disrespect them in any way, they would try to put hands on you or shoot you.

An officer keyed the tank door and slid it open wide and announced "Gentlemen, quiet down. When I read out your booking number, I want you to step out into the hallway and grab a bed roll and sack lunch, you're being moved to a housing unit! So listen up for your number because I will not be repeating it again! If you miss it the first time, then you will be stuck down here in this holding cell for about sixteen more hours if not longer. Zero four two one, zero four two eight, and zero four zero four. That's all for now gentlemen."

I pushed off the wall when I heard my number called last and strolled past Tiny Loc and his boys and said as I was walking out the door, "Tiny Loc, you stay down blood." The entire unit went in an uproar.

"Ah cuzz, you wasn't talking that slob shit when you was in here, punk ass nigga! We would have smashed your slob ass!" Tiny Loc roared angrily.

"Cuzz, we let a slob creep in the tank with us," someone yelled out.

"Loc you should left Tiny Loc alone when he was getting at fool!" someone exclaimed angrily.

As I strolled off I formed a capital "B" with my fingers and held it out toward the Plexiglas window to arouse their anger more. Them fools was steaming hot. If I didn't know better I would have sworn that I seen small bull horns appear from the tops of their heads.

I was taken to a single man cell. I was told by the officer I'm being placed in a High Power Unit, whatever high power meant. I really didn't care what unit they put me in as long as it wasn't that holding cell I just came from. The two white boys that was called out the holding cell with me went to another unit. I tossed the sack lunch toward a gray plastic garbage can and it missed its target by a long shot.

"People! What you doing man with that sack? Don't throw it away, let me get that shit!" a guy yelled from behind a cell door. I turned to see who was asking for the lunch I was throwing away, but found numerous pairs of eyes staring at me through the slit of their cell windows. They looked like a bunch of wolves lurking in the shadows of the night.

I swooped up the bag and held it up in the air with my right hand. A repeated beating sounded off the door of cell three.

"People, that was me who asked for the sack," he shouted so I could hear him over the noise he was making to get my attention.

"Hey guys, let's get it locked up, you can get familiar with everyone later on your tier time," the bubble officer announced over the intercom.

I ambled up to the man's cell and asked how he was going to get

162

that bag.

"Just tie it on the door handle, and thanks people!" he said.

I nodded my head to let him know it was all good and made my way to the cell I was assigned to.

I felt like I couldn't breathe in the small cell they housed me in. The sad dim white paint on the brick walls only added to my bitterness and depression. The slab of steel and thin mattress insulted my integrity, and the one piece stainless steel sink and toilet offered a disrespect beyond my reality. I glanced at the steel desk and turned my head from its sight to keep from being offended a fourth time.

I knew I had to get out of jail immediately because the cell had already began playing tricks on my mind. I unfolded my mattress and covered it with the dingy white sheet from the bed roll. Then laid down using the blanket for a pillow.

I stared up at the ceiling measuring its height while listening to the droning sound of the air conditioner thrusting its breath through the vent violently. My heart felt heavy in my chest as if its weight was applying great pressure against a part of my respiratory organs making it harder for me to breathe. I assumed part of the reason why I might be feeling so short of breath was due to the small brick room I was being held captive in. It imposed a congested boundary to my civil liberties. I raised up and began to pace the length of the cell only to find myself able to take four single steps before having to turn around and retrace those same steps.

My mind was on Jewel and the kids wondering what they were doing. I was missing them greatly and I was sure they were also missing me as much.

I paced back and forth for hours covering a great distance on my imaginary journey, fumbling with the plastic red wristband around my left wrist. The red band was a bar-coded device the Los Angeles County Jail issued to all inmates as their identification card.

I tapped on my cell door to get the attention of the officer who was ascending the flight of steps to the second tier. He turned his head toward the sound, then raised an open hand in my direction to indicate that he heard me. I watched as he turned around and strolled toward my cell.

"Sir, what can I help you with?" he asked.

"I was just wondering if I could come out to make a phone call. And also be put in a bigger cell than this? I'm having a difficult time breathing in here," I said.

He gazed at me sharply, his eyebrows arched in curiosity. I noticed his eyes were laughing and his lips parted to speak before licking them. "Sir," he began, "I'm going to assume this is your first time in jail?" I nodded my head and he continued. "Well sir, there's nothing I can do for you as far as the cell exchange. You are housed in a maximum security unit for whatever reason classification placed you in here. All the cells in here are the same size, you shouldn't have any problem breathing in there because plenty of air is coming through the vents. It only seems like you can't breathe because you are not used to being cooped up in such a small space, but you will be fine. As for a phone call, you just came in today, right?" I nodded my head

He raised his head to look at the number above the cell door, then gazed down at a folded sheet of paper he had in his right hand. "Sir, your ID number is 0404, am I correct?" he asked.

I looked at the number on the wristband to reassure myself that it was before answering, "Yes, sir", I replied.

"Well sir, you are up to be transferred to a different location. You are not allowed to use the phone," he said, then strolled off before I could ask any more questions.

"Transferred", I snapped out loud just to break the silence in my cell.

I wonder where I would be going now? To a different unit, a different jail? Maybe home after they realized they got the wrong person, or maybe they were going to take me back to Las Vegas. My mind was racing on the many possibilities trying to guess where this transfer would lead me.

A full week had quickly come and gone and I hadn't yet been transferred to a different location. I hadn't even heard from Jewel, no visit, no letter or nothing. I had no stationary or I would have wrote Big Dee and Jewel's father. I hadn't showered in seven days because of the twenty-four hour lock down they had me on due to the transfer order, but I took bird baths out of my cell sink twice a day, but what good was that without soap and deodorant.

I was becoming more than restless. I was infuriated from the treatment I was receiving. Being denied a shower, hygiene, outside recreation and all means of contact to the outside world had to be some type of violation of my constitutional rights. I was illiterate to the law and so were the rest of the inmates housed in the unit. They all seemed old enough to be my father and they were repeat offenders of the California Prison System. They sported their jail house tattoos with pride, yelled out gang slogans, strolled with a bounce in their step, displayed intimidating facial expressions, talked the tough and tall timber talk, quick to advocate violence and to complain about the injustice of their treatment of incarceration, but yet none knew anything about criminal law.

What a useless degrading life to live, I thought, feeling more frustrated with the inmates than my situation.

The officer who came into the unit to conduct the hourly count ignored my questions and concerns. He just continued on with his duties as if I didn't exist. So I found a way to get some attention. I flooded the tier, but they quickly got smart and cut off the water to my cell. I hadn't anticipated that, not knowing that cutting off the water was even possible without depriving the entire unit of water, but how wrong I was. I felt like a fool afterwards because I had basically punished myself. Now I had no running water in my cell and just the thought of it made me thirsty. I decided I would go lay on my bunk and rest my nerves since I hadn't accomplished anything but another problem that affected me and me only. I lay staring at the brick wall painting imaginary pictures.

The tray slot in the middle of my cell door opened and it thundered with a sound that took me by surprise. I sprung up to my feet quickly and turned toward the door for action, not knowing what was going on. I believed that I dozed off to sleep. I noticed three officers standing in front of the cell door. My heart was pounding hard and I was panting. I gathered my breath.

"Yeah what's up?" I asked the officer who was peering into the window watching me.

"I need for you to roll your stuff up because you're being moved," he said.

I told him I didn't have no personal property. He instructed me to back up to the tray slot so I could be handcuffed. I complied without any hesitation. I was ready to shake the spot anyway, being up around a bunch of idiots was cramping my style.

CHAPTER 11

I was transferred to the San Bernardino County Jail. The sign as we entered the parking lot read: West Valley Detention Center. I was re-booked on the six trumped up charges: two counts of murder, second degree robbery, one count of possession of a firearm by a felon, resisting, obstruction and delay of a peace officer which is pure, complete and utter bullshit, but I wasn't trippin'. I just wanted to get to a phone. I had to go through the whole process again, being finger printed, searched and photographed.

San Bernardino County was lot different from Los Angeles County. It was cleaner and they didn't issue ID wristbands but a hard plastic ID that featured a ten digit inmate number with full name and picture on the front. On the back side it featured your race, date of birth, age, sex, height, weight and the color of your eyes and hair.

"Say folks, where you from homie?"

A deep voice spoke out from a crowd of eight inmates who were being booked into the county jail. I made no attempt to respond to the question. My mind was focused on getting to a phone. I strolled inside the booking cell and made way toward the phone that was being occupied.

"Say, Ese, let me get next on that horn?"

The Mexican nodded his head. I took a seat on the wooden bench next to the phone waiting impatiently for my opportunity to use it.

"Say folks, where you from people?" the same deep voice asked the question. I raised my head and noticed a stocky built, light complexioned tall man walking toward me.

I swiftly stood up, now making eye contact with the man.

"Say Negro, what's it to you where I'm from? That any of your business?"

"Hold up bruh! I didn't mean nothing by that," he held out open hands. "I was just trying to find out if you was from Dino, that's all."

"Nah, I'm not from San Bernardino or nowhere from California. I'm from Las Vegas, playa! Anything else you might want to know about a gangsta's business while you playing detective and shit? If not, then give me fifty feet and do like Michael Jackson said, Beat It, cause I'm not trying to make no friends."

"Peace, bruh! Peace!" the man said, holding up two fingers, strolling off across the room to make conversation with another inmate.

I turned toward the Mexican on the phone. "Say Ese how much longer are you going to be on that horn? I have an emergency call to make. I'll appreciate it if you give me some action right away to call my people."

The Mexican looked up at me and squinted his eyes, then frowned.

"A homes uno momento, por favor."

"Man, do I look Mexican to you? Speak to me in English, comprendo? Do you understand that?" I said.

Although I spoke Spanish and understood it well, I was not about to expose game to him. My home girl, Big Dee, always told me to keep that as a secret for my own benefit and protection, and I had every intention of doing just that.

"Mi hija, yo te hablo tu maana, buenas noches." The Mexcian turned toward me. "Say, loco, what's your problem, holmes, disrespecting me and my familia? Do you have a problem with me, Ese?"

"Ha, ha," I burst into laughter. I couldn't help it, but I found the Mexican's aggressive stance to be hilarious and untimid.

"Ese, what you laughing at, ey? Do you want a piece of me Ese?" he asked aggressively.

I couldn't stop from cracking up. I found the Mexican to be so funny. The more I thought about how could I ever allow a four foot three inch midget whip me, it became more comical. I liked the little guy's fearless attitude, but honestly, he was barking up the wrong tree and if he stepped too far out of line I would be forced to open up a fresh can of Rodney King and kick off in his ass.

"My friend, I have no problem with you," I said with a smirk on my face. "I just need to make an important call and you can get the phone right back, playboy."

"Okay, Ese. Next time don't be pushing up on me like that," the midget said with authority, then pulled his pants up to his chest. I smiled and nodded my head to give the little guy his respect just to make him feel good. I even shook his hand before getting on the phone.

A recording of a man's voice came over the phone. "Press one for English," I pressed the number one and got a dial tone. The recording came on again. "Please dial the number you are calling." I quickly punched in Jewel's grandmother's number. The recorder came on once more, "Please enter your pin number followed by the pound key." I looked at my ID card that I had clipped onto my left shirt sleeve and punched in the ten digit number. "Please hold," the recorder announced. Then there was a few seconds of silence before I heard a ring on the line, then someone answered. "Hello?" I immediately recognized the voice, it was Jewel. My heart pounded furiously against my chest. The sound of her voice seemed to have erased away my troubles.

"Baby, what's up?" I said excitedly.

The recorder came on again, "You have a call from an inmate at the San Bernardino County Detention Center. If you wish to check the rate of this call, press nine. If you wish to accept this call, dial zero and hold. If you wish to block inmate calls to this number, press five now." Jewel pressed zero and the irritating recording played again. "This is Verizon Select Service." That was the end of the recording. I was put through to my girl.

It took me close to ten minutes to calm Jewel down from crying. She told me Diana, Mrs. Barbra, the kids and herself been trying to visit me, but they was refused every time. She also said she wrote, but the letters was returned. I told her I had been transferred to San Bernardino County Jail and gave her my booking number. She told me how Diana introduced her to some people who made fake identification cards and now she would be able to come visit alone. Also she tried to bail me out, but couldn't because I had no bail. She did go get me a paid attorney and he would be coming down to visit me, but since I had been relocated, she would call and let him know of my new location.

"I love you Boo!" she said.

"I love you more, Jewel," I assured her.

"I want you home now, we miss you." She spoke sadly and I knew the tears would come next and they did, just as I figured.

"Phone check boy!" the sound of a squeaky voice took me by surprise. I knew it wasn't the midget because his voice had a Spanish accent that was distinguishable. This voice sounded like someone who was raised up in the country.

"Ain't this about a bitch?" I mumbled aggressively, turning around to see who the chump was pushing up on me in such a disrespectful manner.

"Whoa! What's up big guy?" I asked quickly, losing the attitude when I seen the huge frame that stood only a foot away staring down on me looking like a big grizzly bear standing on its two hind legs. The man had to be at least 375 pounds and at least six feet, seven inches tall. He resembled a Sumo wrestler, the only difference this guy was white with a long beard that went to the middle of his chest. I sized the grizzly up and took a deep breath, wondering if I should just overlook the disrespect, just this one time, and allow the man to use the phone. I mustered up the courage to speak.

"Say, big guy, did you say that you need to use the phone?"

"Boy, I believe I did. That's what phone check means as ye colored folks would say."

My face took on an unpleasant expression. I could feel the deep wrinkles at the base of my forehead. I didn't take the man's racial remark well, but I also wasn't quick to react to his rude comments either for the big beast of a man was surely an uneven match for me.

"Big guy," I said pausing to find the right word to avoid making the man mad. "Just let me tell my girl I will call her back and you can have the phone."

"A, homes, what about me?" the midget asked. "You forgot that I had the phone next?"

"Keep quiet, little dude! Do you see, I mean hear the man? He said he needs to use the phone, so I'm going to let him use it."

"Homes, you just being punked off the phone, whimp! You scared of that wood, that's what it is. You bitchin' up like a punk?"

"Who's a punk?" I snapped. "I know you not talking to me like that little mini me. I ain't scared of you and that's for sho, you little hush puppy. I'll stomp you into the ground, so you better silence that big mouth you have on that little body quickly before I do it for you," I said threateningly.

"Why you want to jump on little Officer Lee' me so fast?" the midget frowned. "Why don't you fight that big wood who's punked you off the phone? He's the one told you phone check, not me!"

"Didn't I tell you to silence that mouth? Now I'm going to do it for you," I moved aggressively toward the midget.

The husky man quickly grabbed me by the throat with a huge right hand and easily lifted me off the ground. I tried to pry the man's mitt from around my throat, but my attempt was useless. He was too strong for me and he had hands five times bigger than mine. He was tightening his grip at my every struggle for air. He was squeezing the life out of me. I had to think of something to do quickly, but I couldn't think, I had no time to think. So I reacted out of fear and punched ferociously underneath the beasts elbow. I must of hit his funny bone because he quickly released the death grip and swiftly retrieved his hand. I fell to the ground like dead weight, teary eyes and gasping for air. I felt my body being lifted from the polished floor, high in the sky. Then the wind was knocked out of me. I had been body slammed directly onto my back. A thunder of pain rumbled through my body like an earthquake. My head was throbbing and there was the sound of bells ringing somewhere in the depth of my eardrums. I could faintly hear the sound of laughter and ridicules of the inmate bystanders.

Unconsciously I grunted the words below a whisper. "If only my girl Jewel was here, we would down your ass," I was semi-conscious.

I tried to compose myself attempting to crawl to my feet. Somewhere I found the strength to make it up and the will to face my assailant. I stood standing in a fighting stance, facing the huge man. I didn't quite have the full support of my legs under me, they were still wobbly. The man rushed toward me with full force. I knew I would be through with money if I didn't do nothing. So I did the only thing I knew I could and released a right snapping thrust kick into the man's stomach that immediately stopped him in his tracks. Then I followed up with a consecutive left round house kick to the burly beast's left thigh that brought him down to his knees. I wasted no time introducing my fists to his fat face with a flurry of lefts, rights, uppercuts and hooks. He was unconscious before he went crashing down to the floor like a sack of potatoes. I wasn't taking any chance of him getting back up, he might kill me for sure this time. So I followed my own rules of fighting as I taught Jewel and the kids to do to disarm their opponents ability to fight. I kicked the man repeatedly to the head and rib cage.

"Hey you, move away from that guy, now!" a deputy shouted with authority when he noticed what was taking place.

I ignored his demand. He must have pushed the button that rested on the side of his utility belt because the emergency alarm sounded off.

I paid it no mind and continued laying feet on the chump. The deputy's backup team arrived quickly and commenced to spraying me with their OC Pepper Spray in hope of stopping my assault, but the bystanders seemed to have also been affected by it because they hustled to one side of the room far away from me coughing and spitting up.

A sergeant stepped out the shadows of the crowd of deputies moved in range, aimed a block gun and fired without warning. The hard rubber projectile struck me in the chest area. I jerked up in the air as if I had just pulled the rip cord on a parachute. The deputies wasted no time, they trampled in on me introducing wild knees to my face, back and rib cage. They worked me over until they were winded. Then tirelessly handcuffed my hands and shackled my legs. I was hauled out the holding cell and tossed into a rubber room. I felt my clothes being stripped away violently, then the handcuffs and shackles. The thump of a door closed. I slowly turned my head, moaned from the excruciating pain I was in. I was surprised to be still alive. I noticed the room was empty of the deputies who had left me laying nude on the rubber floor. The toxic fumes of the OC Pepper Spray began to take effect. Its chemical substance slowly burned my skin and congested my lungs forcing me to gasp for air.

"I can't see!" I cried out. "I can't see, my eyes are burning deputy!" I yelled panicking. No one came to my aid. I began tracing the floor in a crawl, feeling around for a toilet which I knew if I found, there would be a sink nearby. Then I could flush my eyes with water. There wasn't either in the cell. I crawled around every inch of the small padded room. I began yelling for the deputies again.

"I can't breathe and I can't see, get a nurse down here." Within minutes my cries became silent. A deputy decided to check on me. He slid open the metal flap that covered the small slit window and looked in. He noticed I was lying flat on my face not moving. The deputy called out my name, but I couldn't respond or move.

"Mr. Leonard James Weems! Can you hear me?" There was no response.

He called in over his hand held radio for backup before keying open the cell door to enter. The deputies handcuffed me and carried my unconscious body to the nurses' station. My eyes and throat were swollen and my skin turned a bruise red. Two jail house nurses was waiting when we arrived.

"The handcuffs have to come off this man," the senior nurse ordered. "Fetch an oxygen tank and a number two size mask," she requested of her assistant, then turned toward the deputies. "What happened here deputies?"

One of the deputies blurted, "He was sprayed with OC Pepper

Spray."

The senior nurse frowned up at the deputy with a skeptical look. "It looks to me like he was sprayed with more than pepper spray," she offered and added, "This young man is having an allergic reaction and the swelling at his neck is shutting down his cardiovascular system. It's good you brought him down when you did. If you hadn't, you would have a death on your hands. The medicine I've just injected him with will immediately start to take effect, and it will bring down the internal swelling, but what I'm concerned about is how that bruise in the middle of his chest got there?"

The deputy shifted his weight from one leg to the other and turned his stare from the nurse to the bruise.

"He was shot with the block gun during the altercation," he replied.

"Well, that explains it," the senior nurse began. "That's why I was asking you what happened to this man. We must take him to the outside hospital for x-rays and appropriate medical treatment that I am not authorized to offer. This man needs a doctor."

"Yes, ma'am, I'll inform the captain concerning the matter."

I was transported to Arrowhead Regional, a hospital in Colton, California. There, I went through an extensive examination. Every part of my body had been scrutinized, even my manhood, and if I didn't know any better, I would have sworn on a stack of Bibles in front of a Sunday morning congregation that the female doctor was astounded by the size of my swipe because she held on it as if it was a draping snake, massaging its belly with gentle movement of the fingers. I was in too much pain to feel embarrassed from my erection that had swelled in the soft hand of the doctor. The doctor ordered her assistant to take me to the lab for x-rays so she could be assured that I wasn't suffering from any fractures or internal bleeding. After several hours of undergoing examinations, I was only diagnosed with minor abrasions and bruising and released back to custody.

I was now conscious, fully aware of my surroundings. I wondered how I ended up in a cell. I couldn't remember how I got there. I took a quick inventory of the cell and noticed it wasn't padded like the one I recently been in, but similar to the cell I was housed in at the Los Angeles County Jail. The only difference was this cell was twice its size and had two huge Plexiglas windows built into the steel front door. They were separated by the steel tray slot. I swung my legs off the bunk and slowly stood fighting against the stiffness of my body. I reached out for the ceiling, teeth clenched and jaws flared in an attempt to stretch my back, but that wasn't going down.

I stumbled sleepily toward the stainless steel toilet and gazed at myself through the stainless steel fixture bolted above it.

What type of mirror is this? I wondered. I noticed how swollen my eyes were. The left eye was bruised and blood shot red. I felt underneath the eye and it was tender to the touch. "Oh, this is how we getting down?" I mumbled angrily at the sight. "These pigs want to play like this? Just wait until I get out and get back up around my girl, and then we will see if they want to play. We will make them feel pain and teach them to respect my mind, damn bastards!"

I frowned up at my reflection before ambling off to lay back down. I was still a little dizzy from the medication. I closed my eyes in hopes that it would stop the spinning that was going on inside my head. Then there was the sound of tapping in my ears. I opened my eyes as if that was the remedy to bring the noise to an end. Then I heard it again, a lot clearer than before. The sharp thumps rambled against the steel. I turned my head toward the door and noticed a light complexioned, bald headed man peering in on me. I rolled over out the bunk to my feet without showing the slightest sign of stiffness and moved toward the door where the man stood with his right hand in his pants groping his crotch and his other curled around a black plastic mug. Whatever he had in the cup, I could see the steam rising from it.

"What's up African?" he asked and continued before I could reply. "My name Wilson homie, what they call you brotha?"

"Boo, dawg."

"Boo dogg, listen."

"Naw dawg, my name is not Boo dogg, it's just Boo," I corrected him.

"Oh, aight, Boo, where you from brotha?" he asked.

I thought to myself here we go again, another chump being nosey, sticking his nose in places it shouldn't be. I had always been told growing up if you stick your nose in places it don't belong, you might end up with shit on it. I had a complex about people I didn't know asking me personal questions. What is up with these California cats wanting to know where a person was from? What difference does it make? I wondered to myself. But I figured what the hell, I'll answer his question since his words don't seem to have a demanding edge to them.

"I'm from Vegas, folks."

"Oh yeah?" His eyes smiled with excitement but quickly went cold again. He lifted the mug to his mouth with caution and carefully sipped at the hot liquid. I assumed it was coffee he was drinking, but later found out it was nothing but hot water. He offered no explanation to why he liked to drink hot water and I didn't ask for one.

"Well let me lace you about the get down in this unit and how other races get down out here in these stoops." Wilson began, then paused to take another sip from the mug before he continued. "It's obvious that you never been locked up before because you was laying down in your bunk when I pulled up to the door. You will notice after breakfast every race roll their mattress up and stay up until the lights go out before they lay back down. It's a reason behind that, you don't want to be caught slippin'. If it happens your door pops open and an enemy is out on the tier"

"Enemy" I said harshly. Wilson's eyebrows buckled into a sudden frown, then he let out a breath with a hiss and snapped.

"Yes, enemy. You are black homie," he spoke in an aggressive tone. "You have enemies because of the shade of your skin, African. The whites and Mexicans out here in Cali is pushing a cold line on their people. They are on some racial and political bullshit. They also ride with each other against the blacks. This unit that we are in," he paused to catch his breath, then lifted the mug to his lips, but this time he didn't take a sip. He just held it at his mouth in silence by the weight of a sudden thought. Then he lowered it waist high and added.

"This is Unit 5-A, the High Power Unit. The place where they house their most dangerous inmates. That is why we are dressed in these red jump suits, so the deputies won't get us confused with the inmates in general population who wear orange jump suits. This is also why we all are single cell and come out on the tier one at a time for thirty minutes a day. It's only sixteen rooms in this unit and out of sixteen people there are only four Africans in here. A brotha name J-dogg from Du-Rock Crip and the other is Tray-dogg from Four-tray gangsta Crip. Then it's me, and now you. When they come out for tier time they will be over here to holla at 'cha. It's no set trippin' among us Africans. We only have each other up in here. The rest are Whites and Mexicans. Mostly Mexicans now, they call themselves the Mexican Mafia, and the Woods are Aryan Brotherhood. Everyone in here is facing the death penalty or life in prison so they don't care about catching another case by trying to kill you. There have been incidents where a Mexican cut out the bottom window and came out on a brotha,

175

and a wood popped a brotha's door with a paper clip when he was sleeping and ran in on him and stabbed him. These woods are very crafty when it comes to picking locks and the Mexicans are super sneaky. So you stay on your P's and Q's.

"There is only one TV in here, so we share it. The Africans watch what they want one full day, the next day is the Mexican day and then the Woods. We keep it alternating like that. We have an agreement to go check on everyone on the tier to see if they need hot water or something passed. We give each other the common courtesy and respect behind these doors, but we all understand if either one of us was to get around each other, it's on and crackin'. We all have to live in here together and it's no use for anyone to be wolfin' behind these doors. By the way African, how old are you? If you don't mind me asking? The reason I ask is because you look young."

"I'm only fifteen," I offered in a prideful and confident voice.

"Fifteen!" His face contorted with bafflement as if the answer was a lie. "Man, you are only fifteen?" he asked again to assure himself that he heard me correctly the first time.

"Yep."

"Youngsta, you don't supposed to be in here. They supposed to put you in Juvenile Hall. You must be eighteen and up to come to jail. Do you know if anything happen to you, they are going to be in a world of trouble. And what's up with the black eye you have?"

I lifted a hand and felt gently at the eye. Thick emotions dulled my speech when I spoke. "I had to put hands on a fool in the holding cell and the pigs ran in on me to get me off of dude. Them chumps blasted me with the block gun and then tried to stomp me out. That's why I'm all swolled up like this," I told him.

Wilson offered his advice on how I should handle the situation. He insisted that I contact my family on the outs, or my lawyer, and let them know what has happened and also let them know I'm being housed in a jail and not a juvenile facility. He walked off and quickly returned to my door. He slid me two Ebony magazines and three reading books. I glanced at the titles, "Cold as Ice" by A.C. Bellard, and "Three Strikes" by Crucifix. The third book was called "Prison Secrets."

Now that was the book to read. It gave up the inside scoop about prison life and the gangs, raw and uncut with no holds barred. Everything I needed to know about prison and more was inside that book. I studied it for weeks learning how to make weapons and how other groups function and what to keep my eyes open for. Also I learned the prison terminology and what different words meant. I was now educated enough about what type of individuals I would be forced to deal with. Wilson had given me some hygiene items, a half stick of deodorant, one bar of soap, a new tube of toothpaste and a toothbrush that was the size of a thumb in length.

J-dogg and Tray dogg both gave me canteen items when they came out for tier. They turned out to be some alright brothas. Neither of them were like the mental picture I envisioned them to be. My visualization of their appearance and character was totally contrary to the images I conceptualized. I expected to be approached by two contorted, grimaced mugs that offered the threatening edge of a psychopath as Wilson's persona had. I was wrong. Tray dogg was all smiles with even white teeth. His hair was long in braids going toward the back in corn rows. He had the pretty boy look with hazel gray eyes and a butterscotch complexion. Even his stroll fell in compliance with his cool cat demeanor. I noticed he kept his fingernails long and manicured. My first impression of him I assumed he was a pimp. He didn't fit the description of a gang banger.

J-dogg was a different story. I was positively sure he was a gang member the moment I laid eyes on him. He had the physique of an athlete, a hard muscular body of a gymnast. He was tall, dark and handsome with a shaved head. He sported a shadowed goatee that offered him the resemblance of Taye Diggs, the brotha who played in the movie "How Stella Got Her Groove Back." The only difference was J-dogg had three shaded tear drops tattooed under his left eye. The marking of each tear drop represented a murder he had successfully committed, from what he told me. I wondered how he planned to add the other eight teardrops to his collection that he was now fighting the death penalty case for. It was just an unspoken curiosity of my own that I didn't attempt to bother asking. Just like most Crips I've seen, he sagged his pants below his butt.

I also come to find out that Wilson was a serial killer, just as I assumed from the very moment I gazed into the windows of his past. His eyes told his story. I was always good at reading a person and my thoughts about Wilson were on the money. But regardless of his fetish for killing, he was a real cool cat. The coolest thing since ice cream and I had taken a liking to the brotha because he was down to earth and straight forward. But regardless of how much I liked him, I was positive we would never be friends past these walls for safety precautions, and even now I kept a keen eye on him not trusting or knowing when the craving to kill will resurface within him.

The days were zooming by fast. Three weeks had already gone by and not once had my attorney come down to visit me. Jewel and the kids visited me regularly. The visiting only lasted thirty minutes and it behind Plexiglas. Most of that time was spent talking to Benny and Tasha, they were my legal aids in helping me understand the law and what action I must take.

Jewel had sent me ten legal books to study and I spent my time being intimate with their pages. The kids turned out to be my legal advisors and they worked together as a team. Kevin, Jewlean and Lisa found the case law and gave it to Benny. He shephardized it to determine if the case was still good law that could be relied upon in the courts. Tasha drafted up pretrial motions and petitions and Jewel typed and mailed them to me. I really wasn't able to grasp the full fundamentals and understanding of the law because in one case it would have a totally different ruling and I was becoming frustrated from all the rules and legal jargon.

Tasha insisted that I stay focused. The three hours a week I received on the rec-yard was spent on the phone with Tasha going over the law. The recreation yard was small, towered and enclosed by cement bricks and fenced at the top. A wire mesh cage set to the side on the concrete foundation enclosed a pay phone attached to the brick wall. A stainless steel toilet stall and a workout machine which offered nothing more than dips and a pull-up bar decorated its interior. Only two inmates were allowed to occupy the yard at a time. One inmate would be locked in the mesh cage and the other one in the outside area. I always requested to be placed in the cage for I had no need for the bigger area, being that my full rec-time would be spent on the phone.

Jewel had put money on my account when she came down to visit so I was able to go to canteen every week. We was only allowed to spend seventy-five dollars per week, and that didn't buy much of nothing. The price of the vending machine size items were overpriced, three times what they were worth. Every week I made a spread for me, Wilson, J-dogg and Tray dogg. The store went quickly because I freely shared it with them. Sometimes their money was funny and wouldn't be able to make it to the store. So I had my girl drop five franklins on each of their accounts so we all could go for seventy-five and eat good for the week. Things was running a lot smoother in the unit than I thought it would be. I guess that was only because the Mexican and

Whites was too busy getting high off of heroin they smuggled in through the mail and legal visiting room.

There was a guy by the name of Wizard. A very funny character in all that he does. He claimed to be Indian, but he possessed no features or characteristics of such. He looked like an average white boy with a shaved head and protruding mustache. He was short and small in size and had a long pointed nose that seemed not to fit with his other facial feature. He catered to the Mexicans more than he did his own people and spoke broken Spanish just to win their acceptance. Even though the Mexicans didn't accept any other race among them, they would string him along and used him as their flunky, which was only obvious, but from the look of it he didn't mind for he complied with every request with a smile plastered to his face and without objections. He freely made a weekly canteen contribution to the Mexican organization which was half of his weekly order. I assumed he took it upon himself to give up half of his store feely before the Mexicans got around to demanding it. That way he wouldn't feel he was being taxed and pressured out of his canteen.

For some apparent reason, the Mexicans had taken a liking to me, except for one who called himself 'Green Eyes'. He would always go out of his way to give people the impression that he was someone to be respected and dangerous, but I wasn't fooled. I seen the fakeness right through the cloud of smoke he was kicking up, and come to find out he wasn't even a part of the Mexican Mafia or yet alone a gang member for that matter. He is a wannabe, lame, that's what I was told by Chino, the key holder for the Mexican Mafias in that unit. So I shine Green Eyes little acts off and paid him no attention for his barks were harmless.

I took a liking to Chino. He was a good story teller about the life of prison that he'd known all too well. A place he gave thirty-three years of his life to and now would be heading back to spend the rest of his life there. A place he told me he'd rather be than in the free world. I couldn't quite relate to that, but after he explained to me prison life is all he's known, and the free world was too big and confusing for him and required too many responsibilities, then I kind of understood what he was telling me. He was basically institutionalized. I had learned a lot from that old Mexican gangster, even how to make county jail wine out of oranges, fruit cocktail, kool-aid, Jolly Rancher candies, sugar and bread. The ingredients that were required for the concoction. He would become very talkative when intoxicated off that jumble juice.

That's when I would be freely exposed to their gang politics and what the Mexican Mafia was really about.

He would say, "We control the Mexican gangs inside and outside the prisons. We are the big homies of the Southern Mexicans. We lay down the rules that must be followed. They have no opinion or say so when it comes to this structure."

I asked him who are the Mexican Mafias.

He said, "We are Southern Mexicans who put in work for many years to pave the way for the Southern Mexicans and ran neighborhoods. Myself and other Southside Mexican gang leaders in prison got together and started the Mexican Mafia. It was nothing but a prison gang at first. Then we realized how powerful our organization was and how much control we had over the Mexican neighborhoods. So we decided to take it to the streets and bring the Mexican gangs all together as one raza to stop all drive-by killings of Mexicans on Mexicans and to build a strong community."

I enjoyed listening to him because I learned something new every time. Wilson and J-dogg didn't like the fact that I was socializing with the Mexicans, but there wasn't anything they could do to stop me from doing as I pleased.

The unit activity quickly became monotonous. The same thing every day and I needed some entertainment. I was missing Jewel and the kids more than ever now. I stared at the pictures Jewel sent me until I couldn't keep my eyes open any longer. I became restless and couldn't get to sleep on my own. Lights were now out and I lay staring up in the darkness with Jewel's picture resting on my chest for hours.

CHAPTER 12

Three armed deputies escorted me into the courtroom. I felt like the most dangerous criminal in the world. They put me in ankle shackles which had a chain trailing up to a waist chain and a gadget that provided a protective casing over the handcuffs they called the "black box." The box prevented any manipulation of the hands. I noticed I was the only inmate in the courtroom. The jury pews were empty, the prosecutions table had stacks of files resting on its polished mahogany surface and a laptop opened wide with cables trailing from the back of it to some type of photo projector. At the defense table my lawyer was standing as he read from a file folder. He hadn't looked up when I entered. I assumed he was trying to do some last minute preparations. I was seated next to where he stood. I glanced around the room that resembled an art museum with wooden wall panels with nothing more than a clock and the California State Seal on the wall directly behind and above where the judge would sit. My eyes trailed from one side to the other of the raised judge's podium to the lifeless flags that stood on a thin brass pole at each end. I turned to look back into the gallery in hopes that I would see Jewel and the kids, but saw no one other than a group of news reporters sitting in the front rows of the bleachers eagerly listening with a note pad in one hand and a pen in the other. I wondered where Jewel and the kids were.

"All rise, the Honorable Judge Lisa M. Moore," announced the bailiff.

Everyone rose to their feet. The judge came storming in and to my surprise it was an attractive woman underneath the traditional black robe.

Then once the judge took up her seat, the bailiff announced "Please be seated and come to order. The People of the State of California versus Mr. Leonard James Weems in San Bernardino, California, Department five."

The judge then took control. "My name is Lisa M. Moore, the judge who will be presiding over your preliminary hearing. In appearance is the defendant with his counsel, Robert T. Smith, private attorney. The People of the State of California represented by James Tardy, Deputy District Attorney. Clarra L. Penny, CSR Officer, Reporter 9009. In the matter of the People versus Mr. Leonard James Weems, there are two files here: #ABC 666-M and UBN 357-P. I understand these are double filings, Mr. Tardy?"

"Yes, your honor, I believe so and the People would make a motion to dismiss file # ABC 666-M."

"The motion is granted," said the judge. "That file is dismissed, so we will proceed with the case # UBN 357-P. The complaint alleges:

Count One - Murder, Penal Code Section 187;

Count Two - Murder, Penal Code Section 187;

Count Three - Second degree robbery;

Count Four - Second degree robbery;

Count Five - Possession of a firearm by a felon with a prior;

Count Six - Obstruction, delaying or resisting arrest.

How many witnesses, Mr. Tardy?"

"Two, your honor,"

"Any motions?" the judge looked toward my attorney.

"Yes, your honor. Motion to exclude all witnesses," Mr. Smith replied.

"Granted."

"Objection, your honor," I exclaimed. The judge turned toward me with wide eyes, parting her mouth to speak, but I continued before she could. "I requested that my witnesses be here to testify on my behalf and my attorney just told you to exclude all witnesses. He's my attorney and I paid for his representation and I don't feel he can just do what he wants when I told him exactly what my wishes were."

"Mr. Weems, the Court doesn't get into attorney and client privileges unless there is a conflict of interest and that has to be brought to the Court's attention by verbal or written motion and then a date would have to be scheduled on the Court's calendar for both parties to appear back into court for the issue to be heard. Your attorney has a latitude scope of action how he sees fit in the most professional way to present a case that he feels would be beneficiary to his clients."

"Yes, your honor, I clearly do understand that. But I also know if during the course of court, if counsel prejudices the defense by failing to investigate or present material witnesses at court that are available and crucial to his client's case, then his client is being denied his Constitutional guaranteed right to effective assistance of counsel. My understanding of the law is that counsel must make all significant decisions in the exercise of reasonable professional judgment. If counsel fails to make such a decision, then his actions, no matter how you look at it, are ineffective assistance. If I may quote a United States Supreme Case 23..."

"No, Mr. Weems, that will not be necessary. I am very familiar with the law."

"Excuse me your honor, I submitted a motion via mail to the clerk of the court. I was wondering if that motion reached you?"

"Yes, it has Mr. Weems, if you are referring to the 995 motion that you filed in Propria Persona?"

I nodded my head.

"Sir, you must say yes or no by offering a verbal response. My court reporter must type what's being said in the court's proceedings. A gesture of any kind will not and cannot be taken as an answer here in my court, do you understand?"

"Yes, ma'am."

"Your answer to the question is?" the judge asked.

"Yes, your Honor, I did submit a 995 motion to set aside the information for several reasons and I did make the motion pro per because my attorney seemed reluctant to file one on his own. So I took it upon myself to do so," I replied.

"Mr. Weems, I'm assuming you would like to be heard on this motion, correct?"

"Yes, your honor, I would."

"Well, I normally wouldn't entertain such a motion at this stage of the preliminary proceedings and also being that you have legal representation. But with the permission of your attorney after I allow him a few minutes to look over the motion, then I would be willing to hear your argument," she said, turning her attention to my lawyer and added. "Mr. Smith, have you received a copy of this motion your client filed here in this court? If not, I will have a copy made so you can view it and decide if it's in your client's best interest to address the Court."

Mr. Smith raised a hand as if he was in an elementary class asking for permission to speak. He cut his eyes over at me, then stared in the judge's direction and said, "Yes, your Honor, I have received a copy of the motion and if my client feels he wants to speak, then he's welcome to if the Court permits."

"Very well, Mr. Weems, please state your concerns," the judge said.

I felt a frog lodge somewhere in my throat and my legs began to tremble from the nervousness that had suddenly come over me. I was now being put in the spotlight and given the opportunity to speak up for myself. My life was on the line, I can't get scared now, I thought. I found my voice and the words flowed fluently from my mouth.

"One, your honor, the charges in the Information are inconsistent with the arresting officer's crime reports information and there is no showing by evidence that a crime has even occurred. It is my understanding, and correct me if I am wrong being that I am a layman in the law, if an insidious purpose for prosecution was one that was arbitrary and thus unjustified and bears no rational relationship to legitimate penal statutes, then it's unjustifiable standards of the alleged crime.

"Also your honor, we have a constitutional violation because I was not legally committed, and what I mean about that is I was not arraigned until thirty-one days after my arrest. The first day of my arrest constitutes the first day of my incarceration. From my understanding of the law, I had a right to be arraigned and a preliminary hearing in ten court days. If I'm not. charges should be dismissed, especially if there is insufficient evidence to establish a reasonable belief that an offense has been committed by the accused. There is nothing in the Information that comes close to placing me at a crime scene or even indicate that I was the perpetrator mistaken that would be under Penal Code Section 859(b).

"If the delay of the arraignment extends beyond ten calendar days without reasonable cause, the Information should be set aside, dismissed completely, and I believe that the 995 motion is the proper vehicle to entertain such an argument.

"Furthermore, I was not provided the privilege to be physically present at my arraignment. My attorney himself without my knowledge entered a not guilty plea on my behalf, which I also believe is some type of violation of my Constitutional rights. If I had been given that opportunity, I would have made a verbal demurrer motion for lack of jurisdiction and failure to state a public offense under the California Penal Code 1004(1) through (4), and your Honor that is my position in my argument."

"Wonderful job, Mr. Weems, a very professional presentation."

"Thank you, your honor."

"I will address these issues after the matters of this court are over. We will now proceed with the prelim. Now where were we?" The judge paused for a few seconds and shuffled through her notes. "Excuse me momentarily, gentlemen," she said. "Okay, I had granted Mr. Smith's motion to exclude all witnesses and it still stands. So Mr. Tardy, who is your designated officer?"

"Actually, your honor, the People would designate Officer Cobby Lay Well as the investigating officer," Mr. Tardy answered. "The People call Officer Cobby Lay Well."

"Very well, go ahead," said the judge. "Mr. Cobby Lay Well called as a witness by the People. Mr. Well, my clerk will be asking you a few questions. Please answer the questions as clearly as possible," the judge instructed. "Go ahead, Shanta."

"Officer Well, do you solemnly state that the testimony you shall give in this Court shall be the truth, so help you God?"

"I do!"

"Thank you, please be seated. Please state your full name for the record, spelling your first and last."

"Mr. Cobby Well, C-o-b-b-y L-a-y W-e-l-l."

"Thank you," said the judge. "You may proceed on direct examination, Mr. Tardy."

"Thank you, your honor. Mr. Well, what is your occupation?"

"I'm an officer with the California Highway Patrol."

"How long have you worked as a police officer for the Highway patrol?"

"Since my entrance into the academy. Excuse me, since my graduation from the academy, approximately three and a half years."

"Have you taken and completed a post-certified course regarding investigation, report writing and testifying at a preliminary hearing?"

"Yes, I have."

"Wait one moment!" said the judge. "I'm going to stop the proceedings and inform the defendant of his rights. Mr. Weems, during the hearing your attorney needs to listen to the questions, make objections, and I need to hear the witnesses and the reporter needs to put down what is happening. Hold your thoughts, talk to your attorney after the hearing. Do you understand, Mr. Weems?"

"Yes, ma'am," I replied shifting in the seat trying to get comfortable.

"If you need time, write notes to him and he will stop the proceedings if there is a need for it. Do you understand, Mr. Weems?"

"Yes, ma'am."

"Go ahead, Mr. Tardy."

"Thank you, your honor. Where was I? Oh, were you on duty on April first of this year?"

"Yes, I was."

"On that date at around 11:00 in the evening were you on patrol near the area of 19th Street?"

"Yes, I was."

"Is that located in the County of San Bernardino?"

"Yes it is."

"Were you in uniform that night?"

"Yes, I was."

"How is the patrol car marked?"

"It's a black and white patrol vehicle. It has the CHP star on both doors and it indicates 'Highway Patrol' on both doors as well as the trunk. I activated my forward red light and my wig wag lights and also the driver's side red spot."

"Did you activate your siren at any point?"

"No, I didn't."

"So you never activate your siren, is that correct?"

"Yes, that's correct."

"Well, let's skip to the actual scene of the attempted arrest of Mr. Weems."

"On my way back to the patrol car, I followed the same path that I pursued after the defendant."

"Objection, your honor," I exclaimed angrily springing from my seat. "I don't have a clue what this officer is talking about. He can't be talking about me, I've never been in San Bernardino, I'm from Las Vegas."

"Mr. Weems, take a seat. I will not have outbursts in my courtroom!" the judge roared. "Didn't I make myself clear who was to make objection for the defense? I will not have any more outbursts like that out of you." She shot me a threatening stare.

"But..." She cut me off.

"But nothing! Close your mouth and zip it," then turned to the officer. "You may continue."

"As I was saying, I pursued after the defendant. I then noticed a black handgun lying on the ground. I noticed the clip was not in the gun. I also found a black stocking cap several feet away on the same path. Several days later when we arrested Mr. Weems, I conducted a body search and found numerous denominations of money in his front pockets."

"What!"

"Mr. Weems! Don't you start," the judge threatened.

I was hot as fire now. Listening to the pig sit up on the witness stand lying between his teeth. I hadn't been out this way for one, and two, if I was the actual perpetrator, he sure as hell wouldn't have been doing no chasing me. I would have turned his ass into a strainer. I wondered what he meant by he found numerous denominations of money in my pocket? I only had a wad of franklins. I began to get the feeling that the pigs done pulled a jack move on my bread and replaced it with something small. I'm sure that's what they have done, I convinced myself.

"Your honor, I have no further questions for the witness," Mr. Tardy said.

"Thank you, Counsel," the judge spoke. "Mr. Smith, you may now conduct cross- examination."

"Thank you, your honor. Mr. Well, I have only two questions. The first one is when you found the alleged money on my client, what did you do with it? Did you show my client the items you allegedly found?"

"When I conducted a body search, I found the money. I questioned Mr. Weems about the money. He told me the money was his and I placed the money back into his pants pocket and had my partner place him in the patrol car."

"Now my second question is you chased after my client and at that point in time you never lost visual contact, you never saw him throw anything down, is that correct?"

"That's correct."

"Your honor, I have nothing further."

"Well gentlemen, anything else?"

"No, your honor."

"Mr. Tardy, are you going to redirect?"

"No, your honor, the people don't wish to be heard anymore. The people move the defendant to be held to answer to any and all crimes established by the evidence."

"Well as the hearing judge, I see the defense has no affirmative defense and both parties have rested. So it is made clear to me that the people are not going to call the second witness as the Court was informed there would be."

"Excuse me, your honor, I wish to be heard briefly, if I may" Mr. Smith asked. "With respect to all counts I ask the Court not to hold my client to answer. There's been no evidence offered at all concerning that Mr. Weems, in fact, was not the person who was or had committed the allegations. You heard no testimony of these crimes even happening within the hearing. With respect to Count One through Six, the police officer did not activate his siren. All that he had done was turn on his lights and as a CHP officer, so given his experience and background, was that Mr. Weems was possibly driving under the influence of alcohol in his police report. Officer Well was going to follow him for a period of time to basically buttress that opinion and therefore there was no evidence that Mr. Weems was even in fact the suspect driving.

"And with respect to Count Five, possession of a firearm by a felon, I ask the Court not to hold him to answer and to view the FBI identification records. That alone would clear up this misunderstanding, because my client is not a felon. Additionally, there is no evidence that Mr. Weems actually had possession or actual constructive possession of the gun. The officer's testimony was that the alleged suspect, who he believes is Mr. Weems, exited the vehicle and he, the Officer, saw Mr. Weems immediately start running and he, the Officer, pursued Mr. Weems and had done so in a direct line. He had never observed Mr. Weems throw or toss or drop anything. There is no evidence that the gun had recently been placed there. There's no evidence at all that it was used in a murder or yet multiple murders. The gun could have been there for a long period. There just is no evidence at all, without speculation, that this Court can use to tie that gun to my client or any of these charges. Therefore we ask the Court not to hold him for that. We will also move this Court to dismiss all charges for insufficient information to support a crime and lack of jurisdiction to be held to answer in this adult court. Thank you, your honor."

"Mr. Tardy, would you wish to be heard on the matter?" the judge asked.

"Your honor, it's actually very clear as to what was going on this evening, the evening of April first. The defendant was in the area in very close proximity to the Wells Fargo Bank."

"Objection, your honor, that speculation assumes facts not in evidence," Mr. Smith exclaimed aggressively.

"Overruled, you may continue Mr. Tardy."

"Thank you, your honor. The defendant ran from the police and ultimately crashed his car into a boulder. Yes, he was successful in fleeing capture that day. A gun was found at the scene when the defendant was apprehended several days later at the Los Angeles Airport trying to flee the state. He resisted arrest, plus he had a large sum of money in his possession. It is very clear that the individual is the one who robbed the bank and murdered the employees on that evening and we, the people, would ask the Court to hold him to answer on all counts. The people submit these arguments."

"Objection, your honor," I stood up and shouted. ."

"Excuse me Mr. Weems, but didn't I tell you for the life of me, you can't make any objections. That is what you have an attorney for, to make the objections" the judge said furiously.

"Well your honor, I believe that I have a constitutional right to address the Court personally."

"Not in my courtroom you don't and I refuse to have any misbehavior or I will have you removed from my courtroom."

"I have a right to speak and I want to exercise that rights. This is my life that we're talking about," I snapped.

"Calm down," my attorney whispered into my ear, resting a hand on my shoulder.

"Bailiff, remove this gentleman from my courtroom. I will not put up with anymore disrespectful outbursts," the judge announced harshly.

As the bailiff escorted me out of the courtroom back to a holding cell, I yelled at the top of my lungs, "I have a constitutional right to be present during the proceedings." The bailiff returned back to the courtroom and informed the Court I was secured.

"Thank you," the judge said and turned toward the attorneys and added, "Now let's get back to court business. I have completed my deliberations and I am ready to rule on all counts. The Court finds that after hearing the evidence in this hearing, I have serious difficulty as to all counts and obviously Count One and Two. I have heard nothing that indicates that Count one, two, three, four and even five happened. We know a crime was committed, but from what I see, evidence does not point toward the defendant. I have heard nothing that links this defendant to the firearms, even for purposes of the preliminary hearing. And I hope that there is no gun on my path when I go home today because if a gun is found on my path of travel, it doesn't mean it was my gun. Unless you have something else that I missed, I will not find any evidence to sustain the count. That's a clear cut decision.

"As to all other counts, as far as the felonies are concerned, actually you have not only the problem of the siren being activated, you don't even have a violation of traffic. I don't see it. As for the other remaining counts, the Court finds that there is not enough evidence in this hearing sufficient enough to forward the case to a superior court. The money wasn't properly placed in the chain of custody, so that is tainted evidence. Furthermore, I heard no evidence concerning the murders or the robbery. So I am dismissing all charges."

"Thank you, your Honor." Mr. Smith said.

"Your honor, but this man murdered two bank employees," the District Attorney pleaded.

"Mr. Tardy, I have made my ruling and it's final. The evidence you presented to me was insufficient in its totality. Also, you were blind to the fact that a juvenile must be processed through the proper channels before being charged as an adult and held to answer in the adult courts. Your ignorance has placed the state at risk for a law suit! Mr. Weems is only fifteen years old per his birth certificate that was provided by the Federal Social Security Department. Clearly he never has suffered any prior criminal convictions let alone been accused of any crimes. So I don't want to hear anymore from you about this or you will be pulling out your checkbook because you will be sanctioned. I am not happy with how you made a farce out of the Court today, Mr. Tardy."

"It's not over, I'll get him, juvenile or not, I'll get him," Mr. Tardy grunted angrily under his breath. He snatched his briefcase and the laptop from the mahogany table and stormed out of the courtroom.

"Good job Counsel," Mr. Smith said sarcastically.

Mr. Tardy spun around on his heels. His anger was evident. His face was flushed cherry red and displayed an unspoken hatred and offered harshly, "I will get him for something if that's the last thing I ever do."

"Don't count on it guy, not as long as he has me as an attorney,"

Mr. Tardy dropped his briefcase on the floor and swiftly got into Mr. Smth's face and spoke in a low angry voice. "I see you want to challenge me. Well we can battle if you think that your client is about to walk, think again. I'm about to go refile on the murderer and I have deputies who will file assault charges on him during his little tough guy spree in the jail, plus there is an inmate who he assaulted. They will testify against him."

Mr. Smith moved forward taking up the rest of the space that separated them. "Now listen here peon. I could not care less about your frivolous threats. You are not in my league, you can't beat me at anything. I can't see how you ever passed the bar exam because what you showed me today in this courtroom is pure comical. You are nothing but a comedian, a real clown with all the facial features. You're a beginner and you're playing ball out of your league. So do what you must because you really haven't seen me in action, chump! When I hit you and the state with the lawsuit I'm filing on behalf of my client for false imprisonment, assault charges against the deputies and everything else I can think of, you will be out of a job for putting a kid's life in danger. My client is only fifteen, never should have stepped a foot into jail let alone be housed and assaulted by officers. I have copies of the medical reports. Now please excuse yourself and get out of my face, Mr. Tardy, before my past instincts resurface and you find yourself being acquainted with the floor."

Mr. Tardy took three steps back.

"Thank you. Now let me do what I was paid to do. Go see my client to let him know that he's getting out today," Mr. Smith said, straightening his suit jacket before ambling off to inform the bailiff he would like to speak with me.

The bailiff escorted my attorney to the conference room and then I was escorted to the room. I was still angry and highly frustrated when I was seated cross from my attorney who had a slight smirk on his face.

"How are you holding up?" he asked. I didn't respond but gazed past him as if he wasn't there. "You did a fine job on your motion and the presentation was outstanding. Better than most practicing attorneys I know. You would make an exceptional criminal lawyer. So are you not talking, huh? Well that's too bad because I guess you don't want to know the outcome of the prelim?" he asked.

I didn't respond, but he continued to speak despite my silence.

"Well then, when you feel like talking, just stop by my office after you get out today. I got the case dropped for you and you should be released in a few hours once they get the order and paperwork processed. I'll see you bud," he said raising to his feet. He tapped me on the right shoulder as he exited the room.

I sat in silence wondering if I heard him correctly. "Home?" I asked myself. Tears clouded my eyes and I wiped at them with the back of my hand before they could overflow and fall onto my cheeks. I was elated knowing that I would be in the company of Jewel and the kids today and out of the devil's den where people are waiting patiently to learn their fate or demise, whether it's by life in prison or lethal injection. In my eyes both are a sure death. For the first time in my life I thought about going to church and turning my life over to God. The life behind bars was not for me, and being away from those I love made the time twice as unbearable. I had been told that firsthand experience was the best teacher and I was now a true believer that it was. This would be the opening and closing chapter to my life behind bars, for my life was now as it should be, free and with my family. It was time to hit up the Big Apple to see what it had to offer. New York City, here I come.

THE END

ABOUT THE AUTHORS

Corey 'C-Murder' Miller is a multi platinum rap star, founder of TRU Records and co-founder of No Limit Records along with his brothers, Percy 'Master P' and Vyshonne 'Silkk the Shocker' Miller, the legendary trio who introduced southern hip hop to the world. C-Murder is the author of *Death Around the Corner* and co author of *Bound by Loyalty, Innocent by Circumstance* and *Red Beans and Dirty Rice for the Soul.* He is from New Orleans, Louisiana.

Eugene L. Weems is the bestselling author of *United We Stand, Prison Secrets, America's Most Notorious Gangs, The Other Side of the Mirror, Head Gamez, Bound by Loyalty, Red Beans and Dirty Rice for the Soul, Innocent by Circumstance, Cold as Ice, and The Green Rose.* The former kick boxing champion is a producer, model, philanthropist, and founder of No Question Apparel, Inked Out Beef Books, and co-founder of Vibrant Green for Vibrant Peace. He is from Las Vegas, Nevada.

BOUND BY LOYALTY

COREY 'C-MURDER' MILLER
EUGENE L. WEEMS

The novel that critics across the nation are raving about and people are eager to read.

C-Murder and Weems constructed an elaborate contemporary urban thriller full of twists and false starts. Bound by Loyalty is absolutely chilling and bursting with surprises.

$14.95   278pgs   6x9 Paperback   ISBN: 978-0991238002
Celebrity Spotlight Entertainment, LLC

RED BEANS and DIRTY RICE FOR THE SOUL

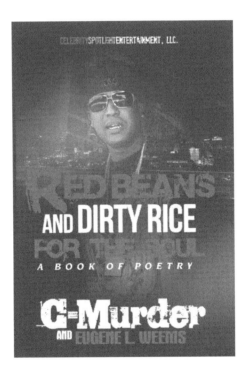

COREY 'C-MURDER' MILLER
EUGENE L. WEEMS
CLARKE LOWE

Tread the gutta' life with **C-MURDER** in this gripping compilation of poetry that is deeply rooted in the streets and behind prison walls.

WARNING! May cause a severe reaction or death in people who are square to the game. If an allergic reaction occurs, stop reading and seek emergency counseling from your local priest.

$14.95   103pgs   6x9 Paperback   ISBN: 978-0991238019
Celebrity Spotlight Entertainment, LLC

UNITED WE STAND

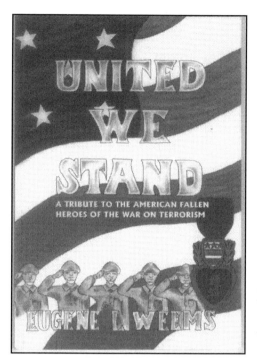

A TRIBUTE TO THE AMERICAN FALLEN
HEROES OF THE WAR ON TERRORISM
Eugene L. Weems

United We Stand is a beautiful collection of inspirational artwork and passion-filled poetry created as a living tribute to the American troops who have made the ultimate sacrifice for our country in the war against terrorism.

100% of the proceeds from this book will be contributed to provide care packages for the active duty troops who remain engaged in the war overseas and provide college scholarship trust funds for the children of our American fallen heroes.

$14.95   95 pgs   6x9 Paperback   ISBN: 978-1-4251-9130-6
Celebrity Spotlight Entertainment, LLC

3 STRIKES

CRUCIFIX

Growing up poor, abused and surrounded by violence, Tito Lopez dreamed of becoming a cop. But as fate would have it, his dreams became a series of nightmares and the treachery of life in the hood overtakes him.

When the water gets too deep, gangsters pull Tito out, embrace him and become his family. Unfortunately, Tito is drawn into a life of crime and gangsterism, which involves the Mexican Mafia and corrupt cops.

This gripping reality takes you on a journey leading to betrayal and a Three Strikes life sentence.

$14.95   187 pgs   6x9 Paperback   ISBN: 978-0-9912380-3-3
Celebrity Spotlight Entertainment, LLC

PRISON SECRETS
2nd EDITION

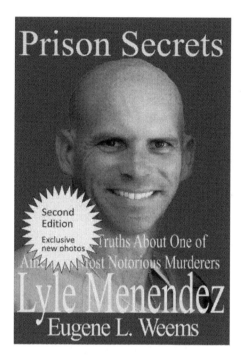

EUGENE L. WEEMS

Once recognized as a ruthless killer and remorseless criminal, Lyle Menendez remains housed in a maximum security correctional facility with other notorious murderers and gang members. In this level 4 maximum security prison, even one of America's most notorious murderers could be victimized. This novel will unlock the doors to all the prison secrets; weapons manufacturing, drug smuggling, prison rapes, gang politics, officer corruption and much, much more.

$14.95   183 pgs   6x9 Paperback   ISBN: 978-1500934873
Celebrity Spotlight Entertainment, LLC

COLD AS ICE

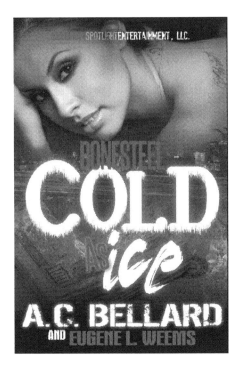

A.C. BELLARD
EUGENE L. WEEMS

Cold As Ice, an urban thriller that reads like a Hollywood movie script. This cutting edge murder mystery has twists, turns, and suspense that will keep a reader's mind intrigued to the very end.

Which character will you root for?

$14.95   212 pgs   6x9 Paperback   ISBN: 978-1500959562
Celebrity Spotlight Entertainment, LLC

THE GREEN ROSE

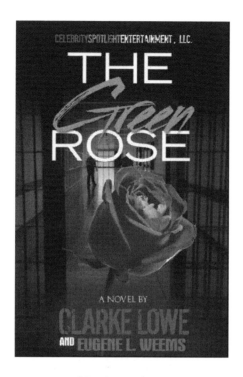

Clarke Lowe
Eugene L. Weems

MaryAnn is assaulted, but saved from harm by an heroic, street-wise stranger. Her hero, Curtis, is not the kind of person she normally socializes with, but she can't help but be drawn to this brave and charming man. In Curtis she discovers love is blind--race, nationality and social class are irrelevant. In him she finds fun, excitement and security she has not felt in years. MaryAnn shares her experience with her best friend Amanda and suggests she meet Curtis's friend Eugene. Unfortunately, he's in prison, but sometimes true love must be sought out in unconventional places. Will they find the deepest, most exotic love of their lives? Will they find The Green Rose?

$12.95   100 pgs   6x9 Paperback   ISBN: 978-1503357044
Celebrity Spotlight Entertainment, LLC

Made in the USA
Coppell, TX
01 April 2022